Praise for the Men of Mercy Series

"Lindsay Cross delivers high-powered action, alpha heroes and an exciting conclusion!"

- **ELLE JAMES**
New York Times and USA Today bestselling author

"This is one of those books that the phrase sit down, shut up and hang on would be used because it's a wild ride from page one to the end."

- **5 Star Goodreads Review**, Redemption River

"This book was wall to wall action. Once the danger hit, it never slowed down. I was late leaving my house because there was no way I could stop reading."

- **5 Star NetGalley Review**, Redemption River

BOOKS BY LINDSAY CROSS

MEN OF MERCY NOVELS
REDEMPTION RIVER
RESURRECTION RIVER
RECKLESS RIVER
RAVAGED RIVER – JAN 2016
DAVID – NOVELLA
ETHAN'S PROMISE- NOVELLA
AARON'S PROMISE – NOVELLA
ANTICIPATION – MAY 2015

Redemption River

Men of Mercy, Book 1

Lindsay Cross

Copyright Warning

The unauthorized reproduction or distribution of this copyrighted work is a crime punishable by law. No part of this book may be scanned, uploaded to or downloaded from file sharing sites, or distributed in any other way via the Internet or any other means, electronic or print, without the publisher's permission. Criminal copyright infringement, including infringement without monetary gain, is investigated by the FBI and is punishable by up to 5 years in federal prison and a fine of $250,000 (http://www.fbi.gov/ipr/).

This book is a work of fiction. The names, characters, places, and incidents are fictitious or have been used fictitiously, and are not to be construed as real in any way. Any resemblance to persons, living or dead, actual events, locales, or organizations is entirely coincidental.

Published by Cypress Bend Publishing LLC

Cover Design by Kari March

Redemption River
All Rights Are Reserved. Copyright 2015 by Lindsay Cross.

First electronic publication: October 2015
First print publication: October 2015

Digital ISBN: 978-0-9968360-0-5

Print ISBN: 978-0-9968360-3-6

To my family and friends whose unwavering support saw me through the tough spots.

DOSSIER

TASK FORCE SCORPION (TF-S)

A branch of Joint Special Operations Command (JSOC)
Ft. Grenada, MS

MACK GREY: Detachment Commander, Captain
  - ➤ Recruited from the 75th Ranger Regiment, Ft. Benning, GA
  - ➤ Specialized Skills: direct action, unconventional warfare, special reconnaissance, interrogations specialist, psychological warfare
  - ➤ First in Command. Responsible for ensuring and maintaining operational readiness.
  - ➤ Height: 6'
  - ➤ Weight: 195lbs
  - ➤ Combat Experience: Operation Gothic Serpent, Somalia. Operation Desert Storm, Operation Iraqi Freedom, Operation Crescent Wind, Operation Rhino, Operation Anaconda, Operation Jacan, Operation Mountain Viper, Operation Eagle Fury, Operation Condor, Operation Summit, Operation Volcano, Operation Achilles

HUNTER JAMES: Warrant Officer, Detachment Commander
- Recruited from the 75th Ranger Regiment, Ft. Benning, GA
- Specialized Skills: direct action, unconventional warfare, special reconnaissance, psychological warfare
- Responsible for overseeing all Team ops. Commands in absence of detachment commander.
- Height: 6'3"
- Weight: 230lbs
- Combat Experience: Operation Enduring Freedom, Operation Crescent Wind, Operation Anaconda, Operation Jacana, Operation Mountain Viper, Operation Eagle Fury

RANGER JAMES: Team Daddy/Team Sergeant, Master Sgt.
- Recruited from the 75th Ranger Regiment, Ft. Benning, GA
- Specialized Skills: direct action, unconventional warfare, special reconnaissance
- Plans, coordinates & directs Team intelligence, analysis and dissemination.
- Height: 6'2"
- Weight: 225lbs
- Combat Experience: Operation Enduring Freedom, Operation Crescent Wind, Operation Anaconda, Operation Jacana, Operation Mountain Viper, Operation Eagle Fur

JARED CROWE: Weapons Sergeant, Sgt. 1st Class
- Recruited from Delta Force, Ft. Bragg, NC
- Specialized Skills: direct action, unconventional warfare, special reconnaissance, Sniper
- Weapons expert. Capable of firing and employing all small arm and crew served weapons
- Height: 6'0"
- Weight: 220lbs
- Combat Experience: Operation Enduring Freedom, Operation Crescent Wind, Operation Anaconda, Operation Jacana, Operation Condor, Operation Summit, Operation Volcano, Operation Achilles

HOYT CROWE: Asst. Weapons Sergeant, Staff Sgt.
- Recruited from Delta Force, Ft. Bragg, NC
- Specialized Skills: direct action, unconventional warfare, special reconnaissance, Sniper
- Weapons expert. Capable of firing and employing all small arm and crew served weapons
- Height: 6'0"
- Weight: 210lbs
- Combat Experience: Operation Enduring Freedom, Operation Crescent Wind, Operation Anaconda, Operation Jacana, Operation Condor, Operation Summit, Operation Volcano, Operation Achilles

AARON SPEIRS: Medical Sergeant, Sgt. 1st Class
  - Recruited from Delta Force, Ft. Bragg, NC
  - Specialized Skills: direct action, unconventional warfare, special reconnaissance, medic
  - The life-saver. Employs the latest field medical technology and limited surgical procedures
  - Height: 6'1"
  - Weight: 195lbs
  - Combat Experience: Operation Anaconda, Operation Jacana, Operation Condor, Operation Summit, Operation Volcano,

RISER MALLON: Asst. Medical Sergeant, Staff Sgt.
  - Recruited from Delta Force, Ft. Bragg, NC
  - Specialized Skills: direct action, unconventional warfare, special reconnaissance, medic
  - The life-saver. Employs the latest field medical technology and limited surgical procedures
  - Height: 6'2"
  - Weight: 215lbs
  - Combat Experience: Operation Anaconda, Operation Jacana, Operation Condor, Operation Summit, Operation Volcano, Operation Achilles

MERC: Engineer Sergeant, Sgt. 1st Class
  - Recruited from Special Operations Group (SOG) of the Central Intelligence Agency (CIA)
  - Specialized Skills: direct action, unconventional warfare, special reconnaissance, Demolitions, psychological operations
  - Demolition expert. Trained in psychological warfare, conducts field interrogations.
  - Height: 6'5"
  - Weight: 250lbs
  - Combat Experience: Classified

ETHAN SLADE: Communications Sergeant/Commo Guy, Sgt. 1st Class
> - Recruited from the 75th Ranger Regiment, Ft. Benning, GA
> - Specialized Skills: direct action, unconventional warfare, special reconnaissance, communications
> - Communications expert. Employ latest FM, multi-channel, and satellite communication devices.
> - Height: 6'0"
> - Weight: 200lbs
> - Combat Experience: Operation Condor, Operation Summit, Operation Volcano, Operation Achilles

SHANE CARTER: Weapons Sergeant, Staff Sgt.
> - Recruited from the Marine Corps Forces Special Operations Command (MARSOC), Camp Lejeune, NC
> - Specialized Skills: direct action, unconventional warfare, special reconnaissance, weapons expert/sniper
> - Weapons expert. Capable of firing and employing all small arm and crew served weapons
> - Height: 5'11"
> - Weight: 180lbs
> - Combat Experience: Operation Iraqi Freedom, Operation Condor, Operation Summit, Operation Volcano, Operation Achilles

CORD CARTER: Weapons Sergeant, Staff Sgt.
- ➤ Recruited from the Marine Corps Forces Special Operations Command (MARSOC), Camp Lejeune, NC
- ➤ Specialized Skills: direct action, unconventional warfare, special reconnaissance, weapons expert/sniper
- ➤ Weapons expert. Capable of firing and employing all small arm and crew served weapons
- ➤ Height: 6'1"
- ➤ Weight: 210lbs
- ➤ Combat Experience: Operation Iraqi Freedom, Operation Condor, Operation Summit, Operation Volcano, Operation Achilles

MR J: CIA Liaison, Embedded with ISA
- ➤ Special Activities Division (SAD) of the Central Intelligence Agency (CIA)
- ➤ Specialized Skills: Classified
- ➤ Training: Classified
- ➤ Height: 5'10"
- ➤ Weight: 170lbs
- ➤ Combat Experience: Classified

Chapter One

Delta Force 2007
Somewhere outside of Karachi, Pakistan along the Indus River

The desert moon highlighted every tree and piece of brush along the Indus River, but it did not touch Hunter James and his men. The small contingent lay on their stomachs in the sand, blending with the camouflage of shadows, legs in the water behind them.

The cool night air was a welcome reprieve from Satan's hell-on-earth heat. Long, dark strips of clouds cut across the ominous sky, slicing the crescent moon in half, and the shadows shifted across Hunter's face. A crisp wind swept sand across the ground, but Hunter didn't blink. Didn't take his gaze from the high-powered night vision binoculars or NVGs.

The only things that moved were the corpses.

Limp bodies hung from ropes in irregular intervals along the twelve-foot concrete wall surrounding the newest compound of the terrorist organization ISA, the Islamic State of Afghanistan. Men. Women. Children. Each of them decorated with blood-painted signs. Traitor. Whore. Infidel.

A normal person would have vomited at the gruesome sight. But not Hunter. Not any member of the team he led—Task Force Scorpion or TF-S. Death hadn't fazed them in a long time. It couldn't, not in their profession.

"Son of a bitch. What kind of man decorates his home with dead women and children?" Ranger, Hunter's brother and second in command, spoke through their team's internal communication system. The remote mic system allowed them to communicate within a thousand yards of each other.

"Not a man. A monster. And I plan on fitting him with his own personal noose, right after we play a little game of dull knife, dull spoon." Jared, an elite scout sniper, shifted forward, careful not to break line out of the bushes.

"Aw, hell no, man, you always get to have all the fun. It's my turn this time. Plus, Mr. J already put you on probationary status after the Congo mission," said Hoyt, Jared's brother.

"No one is killing Al Seriq tonight. That's not the mission. We're here on a capture and carry only." Hunter tilted his head to the right, narrowing in on the west tower with his binoculars. A lone guard stood watch, his AK-47 clearly visible against the sky.

"But Top, that could have changed, you don't know. Mr. J hasn't checked in. Could be command invoked a kill order," Hoyt said. Top, or top dog, was Hunter's nickname for being the first sergeant in charge of the group.

Hunter sighed, not bothering to hide his irritation. Hoyt was a mischief-maker, his blond, curly hair and bright smile a constant source of attraction for women no matter where they were stationed. It only meant Hunter had to be more of a hard-ass.

"You heard him. Besides, you'd puss out before you even started on his eyes," Jared said. He was the more serious of the brothers, with darker hair that matched his grimmer personality.

"Give it up. You know Top doesn't break orders," Ranger said. He leaned left and his shoulder brushed Hunter's as he swept his binoculars in a constant motion, keeping an eye out for new combatants.

"You four sound like a bunch of women. Why don't y'all go ahead and have a cat fight and get it over with?" Shane Carter said. Though not related to either set of brothers by blood, Shane might as well be family. He and Ranger had become best friends at ten years old, and the two had been a team ever since.

Hunter's Task Force Scorpion was a group of nine men. All of them highly intelligent. All of them deadly. All of them fearless.

Years of training together had honed the men to the sharp precision of a finely crafted blade. A blade the government wielded when the broad sword of the army failed. A blade that could slice the head off a terrorist organization, leaving the body in a pool of blood before the group even registered its death.

If they were caught, there would be no rescue. No air strike. No news anchor demanding their release. According to the US government, TF-S didn't exist.

"Speaking of women, if you don't hurry up and nail that redhead back home at The Wharf, I'm gonna do it for you," Hoyt said to Ranger.

Hunter stilled. Evie owned The Wharf, which

just happened to be Mercy, Mississippi's only bar.

"Trust me, you couldn't handle a woman like her if she jumped into your lap," Ranger said. "Anyway, I like to appreciate my time with women, take it slow."

"Yeah, appreciate them right into a nursing home. You haven't had a woman in three years. How much appreciating do you need?"

"Enough. You two can compare dicks later. Eyes on the tower." Hunter leveled his voice, fighting to keep his memories locked down tight. They needed to focus. Their mission was to capture a murderer. Not daydream in the sand.

Muhammad Al Seriq, the new leader of ISA, murdered innocents with a ferocity that made his predecessor look like a GI Joe doll. After a Pashtun drug lord murdered his father, he joined ISA and quickly jumped up the ranking order. When the last leader of ISA had been murdered, Al Seriq took over, and moved the organization into Pakistan.

Intel suspected Al Seriq was acquiring a massive shipment of weapons from a source unknown to the CIA. A source that had to be discovered before more of their weapons were used to kill more innocents.

Hunter scanned the towers again, marking the guards' routine, nailing down their weaknesses. "Intel has Al Seriq in the central compound. Remember, we're here for extraction. Mr. J wants him for questioning." They could all hear him, of course, but Hunter turned his head to look at them. "They can't question a dead body."

Mr. J was TF-S's liaison with the CIA and the only man to successfully embed with ISA. Ninety percent of the intel on ISA had come directly from him.

Shane's voice clicked on in Hunter's ear. "Got it, Top. They won't even know he's missing until tomorrow's call for prayer."

The rest of his men sounded their agreement. "All right, order of march is myself, Ranger, and Shane is trail. Jared and Hoyt, provide over-watch." Hunter checked his SEIKO watch and then spoke into the comm system, "Team two, plan to meet at extraction point A at 0130."

"Roger." Merc, recon expert and leader for Team two answered. TF-S had broken into two groups for this mission. One for invasion and one for extraction.

"Moving." The brothers spread out, rolling away from the group, careful to keep to the underbrush. Hunter held up the binoculars again, watching the guards again. The east tower guard dropped his AK over his shoulder and lit up a smoke.

Hunter eased forward, his heart rate calm, his hands steady. The cold, comfortable weight of training settled over him. He smiled. This was what he lived for. The adrenaline rush of going into a situation and knowing he might not come out. And the pride of knowing there was no better way he could serve his country. Just like his old man.

Al Seriq's twelve-foot concrete walls were topped with guard towers at each corner. Desert surrounded three sides. The gate was four inches of solid iron. Impenetrable even with a 50-caliber. It was a terrorist's dream and a siege team's nightmare.

Their saving grace was the river, which ran

straight up to the southern edge of the compound, with vegetation growing thick along the banks. That was all the concealment Hunter's men needed to make a successful breach.

"Careful, Top, he's turning," Jared said. Hunter continued forward, slow and steady, until he halted directly beside the east tower. He took a deep breath and rolled to his back. A blanket of stars spread out over the night sky, but he barely even noticed their beauty. His focus was on the tower. Watching. Waiting.

His muscles drew tense and ready. His heart rate slowed.

"Go." Jared's voice came through. Hunter didn't hesitate. He threw his grappling hook; the metal chinked quietly into the concrete. He ascended the rope, ignoring the stench of the rotting bodies, and pulled himself over the wall, landing in a crouch on the balls of his feet. The oblivious guard took another drag off his cigarette, and Hunter snapped his neck.

The night remained quiet, the only sounds the cadence of water and the whirring of insects. Ranger signaled him from the west tower. Phase One was complete.

As Hunter looked out across the empty courtyard, a chill of unease slipped icy fingers down his neck. Nothing moved. It was too silent.

Jared cleared the tower and donned the fallen guard's jacket and hat, resuming position for the dead man.

"Clear." All his men were in position now. Hunter peeked over the edge, surveying the compound below.

"Hold." Hunter issued the command.

"What's wrong, Top?" Shane asked.

"Too quiet. Something's wrong." Most of Al Seriq's followers were fanatically loyal, to the point of suicide, and those who weren't, were loyal for fear of death. Hunter poured over the satellite images in his mind. There were always roving patrols. Always.

Unless this was a trap, and Al Seriq knew they were coming. "Jared and Hoyt, take watch. I'm going to radio in to command. Something doesn't feel right."

Normally he wouldn't pay any more attention to his feelings than he would a gnat hovering over his plate, but his instincts were screaming. And they had saved his ass more times than any CIA intel.

Hunter dropped to the tower floor and pulled out his radio. "Apache Main, this is Mary. Over."

"Mary, this is Apache. Over." The rough and unfamiliar voice that came through the comm only intensified the trickle of unease inside Hunter.

"Where's the Wolf?" Captain Grey should have been on the other end of the line.

"The Wolf is in the woods. This is the Cottage. Over." Shit. Captain Grey would be absent for only two reasons: a major screw-up or death. Something was definitely off.

"The Shepherds aren't at home. I repeat, the Shepherds aren't at home." Hunter controlled his breathing, fighting to keep his mind clear and focused.

"Copy, Mary. Stand by."

Hunter rose to his knees and surveyed the courtyard with his night vision goggles. No movement. Everything about this place looked normal, but his gut screamed ambush.

"Mary, this is the Cottage. What is your recommendation?"

"My recommendation is to abort the mission until we have further intel." Hunter leaned his forehead against the radio. He knew command would ignore his advice, just like he knew his men would be the ones to pay for their decision.

"Stand by." The radio clicked off. Static sounded through Hunter's earpiece, replaced by Ranger's voice, "Top, you know they ain't gonna call it off." Ranger didn't possess the ability to turn off his mouth.

"Ranger, you know, Dad gave me a good piece of advice when I was young."

"Yeah, what's that?"

"Shut the hell up." Hunter looked again. Still no movement.

The radio crackled back to life. "Mary, this is the Cottage."

"Go ahead."

"We need you to bring the Little Lamb home if it's on site."

"Roger." Shit. Hunter dropped his head and took a deep breath, ignoring the vise tightening around his chest. He took a quick exhale to release it. They were going into a potential massacre, but then again, Task Force Scorpion didn't get called in for pansy-ass missions.

"You get that, team?" Hunter asked. They had all heard his communication with headquarters over the remote mic system.

"Roger. We're with you, Top."

Really, he couldn't blame HQ for asking them to continue. This was the first time they had come anywhere close to having solid intel on this terrorist fucker. And it might be the last. Two months ago, Al Seriq and his men had begun committing mass genocide on the Pashtuns. So far only a few pictures had made it out of the Indus Valley Desert, but they had been gruesome, even for him.

Corpse after corpse. People. Animals. Nothing and no one had been spared. And the bodies hanging from the walls of the compound...

No. They couldn't call their mission off. Not now. "It's a go. Follow the plan. But be on alert; I don't like the feel of this."

Hunter descended the primitive wooden ladder to the bottom of the compound and took off running before his feet had a chance to sink into the sand. Ranger and Shane followed, each backing into the first outbuilding, weapons raised.

The compound was built like a bull's eye target. Single-story dwellings ringed the concrete wall, and the ISA leaders and their families were housed in the two-story bunker that sat in the center. That bull's eye was their target.

Hunter peered around the corner, down an opening between two of the squat buildings. The pathway was dark and empty. Hunter lifted his hand, motioning his men, and they moved forward in a crouched run. Cleared the next path. Crossed to the central compound and ducked down next to the entry.

Hunter checked the door, found it unlocked, and moved to breach. The wood door swung open soundlessly, so he moved in, gun raised. The dark room swallowed all the light from the moon, but the people littering the floor were clearly visible through their NVGs. And clearly dead.

Unease returned full force, and a cold sweat broke across Hunter's brow. He ignored it, determined to get this mission finished and get the hell out. Anxiety was a luxury he couldn't afford to entertain.

He signaled to the others to follow him and they moved silently to the staircase along the west wall and eased up the stairs, emerging in a short hallway lined with five closed doors.

They moved with the efficiency of a machine, clearing the rooms in order. Hunter and his men re-grouped in the hallway and moved to the second to last door. Hunter led, Ranger following close behind. Men lay scattered on pallets on the floor, some at odd angles.

"Why would Seriq kill his own men?" Ranger knelt down and prodded the nearest form with his weapon.

"Fuck if I know, but I'm getting the itch." The itch that some bad shit was about to go down. Hunter kept watch from the doorway.

"Shit, this isn't good."

"Fall back. Now. We need to evacuate." Hunter's nerves were on full alert.

"But what if Al Seriq's in the last room?" Shane crept to the door at the end of the hall before Hunter could stop him.

Hunter's radar blasted to full alert, blaring in his ears. "Shane, fall back. Now."

But it was too late.

Shane opened the door, his rifle raised. Hunter ran to back him up, weapon at the ready, and came to a stop in the doorway. A mutilated man sat tied to a chair, the light of a single bulb illuminating what was left of him.

"Oh shit, I'm gonna puke." Shane coughed and covered his mouth with his arm.

"Can you ID him?" Ranger approached the

room.

"With what?"

Hunter inched forward, realization dawning fast and hard. The black bag pulled down over the corpse's head was tied off at the throat with barbed wire. Dried blood had tracked uneven paths down his naked shoulders, but not enough to camouflage the word carved into his chest. *Traitor.*

His intestines spilled into his lap below the word. But his eyes weren't focused on the inside-out guts so much as the black ring on the corpse's right hand. A ring Hunter had seen on a hand lifting a beer, casting a fishing rod back home, training for combat.

Ice-cold rage unleashed inside Hunter, but he held still, welcoming the beast inside him.

"It's Mr. J. Fall back. Fall back. It's a trap." Their CIA contact, the only person to ever get inside Al Seriq's circle, was dead.

Hunter ran down the hall, his feet fueled by adrenaline and anger. He took a breath and released it, forcing the raw emotions out with it. Now wasn't the time for grief. He had to get his men out of the compound, fast.

They pounded down the stairs, not bothering to keep quiet now, jumped over the bodies on the first floor, and backed up to the front door. A bullet slammed into the doorframe a couple of inches from Hunter's face. "Shit!"

"Top, we got a shit-storm stirring. This situation is about to get FUBAR on our asses if y'all don't get the hell out," Hoyt said, his voice urgent.

"How many combatants you counting?"

"Fifteen. More coming. Got five behind the

building. Ten in front. We can take out some from the towers, maybe provide some distraction."

"Okay. On your signal." Hunter nodded to Ranger and Shane across the doorway. A few seconds later, the compound rang with the sound of bullets sinking into flesh, followed by screams.

"Top, more coming. Y'all gotta get out *now*." The sound of more gunfire punctuated Jared's voice.

Shane eased his head up over the open window and jerked back down in time to avoid a bullet. "Damn, I'm tired of getting shot at."

Hunter forced himself to focus. They had plenty of ammunition, but they were running out of time to get out of the middle compound. "Shane, can you get eyes on the house to the right?"

"Hell, yes."

"Ranger, house on the left?"

"Got it."

"Hoyt, Jared, clear a path up the middle. We're coming out—going left."

"Roger."

Hunter threw his M-18 grenade through the open door, and within seconds, violet smoke filled the area, concealing their movements.

Hunter radioed to their over-watch in the towers. "Moving."

Hunter and his team rushed through the door and headed left, picking off targets as the opportunity arose. Combatants swarmed from the surrounding buildings like ants. Gunfire erupted like a Chinese fireworks show. The sharp gunshots transformed into sick *thumps* as the bullets sank into flesh.

The *tat-tat-tat* of an AK registered right before

searing pain drilled into Hunter's thigh. "Argh." Hunter hit the sand only a foot from the cover of the nearest house and grabbed his leg, blood soaking his hands.

Shane dragged him the rest of the way to the compound wall before stopping to inspect the wound. "Through and through." Without missing a beat, he ripped open Hunter's first-aid pouch and applied a pressure dressing.

Fuck.

Ranger backed towards them, providing cover fire. Militants continued to swarm the compound, seeming to come from every direction.

"Top, you gotta move now. I see headlights on the horizon, maybe a click out." Jared said.

"Team two, we need early evac. Extraction point A. Will be coming in hot," Hoyt said.

"Roger."

Someone set them up. Hunter's hands shook. Pain screamed through his leg. Blood had already saturated his BDUs. *Breathe. Think.* Hunter forced his body to go still.

"You okay?" Ranger pulled him back from the brink. *Focus on the mission. Get my team out.*

"You think some puny bullet is gonna stop me? Remember Sudan?" Hunter forced laughter into his voice.

"Why you gotta bring up Africa?" Ranger asked, clearly offended.

"You think I'm going to let you forget that?" Hunter knew Ranger was trying to distract him from the pain, and he appreciated the effort.

"Are we gonna sit around reminiscing or are we going to get the fuck out of here?" Shane cut through their conversation.

Ranger pulled Hunter's arm over his

shoulders and got him to his feet. Hunter gritted his teeth as the pain shot through him. "Dammit."

"I thought you said Africa was worse," Ranger said.

"You know I'm full of shit."

Men shouted behind them. They didn't have more than ten seconds to get to the west tower or they'd all be dead. "Ranger, drop me. Get out of here, now."

"Hell no. Shane, cover me. I'm gonna get Hunter up that ladder."

"Roger."

Ranger pushed Hunter above him, giving him no chance to argue, while Shane stayed at the ready, gun in hand. He had fired off two more shots by the time Ranger called down for him to follow.

Hoyt helped lift Hunter into the tower. "Come on, Top, I'll carry your fat ass down."

"Better watch it, he's pretty sensitive about his weight," Ranger said.

"Move." Hunter dropped to the floor, his bad leg taking the brunt. His vision darkened for a minute. Warm blood trickled down his calf and into his boot.

"Shane, get your ass up here," Ranger yelled again over the gunfire. The shots grew louder. Ranger fired his weapon in short bursts to provide cover for their friend.

Someone screamed. Hunter heard a thump.

"Shane!" Ranger shouted over the gunfire and yelling.

"He's not moving." Jared's harsh voice ripped through the com, along with more gunshots. We gotta evac.

"Ranger, get the fuck out of there now or

we're all dead." Hunter said. Ranger just continued firing.

Hoyt helped Hunter over the wall, his leg useless. Hunter grabbed the rope and dove, his body swinging wildly from side-to-side as he descended the rope, ignoring his burning palms. He slammed into a corpse on the way down and found himself face-to-face with a once beautiful young woman, her eyes frozen in horror. His stomach knotted, and he froze for a moment, lost in a haze of pain and rage.

"We gotta go, Top." Hoyt was right above him, waiting on him to move.

Hunter slid the rest of the way down, pulling his bad leg back at the last minute so he fell on his good side. A second later Hoyt was beside him, scooping a shoulder beneath his arm and dragging him toward the river.

Hunter looked back once to see Jared and Ranger bringing up the rear.

There was no sign of Shane.

They dove into the river and swam with the current, back to their meeting point. Hunter half-swam, half-floated, drifting in and out of consciousness, his body cold from too much blood loss. He vaguely heard the roar of an approaching boat.

"Shit. What happened?" Riser, TF-S's medical staff sergeant, hooked his arms under Hunter and drug him into the boat.

"Trap. Mr. J is dead." Hunter coughed, the cold metal floor of the boat stealing what little warmth remained in his body.

"I'm with you," Ranger shouted over the roar of the engine. Though his vision had gone hazy, Hunter's leg seared with pain as Ranger tied a belt around his thigh and applied a new field dressing to the wound.

Hoyt leaned over him, the worried look on his face stark enough to penetrate his fuzzy vision.

"Shane?" Hunter got his lips to move, his voice thin.

Hoyt shook his head. The sky faded, and the roar of the motor grew distant. Just before he blacked out, an image of laughing blue eyes and long, blonde hair flashed through his mind.

Then nothing.

Chapter Two

Evangeline Videl placed her hands on the large hand-carved meeting table and stood. She met every gaze in the room. She didn't blink. She didn't cringe. She didn't back down. As a member of the Mississippi Revolutionary Group, MRG, she knew she couldn't show weakness. After all, the citizens depended on them for protection from the corrupt local government and money-under-the-table law enforcement. "My vote is no."

Lee Brown, Sherriff of Mercy and all around douche bag, stood at the other end of the heavy wood table. "You'd be stupid not to take this deal. He's offering more cash than your little group can make in a year."

Evie eyed the man who'd taken her father's place as sheriff with disgust. Her father, Tom Videl, would never have done business with criminals. Then again, if her father were still alive, Evie wouldn't be involved with a semi-illegal revolutionary group. "I don't care how much money that bastard is paying."

Dale Hendricks, a long-standing MRG member, coughed. "If we don't accept this deal, the money will go to the Lobellos."

The Lobellos were one step down from a cartel, but no less deadly.

Evie's open palms clenched into fists and she straightened. Do business with her abusive ex-fiancé or give up more territory to trash... Decisions, decisions. But as much as she wanted to tell Dale to shut his trap, she couldn't. She wasn't president. "We don't need Marcus. My cousins..."

"Have been promising a deal for six months and have yet to deliver." Dale finished the sentence for her. Evie clenched her jaw tight enough to crack a tooth.

It was true, her cousins, Greer and Rayland Wilde, had yet to deliver the goods. But she'd be damned if she or any member of her group got tied up with Marcus Carvant. "This group has never dealt in drugs. Ever. His money is blood money. And everyone at this table knows that anyone who does business with him ends up dead."

Dale held her gaze, unflinching. Uncaring. Challenging her barely-held position of control. Willing to deal with the devil even if it meant selling what little soul he still possessed.

Evie's grandfather, C.W., founding member of the MRG sat to her left. At seventy years old, the Cajun mountain man was no sweet and coddling Grandpa. He'd taught her to shoot to kill, a skill he'd learned in Vietnam. His black eyes narrowed behind the glasses riding low on his nose. "I side with my granddaughter."

Pride surged through her veins, but she kept her face carefully blank. She couldn't afford to show that weakness.

"I agree." Evie's mother, Maxine Videl, President of the MRG, sat to her right. Her expression was about as readable as a rock and just as hard.

"Are you really going to let this puny little nothing order you around?" Brown turned to Dale, so far his loudest supporter. Another man moving further and further up Evie's shit list.

Evie went cold. Her fingers, already leached of warmth, turned full-on numb. She never envisioned being in this position. Bartering drugs and money laundering with the only law enforcement in town. If only she'd been smart and went to college, but she'd made decisions on a broken heart and half a prayer. A prayer that went unanswered.

She could barely force herself to leave her house some nights, let alone go to work at The Wharf, her bar, and be so close to so many people. Knowing Marcus was out there and that he could walk in at any moment and finish what he'd started two years ago... Well, it was a wonder she could leave her house at all.

Maxine cut her a gaze that could have sliced titanium. Her mother, the housewife turned gangster. She'd managed to step up and take control of her life after Tom died. But not Evie. Evie had been all but forced into this crazy scheme by her less-than-sane grandpa. Maxine turned her attention to Brown. "Better to take orders from a woman than from a filthy pig."

The sheriff tensed. His hand fell to the pistol in his snapped gun holster.

"I guess you're lookin' to lose your hand." C.W. uncrossed his fingers, and in one swift movement, yanked his Colt .44 six-shooter from his hip holster and aimed it directly at Brown. "Maybe you should talk to Marcus about what happens to people who threaten my family."

Evie jerked and clutched the table for support, fighting to keep a neutral expression even though the mere mention of his name sent chills down her spine. The last time Marcus ran into her grandpa, he met the wrong end of a shotgun. He'd escaped without any personal injuries, but his Mercedes had acquired multiple bullet holes.

Of course, gripping the table wasn't exactly normal behavior. She looked around, not taking a breath until she saw everyone's focus was on her gun-toting grandpa.

Brown paled, his overly large Adam's apple bobbing in his long, skinny neck. His hand rose from his holster, empty and shaking. "If you don't do this, you know he'll make you regret it. Every last one of you."

And she did know it. Marcus had already made her regret so much. He'd taken her innocence and used it like an addict used crack, destroying her before she'd realized the damage.

Speak. Open your mouth. Tell him to screw off.

Dale's gaze cut to her, and the knowledge Evie saw in their depths caused her to quake. She wasn't strong enough to stand up to the sheriff. Why was she even here?

Dale's upper lip raised in disgust. But instead of calling her out, he whipped around to face Brown. Before Evie could force her frozen lips to move, Dale pulled back and threw a meaty fist straight into the sheriff's face. The crack of knuckles on flesh boomed. Brown crumpled like a bicycle under a semi truck.

"No one threatens the MRG. Tell Marcus we'll be in touch after the vote." Dale didn't even shake out his fist.

Evie, still immobilized, managed to nod at Dale. He didn't return the gesture, just grabbed Brown by the shirt and dragged him out of the room.

Everyone at the table, all ten members of the MRG, turned to look at Evie. She closed her eyes and gathered what little inner strength she possessed. What would her father say to them?

No one in this room would've dared speak out against Tom Videl. But then again, poor little Evangeline would never be able to live up to the Videl family name.

But she had to try. Wasn't that why she'd finally agreed to C.W.'s idea to re-instate the MRG? It was her last-ditch attempt to recover the part of her spirit that hadn't been permanently crushed by Marcus.

Evie lifted her chin and curled her fingers into her palms. "The MRG was founded on honor and justice. Justice from the exact men who just offered us a deal. Are you all so scared that you'd consider selling out at the first flash of cash?"

C.W. gave her a wink and tucked his pistol back into its holster. Cheri, Evie's best friend and co-bartender at the Wharf, nodded, reminding Evie she wasn't the only one in the room who'd been shit on by Marcus Carvant.

"You realize you could have just kicked a hundred grand out the door." Leftie, their resident white-trash grease-head, had probably needed to bite his tongue to keep silent for so long. If Evie were in complete control, she would have kicked him out long ago, but Leftie was Dale's best friend, and Dale was a founding member of the original MRG in the 70s.

"You do realize he would have killed us once he was finished with us. Even you." Maxine's long red nails clicked slowly, methodically, on the table top, reminding Evie of a cat before it pounced on its prey.

Leftie spat a wad of chewing tobacco on the floor. "You think just 'cause C.W. started this group means you get to make all the decisions. Don't forget. We get a vote. And I vote to take the goddamn money."

Dale re-entered the room and resumed his seat beside Leftie, his look calculating. "I say we take the offer. So we deliver some pot down river, so what? Think of what we could do with the money." He took his time before continuing, looking at each of the people gathered around the table. "I'm hurting for cash. Our group is hurtin' for it too. Evie's been promising her cousins have this big plan, this big deal that's gonna save us, but so far they've produced zero."

Evie swallowed, sinking back into her seat. No matter how much she wanted to call Dale a liar, he was telling the truth.

"Before you vote, think about how much good we can do the community with that kind of cash," Dale said.

Leftie all but rubbed his palms together. The other members started shifting in their seats, looking anywhere but at Evie. It felt like there was a drought in her mouth. "No matter how much money is at the end of the rainbow, delivering drugs, even if it's pot, is not what we are about."

Chairs creaked, more shifting.

"You're talking about one-hundred thousand dollars for our club," Leftie said.

"You mean lining your pockets, don't you?" C.W. said.

Leftie's face turned red, but he held his temper in check. "Lining all our pockets, old man. Think about it."

Evie felt another thread of control snap. She knew she wasn't strong enough to stand up to her people and make them do right.

Mercy, Mississippi was now run by criminals—criminals who wore badges and were led by a corrupt mayor. Marcus Carvant, her ex. As Marcus's former punching bag, Evie had been kept under lock and key, never allowed to bear witness to his 'business' dealings. She'd suspected, though, plenty of times, but never managed to get any proof. Now he wanted drug transport and to launder his dirty money through her bar?

"Anyone else have something to add before we vote?" Maxine stood and Evie sat down. If they voted to accept the deal, she'd have no choice but to work with Marcus. Or step down and give up.

And deep down she knew giving up the MRG would mean giving up on herself.

Chapter Three

Marcus Carvant sat up straight in his Italian leather chair, tapping his engraved pen in precise two-second intervals. He allowed this one small action as his agitation with Sheriff Lee Brown grew. He tapped faster the more excuses the sheriff made for his failure.

"So you didn't get the job done." Marcus kept his tone calm and controlled, denying his mounting desire to hang up on Brown. He wouldn't allow that lapse in control for anyone. Not the man on the phone. Not the mercenary sitting on the other side of his desk. Not himself.

His father had taught him early in life to keep things in order. Not one blond hair on Marcus's head strayed from its combed perfection. Not one hint of a wrinkle dared crease his perfectly tailored trousers. Not one of his employees dared disrupt his carefully laid plans.

Not if they wanted to live, anyway.

"I'm telling you, I did everything you asked. They forced me out at gunpoint. That traitor Dale Hendricks sucker-punched me." Marcus heard the sound of something opening on the other end of the phone line, followed by a crunch and Brown's sigh. He was probably pressing a bag of frozen peas against his face. Something Marcus's ex-fiancée had done on numerous occasions.

"So you not only failed to acquire transportation, but you lost my inside man?"

"No. No, sir. I can get the deal done." Brown's voice waivered, as thin and weak as the man himself. "I'll get that little bitch alone and take care of business. Just like you used to do."

Marcus stopped tapping his pen and laid it parallel with the pad of paper on his desk. Yes, he'd lost control once. Or with one person. One girl he'd never quite managed to subdue. One he planned to reacquire soon.

Evangeline Videl would belong to him again, only this time she wouldn't be at his side. She would be beneath his foot.

When and how Marcus punished her was totally and completely up to him, however, not a bought and paid for Dollar-Store sheriff with a plastic badge.

"I'm not a fan of giving second chances, and I need to decide if you deserve one," Marcus said.

"Listen, I can do it. I've never failed you before. Never. I'll take care of it, right now," Brown said.

"No. I will take care of it. You just do your job and try not to screw up my plans." Marcus snapped the cell phone shut and set it on the rich mahogany table directly beside and in line with the discarded pen.

Nothing in his office or on his person was out of order.

Marcus leaned forward, placing his elbows on the desk, and steepled his fingers. His chair was dark leather, tall and heavy. A throne. It was only appropriate, for he ruled his business with the power and might of a great king.

And he was just as dangerous when pissed off.

The MRG, now led by Marcus's ex-fiancée, would make the perfect scapegoat for his weapons deal. He already had the guns, thanks to a little money and a now-dead guard at Camp Renier stupid enough to steal from the government. He had the contact with a zealous terrorist in Pakistan, thanks to a greedy soldier willing to sell out his country. And he'd figured out a way to get his shipment out of the country without getting his hands dirty, and in the same move, get revenge on Evangeline.

If only Brown weren't an incompetent idiot. The man attempted to tell Marcus that he could finish the deal. That he wouldn't make a mistake again. What Marcus didn't tell the sheriff was that he wouldn't get the opportunity. The deal brewing with the Pakistani was big on an international scale. Millions. His own-personal-island kind of deal.

It would take him far, far from the pissant state of Mississippi.

Lee Brown couldn't handle it; he couldn't even handle a group of pretend revolutionaries. If Marcus had his way, he'd put a bullet in Brown's head right now, but he knew the sheriff might still prove useful at the local level while his plan was unfurling.

No loose ends.

Marcus picked up his pen, studying the gold engraving along its body, using the distraction to rein in the familiar explosion of rage ripping through his body. Control. Precision. Power.

He would win. He always did. No matter if he

had to do some of the dirty work himself.

Marcus lifted his office phone to his ear and dialed his current girlfriend, a former Miss USA. "Colette, dear. How would you like to go on a date tonight?"

"Of course, darling." Her voice was cultured. Refined. The perfect accompaniment for his tastes.

"Good. I will pick you up in an hour. I want to take you to a local bar, make nice with some of the locals."

"A bar? In Mercy?" Her disgust was evident.

"Are you questioning my decision?" Marcus let his tone go soft. Lethal.

Colette immediately stammered, "No. Of course not. I will be ready."

He disconnected the call and went to his master suite. He wanted to look his best, after all, this was the first time he'd seen his ex in over a year. He would show Evie what she'd been missing and then he would remind her of what would happen if she didn't do as he commanded.

* * *

Hunter James sped out of the gas station parking lot and onto the highway, listening as Jared told him about his recon mission on the MRG. It was hard to keep from crushing the steering wheel in his palms. While he was away, his hometown had turned into a hotbed of militia groups.

Why the fuck did their CO have to send them to Mercy? Any other team could have handled the undercover op. Well, any other Task Force anyway. But no other TF had the connections they did. Or the history.

Hunter should never have told Captain Grey about his past with Evie before agreeing to this mission. But then, it wasn't like the Captain had given him a choice. Either go home on assignment or go home. Permanently.

Hunter took a right off the main highway onto Red Fork Road, which led out to his father's property. TF-S had set up headquarters in one of Hank's metal pole barns. Huge cypress trees lined the bayou sidelining the two-lane road, their roots jutting up out of the murky water like giant spider legs. Bugs splattered against the windshield like rain, only instead of rolling off the glass, they stuck, creating a thick, viscous film. He hit the windshield wipers, smearing the remains in yellow and white streaks of goo.

The other half of TF-S was still in Pakistan searching for the terrorist. Searching for Shane in the hopes he might still be alive.

Now Hunter was down four men—five, counting Shane—and on a mission to get close to an ex-girlfriend who'd turned to assisting terrorists.

"Did you plant the bug?" Hunter handled the winding road along the bayou with ease, relying on muscle memory.

"Yep, but not until after the meeting. That old man stayed in the meeting room all day. I couldn't hear what the piece-of-shit sheriff had to say, but when they threw him out, it was easy enough to figure out he pissed them off." Jared adjusted the black skullcap down lower on his forehead. A week's worth of stubble covered his jaw. The thin scar running from his right eyebrow down into his beard made him look like a modern day pirate.

C.W. Videl, Evie's grandpa, was turning out to be one giant-ass thorn in their side. He basically lived in the apartment above the bar, which also doubled as the MRG's meeting room. That left their team almost zero opportunity to get inside and get the intel.

"No shit." Hunter floored the pedal on the last straight stretch before the farm and turned onto a gravel road that disappeared into the woods.

After a minute, the trees thinned and then disappeared as they neared the tan metal building. After Hunter parked, he and Jared got out and headed to the door, where Hunter held a hand up to the state-of-the-art scanner. The deadbolt unlocked with a loud click, providing them access to their new headquarters.

To the right, Ranger was stooped over one of a series of long folding tables covered in every available geotropic map of the area and the Mississippi River. To the left, Hoyt sat at a bank of three computers, not the typical wall of monitors he was used to, but enough he could work his technical magic.

Ranger straightened his posture, his short blond hair gleaming in the fluorescent lighting. "That didn't take long."

Hoyt spun around in his rolling chair, his own blond hair curly and long, his constant playboy grin in place. "Which means he didn't get shit."

Hunter strode to the center table and rapped his knuckles on it. Ranger, Hoyt, and Jared immediately took their seats at the half-empty meeting table. One empty chair loomed larger than the rest. Shane Carter should have been sitting there.

The other four would be filled with the rest of TF-S, as soon as they located Al Seriq, and hopefully Shane.

What was left of his unit was present and accounted for, so Hunter took his seat at the head of the table. "Hoyt, call the Captain."

Hoyt, slid his rolling chair back over to his computer station and clicked a bunch of keys. Captain Grey's face appeared on the wall of monitors a few seconds later. A man they all respected, not because of his title, but because he deserved it. Captain Grey was the best interrogator in the Task Force teams—in the entire military, as far as Hunter was concerned.

"Report." His flat grey eyes matched the steel grey in his beard. Task Force members operated like SEALs in regard to their appearance. They grew their beards and hair as needed to blend in with their environment. A beard, along with sunglasses and a hat, could disguise your whole face, allowing even the more well-known members of the group to move about in anonymity.

"We don't know anything yet. I couldn't plant the listening device until after the meeting." Jared said. Jared and Hoyt Crow looked about as similar as a desert dweller and a Swede. Their light blue eyes were the only outward sign they were brothers.

"So we don't know anything more now than we did two weeks ago," Captain Grey said. Two weeks of knowing Marcus had the weapons and the MRG was being tapped to transport. Knowing but having no idea when or where or how. "Hunter. Ranger. You have history here. What's your take?"

Ranger's gaze slid to Hunter's before bouncing back to the commander. His brother's thoughts were clear as a billboard—Time to man up and move in on your ex.

"Marcus is the youngest mayor in Mississippi's history, but only because his father greased the wheels along the way. He collected enough intel to blackmail all the more prominent locals into controlling the votes. He'll do anything and hurt anyone to come out on top. But he has never operated alone." Hunter completely ignored his brother's look and left out any mention of Evie.

"Which tells me nothing more than I already know." The Captain fell silent. Classic technique to get your counterpart to spill first.

Jared cleared his throat and gave Hunter an apologetic look. A look completely ruined by the death-bringer getup. "We haven't used the girl yet. She will know the info."

Hunter knew that was how the mission would end up, him getting in with Evie to get the intel. But knowing and doing were two totally different monsters. The first he could handle, the second made his gut clench.

"I agree. We've played with our dicks long enough. Either we move soon or we lose the weapons and the evidence to put this asshole away for life." Jared said.

Fucking hell. If Hunter had possessed any doubt about Captain Grey's intentions to use him, he'd just lost them.

"Hunter, it's time. Evangeline Videl is our best resource. If you can turn her to give up Carvant, we can hopefully complete this mission with little risk." The Captain ordered.

Evangeline Videl.

Every muscle in Hunter's body clenched. His jaws locked down. If he could step back from his own body, he knew he'd be able to see his own instinctive physical reactions to her name. *Evie.* He'd hallucinated about her after being shot. Now every member of his team knew he was still hung up on his hometown sweetie. And that she'd betrayed him with Marcus fucking Carvant.

If the look on Captain Grey's face counted for anything, so did he.

Hunter dragged a hand through his buzz-cut hair. "Evie helped Marcus move his political career forward. Her dad was sheriff of Mercy for years, so he had an established reputation. Her position in the community was solid. His connection to her ensured his election." The words were as bitter now as they had been then. When he'd caught them together. Hunter shook off the memory.

Still raw. Still painful.

"Do you think you can turn her?" Captain Grey said.

The Evie he remembered was sweet. Innocent. Loving. Kind. But that was the pretend Evie. The one who cared about animals and volunteered at the Methodist church. The one who had stolen his heart.

The real Evie used people to get what she wanted.

Power. Money. Position.

"Based on experience," Hunter swallowed past the foreign lump forming in his throat, "A hundred grand would be a strong motivator for someone like her. But I can do it. I will do it."

Captain Grey nodded, taking Hunter at his

word. His instincts were almost as notorious as the Captain's interrogation skills.

"Hunter, Ranger, I know you grew up with these people, but the MRG is the enemy. We will operate with the assumption they know where the weapons are and what they're for. Hoyt, I want you on twenty-four hour surveillance. Jared, I want you on Carvant. He doesn't take a shit without me knowing. Hunter and Ranger, you'll work it from the MRG side. Use whatever means you have to get in and get the weapons. The last thing this nation can afford is for Al Seriq to get his hands on that many A-Rs."

"Roger," Hunter answered.

Captain Grey clicked off the monitors and the screens filled with grainy images of Al Seriq and his followers. Hoyt clicked away at his keyboards until images of the Videl family lined the bottom screens. Maxine. C.W. Evangeline.

Evie. His lungs locked. Dammit. But Hunter had enough training to control his reactions. His thoughts. His actions. *Remember the end game. Remember Al Seriq. Remember Shane.*

Even so, the picture on the bottom right monitor seemed to fill his every pore. A candid shot of Evie, surrounded by people, laughing. Her long, blonde hair loose and straight. Her blue eyes sparkling. She looked so innocent.

Hunter clenched his fist in the loose material of his black tactical pants. The memory of Evie in Marcus's arms, his mouth covering her lips, slammed through the barrier Hunter had erected all those years ago.

Innocent, his ass. Evangeline Videl was as innocent as a black widow on the prowl.

Only now, it wasn't a young man's heart at

stake, it was the entire United States.

Chapter Four

Evie crossed her arms in front of her chest and bulldozed through the throng of over-heated dancers crowding the dance floor of her bar, her empty serving tray held tight to her side. The Wharf sat perched over the Mississippi River, whose waters were now swollen to capacity thanks to weeks' worth of unrelenting rain. But the threat of a flood was no deterrent on a weekend night for the residents of Mercy, Mississippi.

One couple spun left, the next spun right, and she countered each, moving like a puzzle piece searching for its place.

Evie almost started to move with the sway and rhythm of the music, but then the dancers tightened around her, cinching an invisible noose around her throat, cutting off her oxygen. Suddenly she remembered to feel out of place, remembered her choking fear of tight spaces.

Tiny, a six-foot, two-hundred-pound biker, staggered into her path and jabbed her in the side, knocking her off center. Evie crashed into a couple two-stepping before his meaty paw wrapped around her arm and righted her.

"Watch it." The stout liquor on his breath

could have flattened a brick wall. She tried to suck in some air, but the stench made her gag. Tiny stumbled forward, heading for the back porch, but the space he created was quickly filled by three more couples. Evie's heart set off on a race to see how fast it could make her pass out. Her lungs locked. The familiar talons of claustrophobia wrapped around her shoulders, sinking its claws deep.

Evie lifted her nose high, sucked in a combination of oxygen and cigarette smoke, and came down choking. *Shit. Dumb idea. Breathe. Just breathe.* Newborn babies could breathe. Freaking chickens could breathe, and they were the dumbest animals on the planet. But Evangeline Videl, wimp extraordinaire, could not get enough air.

Bright multi-colored lights danced before her eyes. *Escape.* The exit sign flashed bright red on the other side of the bar, taunting her. What good would that do her? She was co-owner of The Wharf and head bartender. She couldn't leave. She needed to get behind the bar. Her shield. Her protection.

She forced one leg forward, then another, only to be blocked by more dancers.

She wasn't going to make it. Her rainbow-colored floaters started to fade to black. Then a soft hand encircled her wrist and maneuvered her out of the crush. Evie looked up to see Cheri pushing patrons aside, her bright red hair swishing behind her. "Move it or lose it. We got drinks to serve."

Evie clung to Cheri like a toddler holding on to her momma. She hadn't shaken the fear yet, but she was grateful to be following in the path of a real-life bulldozer. Showing weakness wasn't necessarily a death sentence here, but it could just as easily become a permanent description. And everyone who spent time at this place had seen evidence of it in Evie.

Cheri slammed the half-door of the bar behind them and let loose. "Shit, girl, you gotta figure somethin' out, 'cause whatever you're doing ain't working."

"Hey, are you going to fix me another drink sometime today?" Both women turned to look at the overweight ass in need of a shave sitting across from them at the bar.

"We got a full house, Bill. You see all those people out there? You ain't the only one in here tonight. Now if you know of a better place to drink on a Friday night, you're welcome to it." Cheri gave redheads their fierce reputation.

She turned those flashing gold eyes of hers back to Evie. "Look, you need to..."

"I know. I'm working on it." Evie gave her friend her best impression of an I'm-going-to-make-it smile. Cheri's frown clearly indicated what she thought of her posturing.

But Cheri did the best-friend thing and patted her on the arm. "Okay. Why don't you let me handle the floor and you handle the bar?"

Bless her heart. Restraining the urge to hug her, Evie nodded. Cheri strode back out into the crowd, her rolling hips hinting at hostility.

Bill's gaze snapped from Cheri's retreating backside to Evie's face. He lifted his head and opened his mouth, but Evie held up a hand. Cheri was right. The Wharf was the only bar in fifty miles. If he was that hard up, let him drive. She needed a minute to stuff her irrational emotions back into their titanium-plated lock box.

She gripped the cool edge of the stainless-steel sink and took a deep breath. She took in the familiar scenery, looking for comfort like an alcoholic looked for a bottle.

Stuffed deer heads dotted the walls. A few squirrels and raccoons were mounted on shiny wooden plaques. A black bear stood tall in the far corner, a beer nestled nicely between its outstretched paws and an unlit cigarette dangling from its lips. PETA would say it was inhumane, but she didn't have to worry. PETA didn't come to places like Mercy, Mississippi. No one did if they could help it.

If only she could get the hell out of The Wharf and go home. She could crawl under the covers and go back to sleep. She could lock her doors and keep out everyone and everything...maybe even her past.

She banged a fist on the inside of the sink, the pain in her hand matching the tightness in her chest. Damn Marcus Carvant for making her like this. Afraid of people. Afraid of life. Of herself.

Evie splashed cold water on her face to snap herself out of the pity party of her life. Pouting wouldn't pay the bills. She dried her face on the hand towel, super-glued on a smile, and turned to the first customer she saw.

"Can I help you?" Evie asked.

"Marcus, you were engaged to this creature?" a beauty-queen brunette asked, twining a pale arm around the man at her side.

"Now, Colette, you know I've always had a heart for charity."

Evie's smile froze like instant concrete, rough and uneven. Thor could have dropped down from

Asgaard, hammer in hand, and failed to put a dent in her expression.

Marcus Carvant, her tormenter, her abuser, her ex, approached, resplendent in a crisp button-up, his slim fingers trailing up and down the arm of his companion. So smug with his sideways grin and raised blond brows. His cold grey eyes. It had taken her over a year to figure out smiles didn't always mean happiness.

He was a predator.

Not one of those hulking, obvious predators. More like a water moccasin hanging from a tree limb above your boat. Waiting until just the right moment to plop down, leaving you with no means of escape. Trapped. Helpless. Terrified. All you could do was watch the snake coil and prepare to strike.

Her hands trembled, and she reached down to grab a beer from the cooler. She needed to figure a way to get him out of here.

Colette's red lips turned down in a pout, and she stroked a manicured nail down his clean-shaven face. "You do have a soft heart for those less fortunate."

Evie had a brief flash of diving over the bar and tackling Colette to the floor. Of course, she wasn't the real enemy.

"Now, darling." Marcus took Colette's hand in his limp one, raising it to thin lips.

Evie swallowed the gorge rising in her throat.

She focused on the woman's purple nails. A few years ago, Evie wouldn't have left the house without her Tickled Pink polish gleaming. Now she was lucky if her nails weren't cracked, chipped, and caked with stale beer.

"She did dress better than this with me."

Marcus's grey eyes traveled the length of Evie's body. His lip pulled up with just the barest hint of a sneer.

The woman before her was perfect. Statuesque. Just what Marcus longed for, his own perfect Stepford wife.

Evie glanced down at her loose, torn jeans and long-sleeved T-shirt. Her tight, revealing dresses had been the first part of her Marcus uniform to go. She shook her head. *Get it together.* "What do you want?"

"My sweet Evangeline, I need to speak with your mother. Is Maxine in?"

Evie stiffened. He was the only person who ever used her full first name. The scar on her side burned.

If he was looking for her mom, it could only lead to bad things.

"She's not here." She glanced to her left, praying her mom stayed in the back office. Maxine ran the books along with the bar. She was here as often as Evie, but she kept to the back of the house. Plus she had to make the books look legit, and that took a little more time now that they weren't.

Filtering in the 'extra' revenue brought in by the MRG took finesse. And Evie couldn't think of anyone better equipped to skirt the law than the wife of an ex-sheriff.

Marcus raised his head, regarding her down his thin nose. "Really? My man said she was just here."

"Your man? You mean your rent-a-cop?" Evie swallowed, fear choking her windpipe despite her bold words.

Marcus turned to his date. "Colette, you need

to go to the restroom. Your mascara is smudged."

Colette gasped and all but ran to the bathroom. Marcus turned back to Evie, the polite façade slipping.

"I thought a personal meeting was in order, since you were so rude to the sheriff. You might need a reminder of what happens to people who don't follow orders."

Evie barely restrained her tremble. Barely. She inhaled, deep, slow. Tried to calm her heart before it exploded in her chest. "I think we all know what happens to people you disagree with."

Marcus's smile stayed fixed in place. Perfect. Deadly. "You know, but I think you need to *remember*. For instance, I remember what happened to your father after you left. How he finally got caught dealing drugs and using his badge to cover his mess. Too bad that drug dealer had to kill him."

Evie's racing heart stopped cold. The scorching heat from the packed bar turned to ice around her.

"It would be awful if something like that happened to your mother," Marcus continued. He reached across the bar and wrapped his long slender fingers around her wrist, then yanked her forward. His Armani cologne invaded her nostrils, chocking off her already dwindling air supply. "We wouldn't want that, now would we?"

Evie stood frozen, her limbs locked in horror. She'd worked so hard to block out the memory of her father's set-up. His murder. She'd always suspected Marcus was involved, but this confirmed it.

"Are you threatening my mother?" Evie forced the words through her clenched lips.

Marcus pulled her closer, choking her with his scent. "I would never threaten someone. That's illegal. I am simply reminding you of the importance of manners. A thoughtful woman would give my offer more consideration before turning it down." His gaze held her hostage. "A thoughtful woman would remember to take care of her loved ones."

Evie sucked in a breath, unable to force herself to breathe normally. Marcus released her wrist, all but throwing her backwards.

"A thoughtful woman would offer her ex-fiancé a drink."

Thoughtful. One of Marcus's favorite teaching points. Or, as she remembered, his favorite excuse to cause pain. And here he was. In her bar. The man who'd already stolen her father was threatening what family she had left, not to mention her entire existence.

But she'd grown a little bit of backbone after gathering the courage to leave him. And that backbone stiffened with anger. Evie reached below the bar and pulled open the small refrigerator at her feet.

"You want a beer?" Evie held up their cheapest, daring to edge forward and hold the drink within smelling distance. The bastard before her shuddered and pulled back. Evie couldn't restrain her smirk. The likes of Marcus Carvant didn't touch cheap beer. "I'll take a Peroni."

"Do you have a wine list?" Colette reappeared, her make-up now spotless, and perched on a barstool. She made as little contact with the pleather as possible, all the while petting her boyfriend. Evie didn't bother telling her not to worry. He was the last creature on this planet she wanted to be near.

"I'm sorry. You must be lost. We ain't got none of that highfalutin' stuff." Evie cleared her throat, laying it on as thick as sweet Southern honey. "And we ain't got that beer, neither."

Colette pulled back, probably afraid of being infected with white trash.

Marcus looked pissed. He didn't yell, but Evie could see the hardening around his eyes, the tightening of his lips. Tension roiled off him like air off hot cement. She took a step back.

He smiled and her stomach sank. He knew. He could sniff out fear like a bloodhound trailing a scent.

He took Colette's hand and stood. "Come, dear, I'll take you to Greenville. This barbaric dump doesn't have what we're looking for." Colette turned to leave, but Marcus's grip on her arm stopped her. He stared hard at Evie.

"Tell your mother I have every intention of finishing our conversation. With her, or with you. Whichever she prefers." His gaze burned holes into her brain and she felt herself nodding against her will. Her gaze followed the back of his grey blazer until the glass door banged shut behind him.

She grabbed the sink again and forced her hands to open and close, attempting to get some blood flow to her numb fingers. Anger returned along with her circulation. Her brain decided to function again and all the thoughts of what she would have said to him, how she should have put him in his place, bombarded her. Oh, how she wanted to embarrass him and take away his public golden-boy façade, even if it meant showing everyone the marks he had left on her body.

And yet she had stood there listening to his insults. And she'd done nothing. Absolutely nothing.

So much for the stack of personal growth books on her coffee table at home. Apparently Oprah knew a lot about relationships, but she'd missed the chapter on confronting assholes.

Chapter Five

"Girl fight!" The music stopped, plunging the bar into silence.

Then Evie heard it. First a shatter. Definitely a beer bottle. Next a scream. Definitely a woman. A crash—definitely a table. Tables that cost over a hundred dollars each. *Crap. Not tonight.*

Several people whipped out their cell phones and started snapping pictures, the flash on their cameras like an invasion of lightning bugs. Bill glanced over his shoulder, then turned back to the beer Evie had finally served to him, the commotion only warranting a grunt.

John Redman, an anorexic version of Bill, said, "You know, I heard Mike's Market lost a lawsuit to some chick toting stolen beer in her coat pockets. One of 'em popped out of her pocket, busted on the floor, and she slipped and got cut. Somebody took a picture of her bustin' her ass and she got herself a new Cadillac."

Visions of foreclosure signs flashed through Evie's mind.

Bill chimed in, "Yep, bought her that old mansion on Redwood too. Poor Mike's workin' the gas station down the road. I bet he's gotta pump gas into that purple Cadillac every week."

Evie choked. A liability suit would cost more than she could make in ten years.

"You need a drink, sugar?" John stretched his bony arm out, his own half-empty beer in hand.

Evie shook her head and cleared her throat, "No thanks."

Next the sound of splintering wood reached her ears, and Evie could no longer stay tucked behind the safety of the bar. She rushed into the crowd, claustrophobia prickling her flesh like a thousand fire ants. She elbowed her way toward the screams near the stage, the riot of emotions inside her like a Molotov cocktail. She burst free and barely kept from nose-diving into a girl fight gone wild.

Her grandpa sat on the stage in his army fatigues, swinging his legs and collecting bets. His long grey beard touched the center of his chest, hanging right above the POW lettering on his black T-shirt.

"Grandpa." Evie's tone sounded more like a parent's than a grandchild's.

C.W. glanced up and grinned, fanning the cash like a bookie on a winning night. A pipe hung from his mouth.

"Last call!" He hollered above the crowd. Shaking her head, Evie turned her attention to the two women brawling on the floor. They rolled, and when the brunette landed on top, she pulled her fake-jewel encrusted hand back to crack a slap across the blonde's face. The crowd went from a Prius purr to a Harley Davidson roar. She recognized them both. The brunette was Beverly, the blonde, Sue Ellen.

Evie's heart rate throttled. She held out her

arms, attempting to keep the crowd under control. The only way this was going to end was bad, bad, bad. But hopefully she could avoid a complete disaster.

"You slut. Don't you ever touch my man!" Beverly struck again. Sue Ellen kicked her assailant to the side, and both women scrambled to their feet.

Cheri appeared, much to Evie's relief, and they exchanged a long gaze that communicated a clear plan of divide and conquer. They nodded in unison and charged. Cheri hooked an arm around Sue Ellen's neck and yanked the screeching woman back. Evie grabbed a handful of the other woman's hair, yanked, and came up with clip-on extensions.

Bev staggered, clutching the fresh bald spot, and screamed. Evie shook her hand, trying to remove the clumps of fake hair from her fingers, but they stuck like brown leeches hanging on for their last meal.

Evie took a step back. "Now, let's just calm down. You know we don't allow fighting in the bar."

Bev swung around, her bloodshot eyes glowing wild with alcohol and fury. She lunged to the side and swiped a full pitcher of beer off a nearby table. She pulled back, ready to hurl the contents.

Evie held up her hands.

"You do that and I'm calling the cops!" Her heart rate drummed faster.

A pitcher of her ice-cold finest hit her in the face. She stood drenched, arms out, beer running in thick rivers from her fingertips.

Evie's logic disappeared along with her

sanity. She knew she was about to play road kill to Bev's Mack truck, but she was done playing victim for the day. Springing forward, she latched on to what was left of Bev's extensions and pulled the taller woman down to her own level.

Time slowed.

"Get her, Evie!"

"I want to change my bet!"

Shouts roared around her as she fought to hang on, the fear of being stomped into the ground becoming more of a reality with each passing second. Finally, Bev pulled Evie's fingers loose and Evie stumbled backward.

Bev charged.

But an arm appeared from the crowd and clotheslined Bev, throwing her to the ground in a twisted tangle.

Evie stood staring down at Bev, shock jacking her furious heart rate like she'd shotgunned a fifth can of Red Bull.

"You okay, honey?" Her mother stepped over Bev, careful not to get any beer on her heels.

Evie nodded, unable to form words.

Maxine thundered over to C.W. and stuck a long red nail in her father-in-law's face. "We're shorthanded as it is and you encourage this behavior in our bar?"

He slumped and took a drag from his pipe. "We were just having a little fun. No harm done."

The crowd returned to their tables, the band cranked up, and Bev's boyfriend, Jerry, helped Bev up from the floor. "I'm real sorry, Evie. I swear it won't happen again."

Evie turned, completely soaked in beer, to look at him and his woman. Those two assholes were staring at her like they had only watched the fight—not started it.

"Get the hell out of my bar." The words choked past her clenched teeth.

Maxine spun and closed the gap between them once more, striding on five-inch platforms like they were old tennis shoes. She propped a hand on her hip. "You need to wash up and change. We can't call anyone else in to help tonight."

Evie squashed the little girl inside crying out for a hug. After all, her mom wasn't the butterflies and fairies type. She was pure steel and thorns.

"I'll shower upstairs."

Cheri stepped to her side. "I've got a change of clothes in my truck."

"That's great. All my clothes are back home and I don't want to tend bar smelling like one."

As soon as Cheri left to grab the clothes, Evie grabbed her mom's arm, maybe a little too roughly. Maxine had at least six inches on her, plus another three from her teased brown hair. "Marcus just left."

Maxine's dark brows swooped down, but she didn't seem as angry as Evie'd expect. Heck, she didn't seem angry at all. "What did he say?"

"He encouraged us to reconsider his offer." *Or he'll kill you.*

"And?" Maxine continued to study her.

Fear crept down her spine and Evie resisted the urge to back up a step.

"Doesn't this seem like a problem we need to address?"

Maxine's right brow rose to a sharp point. "When did you decide to grow a backbone?"

Evie was on the verge of stomping her foot, something she hadn't done since high school. Her mother had always been able to pull her strings, but since Daddy's death, she no longer pulled. She yanked.

"When my ex-fiancé decided to show up in my bar. And now my mother is acting like it's not a bad thing."

Maxine pursed her lips into a thin red line. The battle was on. "Listen here, I might run the club, but I don't control it. We go with the vote. If you can't handle it, you need to get out." The club was what they called MRG when they discussed it in public.

Evie took a step back and her mouth fell open. Even though she and her mother didn't always see eye-to-eye, she relied on Maxine to be her rock. But instead of supporting Evie, she was crushing her will.

"Don't look at me like that. I'm trying to save you from more pain," Maxine said.

"Pain?" She fought to control the shrill edge to her voice. "You think ripping my membership away will make me stronger?"

Forget Dr. Phil, this crap belonged on Jerry Springer. Her mother's betrayal, whether it was couched in concern or not, stabbed deep.

"Dammit, Evie. I lost your father. I'm not turning a blind eye to your affairs."

"So you want to work for him? You want his money?" Evie said.

Maxine didn't respond. She didn't have to. The truth crashed into Evie, rocking her to her core.

Her soaking clothes seemed to freeze on her skin. Chills raced down her legs and anchored her feet to the floor.

"You know how I feel about that asshole. But

I don't get to tell him off. We go with the vote. Period."

Where were the tears? The remorse? But Maxine wasn't the type to cry. She was a machine. A machine that didn't care about her own daughter. "How could you do this to me?"

Maxine lifted her chin, looking down at Evie. Just like a mother would a pestering child. "It hasn't been decided yet. Look, I'll tell the club you need a break. I think that is best for everyone." In a show of rare show of affection, Maxine cupped Evie's cheek. "They will understand you need to sit this one out."

"I'll never understand how a mother could betray her own daughter."

Evie spun around, trying to hide the tears. This time she didn't have to fight her way through the crowd. Everyone gave her a wide berth. Her tennis shoes squished with each step, her already-loose blue jeans sagged, and her long sleeve T-shirt clung to her like a spandex glove.

As Evie burst through the back door, a match flared in front of her, the light temporarily blinding her. She stumbled sideways to avoid running into a lit cigarette.

"Hey." His Southern drawl put Matthew McConaughey to shame. Slow. Sexy. And familiar.

Her gaze traveled up the muscled torso to a pair of dark chocolate-brown eyes.

Holy crap.

"Hunter James." His name breathed past her lips on a whisper.

For the second time that night her heart stuttered and her stomach clenched tight.

Hunter blocked her path, his towering six-foot-three frame packaged in a tight-fitting black

T-shirt and jeans that showcased his muscles. His arms had to be twice the size they were the last time he'd been here. His gaze twice as intense. Her reaction twenty times that.

According to the town gossips, he'd been back in Mercy for a couple of weeks, but so far he'd avoided her. And she'd prayed daily he would stay away. Every time he came home on leave, he seemed to make it a point to show up here. At her bar. With another woman on his arm. Making sure she saw he'd moved on. And each time her heart broke a little more.

"Need some help?" he asked.

Her brain took a full minute to kick into gear, then another minute to reconnect to her mouth. "What?"

"You look like you could use some help. Can I do anything?" His serious voice passed through lips that were way too tempting.

She couldn't think. The man standing before her had gone AWOL with her heart over five years ago, like the tail end of a twister after a storm. Part of her had been happy he'd left. The other part had been devastated. Their love had been wild and crazy, but ultimately destructive.

She noticed the knotted wood cane leaning against the table beside him. "What's with the cane?"

Hunter grinned and shifted his weight to the side. "What's with the wet clothes?" He extinguished his cigarette and stepped away from the doorway leading to the upstairs apartment, his limp noticeable.

Evie crossed her arms over her chest, the action squeezing more beer out of her bra. Her lips pressed into a tight line and she forced herself to answer, "Wet T-shirt contest. It's a new thing we're trying."

Evie straightened her arms, clenching and unclenching her fists at her sides in time with the ticking in his jaw. A couple day's stubble graced the hard planes of his face, only a little shorter than the black hair buzzed close to his scalp. He looked as if he'd been chiseled from steel.

Hunter leaned in close and Evie's stomach knotted. Lust built inside her, pushing against her dam of resistance. "I bet you won."

He wasn't staring at her chest, she had to give him that. No, his target appeared to be her mouth. His head lowered to hers and her mind went blank. If she had been thinking like a full-grown woman, she would have jerked back before his lips made contact. But tonight her brain had pointed and aimed but failed to fire.

Hunter's mouth closed over hers. She froze, holding her body still even though she felt like the Mississippi River, swollen with floodwaters, shorelines about to explode with desire.

He deepened the kiss and her dams of resistance weakened, cracking under the pressure.

But something held her back. She didn't let him take over. She swam and fought against the rip current of Hunter James.

"God, I've missed your mouth. I can't believe I stayed away from you this long." His words yanked her back to reality.

Fury exploded through her limbs. "How did you manage?"

"I have no idea." His eyes promised sex. Mind blowing, body numbing, sore-for-three-days sex.

The words were out of her mouth before she

could seal her lips. "Yeah, well if you were expecting a welcome party, you're five years overdue."

Chapter Six

Hunter dangled a cold beer from his fingers and leaned his elbows against the bar. The dim glow from a few hanging Edison lights illuminated small circles along the scarred top. Probably a good thing. Too much light and he might see a cockroach crawl out of the peanut bowl.

Evie had sunk fast after her relationship with Marcus ended. Her fiancé had left her two years ago, upgrading from local country girl to city-born, politician-bred elitist. Then her father had been killed on the job, a hazard of being sheriff. Now Maxine and Evie owned a run-down dump.

How they got involved with the MRG was one of the first things he intended to find out. Hunter was missing one giant-ass piece of a three-thousand part jigsaw puzzle, and fuck all if he'd ever completed a puzzle in his life.

Why the hell had he agreed to this mission? In terms of discomfort, reconnecting with his ex ranked right up there with those getting-in-touch-with-your-inner-feelings classes the government required when demobilizing from deployment.

Maybe he could tolerate this a little more if she hadn't moved on with another man. Particularly such a scumbag.

And here Hunter sat. At her bar. Drinking her beer. And planning the best way to infiltrate her pants.

Gotta love karma, that twisted bitch. He downed his beer and banged the bottle down too hard on the bar. Cheri, a loud-mouthed redhead, jumped and snatched it up. She wasn't some shy virgin, but she backed away from him like he was the Grim-fucking-Reaper.

Hunter could kill an enemy without the slightest rise in his blood pressure. He could target, torture, and terminate with a smile. But right now, the emotional control he so relied upon had disappeared—all because of one woman. One small, blonde memory that had dug a pick ax into his mind and refused to let go.

When Evie had brushed past him in her rush to stop that fight, her fresh scent had nearly knocked him down. He'd watched as she tackled a woman nearly twice her size, ready to go all Superman and fly to the rescue. Just like before. And just like before, she hadn't needed him.

Hunter took a deep breath, forcing his abdomen to relax enough to allow air into his lungs. He clutched his fingers, counted to three, and cracked the closest thing to a smile he could manage. "Sorry, didn't mean to scare you. Rough week. Can I get a refill?"

Cheri paused, tilting her heart-shaped face to the right. Her pupils shrank the smallest millimeter, making her hazel eyes appear almost gold. Careful calculation snapped across her features. "Why should I get you a refill? Every time you come here, you hurt her."

His first thought was, good. He wanted to hurt her, just like she'd hurt him. But he kept that thought to himself. "I don't want that. I came tonight to apologize. For being such a prick."

God, the words might as well be soaked in battery acid as bad as they burned. Liar. He wasn't going to just hurt Evie, he planned to use her and then turn her over to the government.

"Ha, I'll believe that when I see it." Cheri made to turn away but Hunter reached across the bar and grabbed her arm. She stopped, looked at their connection like she would cut his arm off if he didn't let go. And he had no doubt she would.

"Fuck, you're not making this easy. Listen, I got shot, see the cane?" Hunter lifted his prop, a gnarled wooden cane for Evie's best friend to see. "It made me realize how wrong I've been."

Cheri peeled his fingers off her arm, one by one. "I'm not buyin'. You probably been shot before, and that never made you give a flying crap."

"You're right, I've been shot. I've been wounded. But this time was different. This time, I almost didn't make it." Hunter leaned in, making sure to hold her gaze. "And when I was lying there, bleeding out, the only face I could see was Evie's."

Cheri stared, hard. This crap better work. He'd pulled out all the stops. And used a trick he'd learned in training. If you're going to lie, tell a little truth.

Even if the truth like swallowing rusty nails.

"Crap. You're serious."

Hunter nodded. "I am. I tried to talk to her a few minutes ago, but she wasn't in the mood." And that was putting it lightly.

Cheri shook her head, grabbed a beer and

passed it to him. "I've seen the way you look at her when you think she won't see."

Hunter cringed and took a drink. Maybe he hadn't been as cavalier before as he'd thought.

"But I've also seen the way she looks at you. I tell you what, I will stay out of your way. But I swear to God if you hurt her, I'll cut off your balls and use them for fish bait."

Hunter opened his mouth, and then decided better. No need to respond. Cheri moved away to serve another customer.

"Hello, handsome." Tonya Lee Swopes sat down beside him, her long black hair teased and sprayed a lot higher than normal. "Wanna dance?" Her fingers brushed his, stayed a second too long. Her skin was soft, her body temperature a little cooler than his. She leaned forward, displaying a pair of tits to rival a young Dolly Parton's. He knew he could have her in his bed in a few hours. Or maybe even in his truck in a few minutes. But he didn't feel any heat.

The only woman he could picture had blonde hair and impossibly blue eyes.

"No, thanks." Hunter pulled away first and took a swig.

Tonya pouted, but the look only made him cringe. Her red lipstick was too bright. Clownish. "You're not being very nice tonight." Ignoring his fuck-off and go away glare, she slid a hand up his thigh. "Remember the last time we went out?"

Did he remember her drunken advances? Unfortunately, he remembered too well. "Actually, no. And if you don't mind, I want to be alone tonight."

Any semblance of charm disappeared and she stood, shoving her stool back so hard it crashed to the floor. "You don't know what you're missing asshole."

"You are right, and I don't want to find out."

Tonya's blush stained cheeks turned full-on red. She sputtered, and Hunter imagined, she was wracking her brain to come up with some type of come back. Shit. This was not the kind of attention he wanted or needed.

"Back off slut or I will kick you out of here."

Hunter turned to see Cheri pinning Tonya with a lethal glare. Tonya looked like she would explode, but somehow she managed to keep it in. Instead, she stomped off and Hunter breathed a sigh of relief.

"Wow. I would have rescued you, but I swear Tonya stalks me." Ranger righted her vacated stool and plopped down next to him, his dark blond hair sticking out in three different directions. Typical.

About fifty people crowded the room, if you included the bear holding a beer in the corner. Hunter nodded to C.W., Evie's grandpa, across the room. He was straddling a backward chair at a table occupied by nearly half the MRG.

Hunter snorted. "Gee. Thanks. Now I know who not to call in a pinch."

"Hey man, I can handle bullets, but not blood thirsty gold-diggers." Ranger looked over his shoulder, winked at Cheri, and had a beer in his hand in less than a second.

Hunter could have raised his brow, but there was no point. Women always fell at his brother's feet. Literally. One had even dropped to a knee and proposed to him a few years ago at a party. Too bad the only woman his brother wanted was the one married to his best friend.

"Anyway, you seen her yet?" Ranger said.

"Yes, I've seen her." Of course he'd seen Evie. He hadn't been able to peel his gaze off her all night.

"Any progress?"

"Well, since I've got to talk to her for all of two minutes before she told me to basically fuck off, I'd say the answer to your question is no." He'd made contact all right-and lost his ability to think. Kissing her hadn't been part of the plan. Not yet anyway. He sure hadn't planned on the atomic bomb of need that had exploded the minute he touched her.

Ranger cringed, "That bad, huh?"

"Apparently she has some hang-ups. But I'm sure we'll work through them." Maybe with a little light groveling on his part.

"You better. We don't have a lot of time." Ranger nodded at a group of men two tables over.

"No shit." Hunter didn't need a reminder that he had to swallow his pride and basically beg the woman who'd betrayed him to take him back.

"I take it the deputies don't know Sheriff Brown got kicked out on his ass?" The men at the table lazed back in their chairs and while their pressed shirts and jeans seemed normal enough, something about them was not quite right. Their mouths moved in conversation with each other, but their eyes constantly scanned the room, never lingering on one person for too long.

"I'm guessing the sheriff didn't want to tell his cronies he got punked down," Hunter said. The men continued to act casual, laughing and nodding, but not one person walked within a foot of their table. Hunter had been too busy doing recon on the Videls to even notice them.

"Probably right. They've got a really mean streak and if they scent blood in the water..." Ranger let his words trail off.

"The good sheriff will lose his position as head honcho."

Ranger took a long pull off his beer and swerved the barstool around so it faced the mirrored wall behind the bar.

One of the deputies grabbed a girl walking past their table and pulled her onto his lap. She couldn't be older than twenty-one and her expression closely resembled a bunny caught in a hunter's snare.

His hands roamed over her body while his deputies watched the show, doing nothing to help the girl escape his grasp. Hunter's muscles went tense, and in one move he sat his beer on the bar and his feet on the ground.

Ranger wrapped a hand around his arm, barely managing to restrain him. "Don't. He won't do anything in front of everyone."

The young girl finally managed to escape and scurried away, disappearing into a circle of women near the restroom. "Too bad we're on a mission. I'd mop up the shit stains on the floor with the bastard's face."

"Don't worry, I'm pretty sure before all this is over, you'll get your chance."

Apparently everyone in his hometown had a price tag, including Evangeline Videl. The Wharf, the MRG—all around him there was evidence she was in desperate need of funds. And would be willing to do anything to get the money—including betraying their country.

But no matter how much Hunter tried to picture Evie slinging an AR-15 over her shoulder, he couldn't make the image stick. "I hope so. I'm gonna make sure he gets special attention."

Ranger shook his head, his gaze sharp but amused. Hunter had never tried to be the nice one. He hadn't seen the point. Family mattered. His country mattered. Loyalty mattered. Other than that... Sure, he had friends from high school, and he probably would have continued to hang out with them if he'd stayed in Mercy. Shit, he'd probably be working the ranch with his dad, drinking beer every Friday night with the boys.

But Hunter had joined the military a couple years out of high school, leaving behind most of his relationships in Mercy, and he hadn't looked back.

"So where is Evie?" Ranger leaned sideways, his blue shirt pulling tight over his shoulders.

"She broke up the fight and one of the women threw a pitcher of beer on her. She took off out the back."

Ranger's smile disappeared into the first scowl Hunter had seen all evening. "She go home?"

"Nope. Upstairs." They'd been watching the Wharf and its occupants for over two weeks now. The apartment upstairs was where the MRG met.

"Where are Hoyt and Jared?" Hunter asked.

"Back at base. Hoyt's pulling the satellite images of the river and all the points of interest. Jared's going over the intel from Mr. K." Ranger's words were tinged with bitterness. A bitterness that grabbed Hunter by the bones and hung on tight.

Mr. K was Mr. J's replacement. Hunter had yet to meet Mr. K, and he'd avoid it for as long as possible. He'd learned his lesson. Never get too close. Never care.

TF-S had lost two men that night. Mr. J, Hunter's mentor, and Shane Carter. Shane had been secretly classified MIA. His wife knew, but no one else.

"Anything new on Shane?" Hunter asked. So far, they'd found out nothing beyond that Shane was either being held hostage by Al Seriq or was dead.

Ranger paused, his beer halfway to his lips. "No."

Infiltrating the MRG and following the weapons to Al Seriq was their best hope of finding Shane, taking down the terrorist and hopefully saving their hometown.

Hunter lifted his gaze and surveyed the room through the mirror's reflection. His gaze slammed into C.W.'s. Time to implement their plan.

Hunter slapped a hand on Ranger's shoulder and stood. "Go time."

Chapter Seven

Evie pounded up the outside staircase, her footsteps thudding as fast as her heart rate. The old wooden steps creaked and groaned like an old man with arthritis, protesting her mistreatment of their shabby structure. Rain beat a steady staccato on the tin roof covering the stairs and the dock below them, providing some cover for her hasty retreat.

It had been raining relentlessly for weeks now, but rain was always welcome in the summer, when the crops were bone dry and liable to break in a strong wind. As liable as Evie was to break right now. The first time she'd seen Hunter in years and she'd been covered in beer. Shit. This wasn't exactly the kind of look-what-you've-been-missing appearance she would have hoped to channel.

Still, there was the type of rain that fed the crops, and there was the type of rain that caused a flood. The Wharf, built on ten-foot stilts from fifty-year-old cypress wood, fared better than most structures in a storm. But the ground was saturated and the Mississippi was swelling to capacity. Talk of flooding were spreading through Mercy like the flu, apparently multiplying as fast as ex-boyfriends.

Everything she had worked so hard to build could be destroyed in a flood, but there wasn't anything she could do to stop it. Powerless. Once again, she was powerless. She slammed the door to the small apartment over the bar and leaned against it for support. Tonight had taken a lot out of her and it wasn't even over.

But this was no time to fall apart. She could analyze and dissect everything that had happened later. Now she had to get back to work.

Evie stripped out of her soaking clothes and turned on the shower, letting the hot water wash everything away. She braced both hands on the tile in front of her, dropped her head as she struggled for control. Her mother's betrayal almost hurt worse than her father's death, and for it to come on the night she'd run into both Marcus and Hunter... She reached for her safe place, the blank void in her mind where nothing and no one could reach her.

She couldn't find it.

Long-buried tears spilled out and Evie wrapped an arm around her middle, holding in the sob that threatened to wrench her gut in half. She bent forward and sucked in air, trying to tame the tremors wracking her body.

Marcus disgusted her. Just being near him made her want to vomit. His careful elegance hid a monster she'd discovered too late.

Hunter disgusted her too. He'd left without a word five years ago, leaving a void she had barely managed to fill. But instead of repulsion, her body craved his like a crack addict craves a needle.

A hand shot through the shower curtain.

Her heart slammed against her chest like a

two-ton truck hitting a tree at ninety miles an hour. A scream stuck in her throat. She jumped back. Slipped. Her feet shot north and she caught herself just before her ass slapped the bathroom floor.

"Holy shit, are you okay?" Cheri popped her head around the shower curtain, which was when Evie realized there was a bottle of shampoo in her hand.

Evie pulled herself upright, heart still racing, and grabbed the bottle, stifling the impulse to use it to smack her friend.

"You're welcome." Cheri's voice dripped with the sweetness of acid.

As if she would thank Cheri for scaring the holy hell out of her. She popped the top and took a cautious sniff. The scent of spicy vanilla hit her.

"You shoulda kept on your toes. Everyone knows Bev fights dirty," Cheri said.

Evie applied the shampoo to her hair before answering, "I know."

"She could have punched you," Cheri continued as Evie rinsed her hair, apparently content to carry on a mostly one-sided conversation. "You're lucky Maxine stepped in."

Evie cut the water off and yanked a towel down from the rack to dry off. "I know. Believe me. I know. Anything else?"

"Yeah, you need to hurry it up. I left your mom behind the bar."

Evie wrapped the old brown towel around her body and jerked the shower curtain open.

"Yes, ma'am. I know Bev could've kicked my ass. Yes, I'm glad my mom bailed me out. And yes, I know I need to hurry up," Evie said, not bothering to control her volume.

Cheri didn't even try to look apologetic. She strolled into the connected bedroom and plopped down on the bed. "Good. Now that you're through thinking about that asshole, you can get dressed and get back to work." Cheri's lips stretched over her pearlies in a huge grin.

Evie blew out a breath and turned to look at the clothes her friend had laid out on the twin bed. "Where's the rest?"

"You're looking at it." The expression on Cheri's face wouldn't have looked out of place on an Olympian who'd won the gold medal.

Evie regarded her in silence, ready to take her best friend from gold to bronze. The clothes, if that's what you could call them, would barely cover a Barbie-doll, let alone a full-grown woman. Hot pink tank top. Jeans cut so low she'd be lucky if her ass didn't hang out.

"What? This is my cutest outfit."

Evie had one of those moments that felt like it stretched from seconds into minutes and minutes into hours. Cheri was her best friend. End of story. But their taste in clothing was Victoria's Secret and Betty White different.

Maybe she could blow dry her beer-soaked clothes?

"Oh hell no, I know what you're thinking. You are going to put this outfit on right now," Cheri said, rising from the bed.

The halter-top would cover her stomach, and her scar, but put her boobs on major display. "I can't wear that. It's been years since I've worn anything that sexy." Evie trembled and inwardly cursed.

"You listen here. I am sick of watching you hide beneath ugly clothes two sizes too big." Cheri crowded Evie's personal space down to about two inches.

Evie sucked in a breath and gripped the towel tight enough to crush it into a Kleenex. Fear bubbled in her stomach.

"I've stood by for as long as I can, but dammit, you've been hiding for two years." Cheri grabbed her ice-cold hands.

Evie's chest tightened and she pulled away. Jagged shards of memory from her last night with Marcus sliced through her, still sharp enough to cut deep.

"I'm the one who found you. I took you to the hospital. I thought you were going to die." Cheri's words stumbled out in rough stops and starts.

Sobs built in Evie's chest. She swallowed, but her throat just squeezed tighter. She remembered. She wasn't conscious when Cheri took her to the hospital, but her friend's soft voice was what had pulled her back from the darkness. Part of her had not wanted to come back.

"You didn't die, you survived. You survived and started over, but you're still letting him win."

Evie broke. Her legs gave out and she crumpled to the floor. The sobs broke free and she buried her face in her hands. She knew it was true, that she was still dangling from Marcus's puppet strings like a bad replica of Pinocchio. Well, Evie was tired of impersonating herself. Tired of being too scared to draw attention to dress like someone her age. Too scared to let anyone get close. Too scared to do anything.

Cheri dropped to her knees and wrapped her arms around her friend, and for a long moment, the two of them sat there crying together.

"Dammit, what the hell is wrong with me?"

Evie leaned back and wiped her tears.

Cheri grabbed her hand, "Nothing is wrong. I wouldn't expect you to be normal after what happened. But you gotta quit acting like a wimp."

"You can't talk to me like that." Evie sniffed and wiped her running nose with the corner of her towel.

Cheri snorted. "Sure."

Evie had introduced Cheri to the MRG early on, right after her family had started putting the militia group back together.

And her no-shit-no-service attitude was one of the main reasons Evie had asked her. That and the fact that Cheri had family along the river who helped them hide any one from Mercy that the sheriff or Marcus targeted.

"I'm talking about respect. Are you going to keep letting everyone run over you?"

Evie sniffed, rubbed her nose. "It doesn't matter anyway. Apparently I'm not part of the club anymore."

Cheri jumped to her feet, paced out of the tiny bedroom, over to the MRG table and kicked it. "I knew they were up to something. What happened?"

Evie filled her in on her conversation with her mother, holding her hurt in by a thread. "Basically, everyone would rather take the money than hold to the cause."

"No. You're not going to let them." Cheri pulled Evie up and grabbed her shoulders. "You let this happen and you might as well have never left Marcus. Except this time you won't be the only one in his pocket—we'll all be there."

"What choice do I have?" Evie wanted to scream. Shout. But she was too tired. If her own mother was willing to turn her back on her, what was the point?

"You are stronger than this. Think. You can find a solution." Cheri said.

"What can I do? Marcus threatened to kill my mom if I prevent this deal from going through...not to mention the fact that my mom just kicked me out. He *runs* this town! How am I supposed to fix anything?"

"I don't know. We'll figure it out. But you have to want to believe in yourself. You need to put on your big girl panties." Cheri glanced in the bathroom, at the granny-panties hanging over the edge of the bathtub.

"I know." Evie let her head fall into her hand.

Cheri picked the red thong off the bed and dangled it in front of Evie like bait. "The woman who wears this is in control of her life. The woman who wears those," Cheri pointed to Evie's beer-soaked undergarments and shuddered, "might as well move into Magnolia Nursing Home."

Evie snatched the thong from Cheri's fingertips and stood. Her veins heated with something she hadn't felt in a long time. Something she'd pushed to the back shelf in her mind. Something that felt a lot like confidence.

"You're right. I can fix this." Evie forced the words out, her voice still husky with emotion.

Cheri gave her a hug. "That's right. With my help. And after you kick some major ass, I expect to be promoted to VP." She headed to the door. "I'll leave you to it, El Presidente." With that, she left and closed the door softly behind her. Evie dropped the towel. She stepped into the red satin thong, one foot at a time, and slid the panties up, savoring the feel of the sexy material. She'd worn cotton so long she'd forgotten the pure sin of satin on skin. The matching bra with its front closure went on next, followed by the low-slung jeans.

She turned then and strode to her meeting table. The original MRG had carved those letters into the wood many years ago. Before she was born, back when C.W. was a young man.

Evie lovingly traced the worn grooves in the lacquered cedar. This was her family now. This was her life. It was time to take it in both hands.

Evie squared her shoulders, went back to the bed, and pulled on the tiny pink top. Yes, it was time to lay all her old fears to rest and live up to the Videl family name.

First order of business: kick Marcus's offer to the curb, no matter what resistance she faced from her mother or anyone else, and then kick his ass if he had a problem with that. No more missus-nice-gal.

Was she physically strong? No. Brutal? Maybe. Cunning? Absolutely.

Forget Kill Bill. It was time to kill Marcus.

Chapter Eight

Hunter grabbed his cane and approached the table surrounded by MRG. No one rose or acknowledged him with more than a nod. They all looked to one man for guidance. C.W. Videl.

Hunter realized two things. The people at the table weren't all Grandpas. In fact, a few of them were closer to his age. And a few of them weren't men.

"Well, well. If it ain't Evie's very own Houdini. Get tired of the disappearin' act, boy?" C.W.'s voice came out deep and scratchy, like he'd swallowed a bucket of rusty nails for supper.

"Yep."

"What's wrong, boy? Couldn't handle the military?" Another man, this one with long grey hair and a handle bar mustache to rival Sam Elliot's, asked the question.

"Not the military, old man. Just a haji bullet."

"And what, you decided to come home crying? Trying to pull disability, right?" Mustache added.

C.W. had a dip in his mouth, and he looked liable to spit it at Hunter any minute.

Hunter kept his expression blank. The

comments didn't bother him. He knew they were a test. "I don't need disability to handle my shit. But he sounds like he's speaking from experience." Hunter turned back to Mustache. "You must know your way around the system pretty good."

Mustache stood, his face turning dark red. Hunter let his gaze drop briefly to the MRG label on his shirt before lifting it to meet the man's gaze once more.

"What're you sayin' boy?"

"I'm saying only weak, pansy-ass men live off the American tax dollar. And I bet you get your blue check every month."

Mustache kicked his chair back, sending it crashing to the floor. Before he could take a step toward Hunter, C.W. grabbed his arm, stopping him. "Hold on, Lafoy. That boy's messing with you." C.W. spit into the Styrofoam cup in his hand and turned back to Hunter. "What do you want?"

"I wanted to let you know I'm back. For good. And I have every intention of seeing your granddaughter." Hunter knew C.W. from childhood. He knew the man could sniff out a lie from another town. Hunter's best shot was honesty. Or at least part of it. He wasn't home for good, but he would be dating Evie again. And soon.

"Well, now, any of us can 'see' her." C.W. said.

A smattering of low laughter spread across the group. Hunter tensed, and then forced himself to relax. Play his cards right. "I want to date her. I'm just letting you know, out of respect."

"And hoping I'll mind my own business and stay out of your way?" C.W.'s tone was sharp and blunt.

"Yes. After my injury, I realized how stupid I've been. And how much she means to me." Somehow, the words weren't as bitter the second time around. They rang with honesty. An honesty he would never be ready to face.

C.W. squinted at him, and Hunter fought the urge to hold his breath. *Remember, this is just a game.*

The old man spit in his cup, and said, "Close calls make you realize a lot of things."

"Cyprene Willis Videl. I knew I'd find you here."

Hunter turned and stopped cold. Mrs. Trudy Van Meter. She'd been matriarch of the First Southern Methodist Church of Mercy for as long as Hunter could remember.

"Trudy, what the hell're you doin' here?" C.W. stood, his voice a few octaves higher than it had been one minute before. His face had gone a little pale, besides.

"Oralee Bates called me. Said she'd seen you flirting with some hussy." Mrs. Trudy plopped her fists on her generous pale-pink clad hips. Her blazer and skirt were pressed stiffer than Hunter's dress blues. An American flag pin sparkled on her lapel. Her short white-grey hair was sprayed into submission.

Another man from the table spoke. This one was smaller than the rest. Scraggly. His Carhartt jacket was torn in a few places. "What's it to ya, lady?"

Mrs. Trudy's already straight spine stiffened and Hunter could swear he heard wood crack. "Not that it's any of your business, but Cyprene and I are dating. And he made promises."

"How the hell would Oralee know what I was doing in here unless she was here too?" C.W. resembled the proverbial boy with his hand caught in a cookie jar. Only the boy had a long grey beard and the cookie jar had alcohol in it.

"Never you mind that. What do you have to say for yourself?"

Her tone was so sharp Hunter took a step back. He'd learned from an early age to respect his elders. But that didn't mean he had to stand close to a grenade in the form of Trudy Van Meter.

The people closest to where she stood had the same idea and cleared out.

Hunter tipped his head. "C.W."

C.W. didn't take his gaze from his lady. And Hunter didn't blame him. The look in her gaze screamed kill shot and C.W. was her target.

"Now, Trudy. I was just having some fun with the boys. I ain't broke no promises." C.W.'s rough voice disappeared, replaced by the smooth, dulcet tones of a Southern gentleman doing just a touch of begging.

Hunter didn't need to stay around to see the fall-out. He headed out onto the screened-in porch and straight into the summer heat. Darkness permeated the night, but the dingy yellow lights hanging from the ceiling provided enough illumination for him to see metal folding chairs and scuffed up wood tables. The exact place Evie had ran from him earlier this night.

In a normal place, several weeks of rain might take the heat down a few degrees. Not in Mercy. The Mississippi Delta didn't play around. She reached a hot hand down a man's throat and ripped the air right out.

He'd been on missions in the desert for the

majority of the past five years. The temperature in those places could burn your skin in thirty minutes flat, melt the pads off your fingers if you grabbed a metal door handle without gloves. It didn't hold a candle to the South's deadly concoction of heat and humidity.

A few die-hard smokers littered the porch, standing far enough apart so the air circling down from the fan stood a chance at reaching them. Mosquitos battled the wire mesh of the screen for entrance to the flesh-fest.

A flash of bright pink tugged his gaze to the right. When he realized what he was looking at, all the air rushed out of his lungs and the heat on the porch kicked up twenty degrees in the space of one second.

Holy hell.

Evangeline Videl. All five-feet-two inches of sex on a stick. Her shirt was like a flashing neon sign through the haze of cigarette smoke, framing her perfect breasts in a way that had his hands clenching. Her navel peeked out above low-slung jeans that hugged hips made by God himself.

Hunter's body went on instant alert.

He gave the men around him a get-the-hell-out-or-die stare. He didn't speak. He didn't have to. The smokers took one last drag, extinguished their cigarettes, and beat it back inside. Evie pushed through the screen door and stopped.

She stood on the other side of the long porch, clutching the back of a chair. The half-moon cast dingy light across the porch, tingeing everything a washed-out yellow. The sound of rushing water competed with the night crawlers' croaking. Hunter took a moment to study her. And get his shit together.

"I fucked up." The words tasted as bitter as a hot Afghani beer. He didn't want to be here, working this mission and pasting on a fake smile for his ex-girlfriend. She'd been the first, and only, girl he'd ever loved. And she'd torn his heart apart by cheating on him with Marcus. He wanted to be back at his forward operating base at Camp Tajik, playing cards and planning his next operation. Away from all this baggage he'd left behind.

"The understatement of the year?" She studied him a moment and turned away, walking to the porch railing. A part of him felt the loss of her gaze and wanted it back. The other part breathed a sigh of relief. When her baby blues settled on him, he lost the ability to think.

A breeze fanned her long hair sideways, revealing the smooth skin at her waist. He remembered how soft she was all over, how his hands could span her waist as he pulled her close.

Awareness trickled through his blood, heated his veins. Frustration followed close behind. She affected him, no matter how much he wished she didn't. Across a room. Across a country. Across a goddamn ocean.

His plans threatened to evaporate like smoke.

Hunter shook his head. *No.* This was just his body remembering how hot their sex had been. How right she had felt beneath him. There was nothing wrong with attraction, as long as it didn't twist into something more.

"Maybe. Maybe I'm just a little hard headed." He moved around the tables, his leg a throbbing reminder that he hadn't completely healed. Her gaze shot to the wounded limb, seeing more than he wanted. As much as he detested the weakness, it played into his plan.

Her blonde brows drew together. "What happened?"

Hunter stopped when he was a foot away and leaned a hip against the porch rail. "Gunshot. It was a through-and-through, but in a bad spot. I'm taking some time off to let it heal right before going back overseas."

Her blue eyes darkened with concern, despite the mask of indifference on her face. She'd always detested violence. Or so he'd thought.

"Was anyone else hurt?"

Hunter shrugged. He wasn't ready to talk about Shane, and besides, he couldn't reveal classified information. "Nah. I screwed up and took a hit. It happens in combat." *Why was she acting so concerned?* "Anyway, it was bad enough for them to send me home. So here I am."

"Why come here now?" Evie said, her voice subdued, blending with the soft cadence of the river.

"I told you, for the beer." He paused, looked out at the river, not really seeing the scenery. "No. That's not true. I came for you."

Evie shook her head and he could feel her disbelief. Hell, he could feel his own. He was going to have to tread carefully with his words or she would sense his insincerity.

"Hunter, you've been in and out of here on leave. You've made it a point to bring every slut in a hundred miles to parade in front of me. Why do you suddenly want me now?"

Because my CO threatened to send me to guard the French foreign minister if I didn't get into your pants and get information. Even he knew that wouldn't exactly put him in her good graces.

He'd thought about this woman almost every day since leaving Mercy. He'd never thought he'd return home to face her. But in the end there hadn't been a choice. "Honestly, Evie, I don't know. All I know is, the harder I try to forget you, the more I remember. And...the more I want you."

* * *

Evie jerked back, his words sucker-punching her in the chest. In the heart. This was the man she'd dreamed of for years, praying he would come back in one piece. The man who'd stomped on her heart harder than Marcus had stomped on her body. Now he stood right here in front of her. Not more than a foot away, wanting her.

A stray breeze from the fan blew her hair across her face and she brushed it back, her hand shaking. Evie tucked her hand in her back pocket before Hunter could see how much he affected her. The last thing she could afford to do was give him ammunition to use against her.

"I don't believe that," she said. "You left. Not me. And you expect me to think you thought about me once? Do I look stupid?" The shaking in her hands spread upward, past her shoulders, and took over her whole body.

Hunter's dark brown eyes held hers, and she felt like he could see inside her. His hands cupped her shoulders and forced her to face him. "Not stupid. Scared. Just as scared as I am."

Evie scoffed. "You? Scared? Haven't you been off playing Rambo or something?"

Hunter laughed and Evie felt it all the way down to her toes. "Rambo? I'm a thirty-year-old combat veteran with a gunshot wound and what I suspect is the beginning of arthritis in my knees."

As he said it, Hunter leaned forward and rubbed his thigh. She cringed. What if he was telling the truth? What if he had come home to reclaim her?

Did she still want him?

"Maybe you should sit down?"

"I've never let a few aches get in the way of my mission."

The breath left her in a whoosh. From the look Hunter was giving her, it was clear *she* was his mission.

He closed the small gap between them and the scent of earth and raw male power flooded her senses. All she would need to do was lean forward a few inches to touch her lips to his. See if they were as soft as she remembered. As demanding.

Lust tied her stomach into a knot a Boy Scout leader couldn't untangle. Hunter's gaze dropped to her lips. This time when his lips touched hers it was tender. Gentle. Brief. And he was the one who pulled away. But not before his touch unleashed a torrential downpour in her body that left her drowning in desire.

* * *

"Am I interrupting?" Ranger said.

Hunter jerked back and pinned his brother with a deathly stare. The reaction wasn't what he would have expected. Ranger leaned against the back door of the bar, arms crossed, his expression...worried. Awareness tugged at Hunter's conscious. This wasn't just some brotherly jest meant to disrupt Hunter's chance to score with Evie.

On the heels of that thought came another: He had completely forgotten his goal in the space of a second.

Evie was glaring at Hunter, her cheeks flushed, her eyes wild.

He frowned. If she left in this state of mind, he would lose all the ground he'd gained. "Stay put," he said to her.

"I need to talk to you," Ranger said.

"Not right now. We're trying to catch up on a few things," Hunter said.

Evie pushed past him. "Actually, we weren't catching up on anything. I need to get back to work."

He grabbed her arm, pulled her to his side, "Stay. Please."

She ignored him, squirming in his grasp. "You need to let me go. Now."

"But I'm not through talking to you."

"Sucks for you. I'm warning you one last time. If you don't let go, you're gonna regret it."

Hunter ignored the threat. He had no intention of letting her go now. Not when he finally had a clear head again. Not while she was still breathing hard and thrown off balance. "Don't do this."

Ranger cleared his throat, but they both ignored him. Hunter knew he needed to establish control.

Evie's mutinous expression slackened into annoyance, but he held her stare. Her stubborn streak had grown. She held out for another minute before dropping her gaze and nodding.

Hunter relaxed and focused on Ranger. The look on his brother's face added new stress to the situation, but at least Evie wasn't arguing with him anymore.

"Ranger, give me ten minutes. Tops. I won't be much..." Hunter broke off mid-sentence, sucking in a breath as sharp pain stabbed his shin.

"Jerk. You're not my boyfriend. You're not even my friend. I don't know who you are, but you don't control me!" Evie ducked and darted around him. Ranger stepped to the side, pulling the glass door to the bar open for her to run inside.

Hunter rubbed his shin, anger and annoyance mixing with amusement. "I'm going to tan her ass for that."

"I don't know, brother, I'm not sure she'd agree to that particular form of foreplay."

Hunter had been so distracted he'd let a girl get the best of him. She'd fooled him with her innocent look.

Again.

Fury edged out any traces of amusement. This was the last time she'd catch him off guard. His jaw clenched and the throbbing in his ears commanded his attention more than his throbbing shin.

"You sure do know how to get under her skin." Ranger must have sensed the dark direction of his thoughts.

"That's not all I plan on getting under."

Chapter Nine

Ranger paced the gravel and grass lot underneath the bar, eyeing the chipped paint and cracks on the stilts holding The Wharf upright. His T-shirt was soaked from running through the rain, and water dripped from his hair into his face.

The rain poured down in a deafening roar, drowning out all other sound. The mosquitos wouldn't even brave this kind of weather.

Ranger loved to party and he loved being around pretty women. The women especially. But the perfume and cigarette smoke in the bar had turned his stomach three shades shy of soured milk. At first he'd been fine, dancing and flirting and relaxing with Mercy's best. But thirty seconds into the second song, he'd caught sight of a baby-faced kid in dress blues standing by the door.

Maybe it was the navy-blue hat he clutched in his perfect white gloves. Maybe it was the fact that the greenhorn looked about ready to piss his pants.

The kid stood with his shoulders back, chin up, but he was still six inches shorter than everyone else around him.

Ranger dipped his dancing partner, placed a

kiss on her lips, and deposited her back with her friends. He didn't give her time to protest. He turned and headed toward the exit. The soldier stood unmoving just a foot inside the door.

"You looking for someone?" Ranger said, getting his first look up close. God, the military was getting desperate.

"No, sir." He stammered, shifting his feet. "I mean, yes, sir. I am looking for Chief Hunter James. I went to his father's residence and was directed to this place."

Ranger's old man, Hank, had about as much patience with newbies as he did for weeds growing in his fields. Hank tended to take the more direct approach of scaring the ever-living crap out of impressionable young troops.

"Did you just graduate basic?" The light caught the kid's brass name badge. *Specialist Green.* Perfect.

Green turned red and ducked his head. Yep. He couldn't be more than a year out. "My brother is in here. What do you need him for?"

"I'm afraid I can't say, sir. I must speak with Chief James."

"If you want to find my brother you have to go through me, and he is currently occupied." With figuring out how to get in a certain blonde beauty's good graces. She should come with her own warning label: explosive material—handle with caution.

Hunter acted casual, like this mission wasn't a big deal. But Ranger knew his brother. He felt his tension, saw the anger barely banked behind his eyes. Hunter had loved one woman in his entire life. One. And now he had to get up close and personal with her. Use her.

Sure he'd dated other women, but he'd never gotten close again. He said he didn't care, that this was a cake mission, but Ranger knew without a doubt his brother was in for a bigger challenge than any they'd faced on their covert ops.

"Sir?"

Goddamn, was he expected to blindly babysit the kid until his brother was free to talk? The urge to grab the specialist and shake the information out of him pounded in his blood. He acted on the impulse and pulled Green toward him by the lapels. "Why the fuck are you here? Is it because of Shane?"

Even the name tasted bitter on his tongue. Shane Carter. His best friend. The one guy who'd always stuck his neck out for Ranger, who'd always had his back. And Ranger had left him behind.

Green's legs did a little kick, his feet a few inches off the ground, and his hands grabbed at Ranger's wrists. "Please, sir, let me down."

Ranger had been through enough SERE training to read body language. To know what wasn't being said. He pulled Green closer, their faces close enough for their breaths to blend. "Tell me."

"It's regarding Staff Sergeant Carter."

The oxygen disappeared. Ranger's vision tunneled and his body went rigid, his muscles locking down on his organs.

Shane. Suddenly the dress blues made sense. He flung Green away, the need to dig into the specialist turning into the need to escape. He didn't want to hear the news.

"Meet us outside in five minutes, got it?" Ranger didn't wait to see if the boy followed orders. He turned instead to find Hunter. He got one step and collided with his brother. "You need to follow me. Now."

Ranger and Hunter headed out the front door and down the stairs together. Specialist Green paced the gravel and grass underneath the Wharf, obviously nervous.

Now here they were, waiting to hear whatever news the kid had, and Ranger was the one who couldn't hold still. And he wouldn't be able to until he knew about his best friend. If he was alive. If he was being held for ransom. If he was dead.

"We've got some privacy. Spit it out." Ranger eyed Green with venom.

"Captain James, Captain Grey sent me as soon as we received the package," Green said. The boy was stubborn, refusing to cower under Ranger's glare. Any other time he would have given Green props for his nerve. Not tonight.

Hunter stood still. No expression. No response. A fucking statue. He might as well have been waiting on the latest weather report.

Ranger's nerves grew thin, ready to snap like a worn rubber band. He stalked toward Green, ready to do what needed to be done to wrangle the information from their reluctant messenger. Ranger knew it wasn't the boy's fault, but he couldn't help it. It felt like Green had thrown an RPG of information and Ranger was waiting for it to explode.

"What package?" Hunter said, his voice cutting into the killing rage eating away at Ranger's sanity.

"Tell us what the hell is going on with Shane." Ranger crossed his arms and stood tall, looking down at Specialist Green. The boy was just that. A boy. No facial hair, no muscle tone, no height. Even his voice was weak.

The specialist stuttered and turned his hat in circles. When he spoke next, his voice dropped in volume. "I'm sorry to be the one to tell you, sir, but command received a package containing Sergeant Carter's remains three days ago. DNA confirmed it was him yesterday."

Ranger had braced himself for the news, but the words cut into him with razor precision. His ears started to roar, drowning out the rain. The thunder. His heartbeat pounded like small explosions in his head.

His fault. It was all his fault. Ranger turned to Hunter, his gaze helpless. Hunter held up a hand. "DNA? If we received his remains, why did you need DNA to confirm?"

"Ah... We received some of him. Not enough for a positive visual ID." Green's voice sounded weak and wobbly now. He pulled at his collar and stepped back, the rain keeping him caged, but he kept to the perimeter.

"You haven't been to Shane's wife's house yet, have you?" The realization dawned fast and hard, knocking the wind from his chest. Green was here to collect Hunter and deliver the news to Amy Carter.

Ranger threw his head back, neck muscles taut and straining, the blood whooshing through his body so thick he thought he would explode.

He couldn't let Green tell Amy. She would need someone strong to tell her. To be there for her. To hold her.

Ranger raked a hand through his hair, sending a fresh slew of water down his face and neck. The image of Shane falling replayed over and over in his mind. And he was standing there thinking about holding his best friend's wife. What kind of sick pervert was he?

Green cleared his throat. "We also received a video of his execution. The CIA has confirmed its authenticity. They are trying to keep it quiet, but the media will know within the week."

"What?" Hunter said, his voice loud enough to drown out Ranger's bellow of pain. "When can you get me in the air? We're going to kill Al Seriq and every man aligned with him."

"Hunter, call the commander. I can be ready to go in an hour." Ranger needed this, needed to avenge Shane.

"Captain, I need you to come with me before you do anything," Green said.

Hunter and Ranger froze. Amy. Amy needed to be told.

"So you want me to tell his wife, my friend, that her husband is dead?" Hunter moved toward Green, his dark brows rising in two angry arches.

"Fuck, no. He needs a sidekick for this mission. He's too much of a coward to do it himself." Ranger knew his words were harsh, but he was spiraling out of control, so he simply didn't care.

Ranger looked up, the sounds of bass and laughter seeping down to them through the wood planks above them. He had no intention of letting either one of them tell Amy, but then, his brother probably knew that.

"Look, Green, we all need a drink," Hunter said. "It's late, and even though I haven't seen Amy Carter in almost a year, I know she will be getting ready for bed by now. Why don't you wait until tomorrow morning? Ranger can meet you at your hotel and drive y'all out to their ranch?"

Green swallowed, sweat dripping down his temples. "You don't think she would want to know now?"

"You want to take away her last night of peace? She won't sleep for the next six months. Why break her heart this late at night? Ranger prayed the kid bought his logic.

Hunter moved to his side. "I agree. It's better to deliver bad news in the light of day, give her a chance to call her family so she won't have to be alone."

Green nodded. "Of course, sir."

Ranger's gaze cut to his brother, the silent message clear.

"Green, how about I buy you a drink?" Hunter hooked an arm around Green's shoulder and dragged him toward the steps leading up to the bar. Green shot a glance at Ranger before doing what any person with half a molecule still firing would do—following Hunter up the stairs before Ranger lost his shit.

Ranger waited until they disappeared inside and took off at a dead run for his truck, barely giving the engine time to roll over before he threw her into drive and squalled out of the parking lot.

Ten minutes later he turned off the highway and drove down a driveway lined with Bradford pears. All of them were well tended and trimmed to match, the grass mowed short but thick. Ranger slowed when her porch light came into view. Amy always kept it on when Shane was gone.

Ranger squeezed the steering wheel so tight it should have bent off the frame. Sweat broke out on his forehead and he cranked up the AC to full blast. Now that he was here he didn't know if he could do it. Give her the news. Break her heart.

He parked and cut the lights. He put his forehead on the steering wheel and took deep breaths, building up the strength to open his truck door. Dammit, why Shane? Why couldn't it have been someone else?

Maybe he should just drive away and let Green be the Grim Reaper. She might never forgive him for being the bearer of such news. *No.* He sat up straight and focused. It was his duty. His.

He couldn't put off telling her any longer. Ranger walked slowly to her front door, the effort to climb her three front porch steps as taxing as mounting Everest.

He knocked. Waited. Realized how wet his shirt was and wrung some of the water out.

Amy opened her front door, a loose dark robe draped around her. She folded her arms over her front, snagging some of her long auburn hair with her elbow.

Her gaze held him; he couldn't rip away from her eyes' dark brown depths. Her lips had always been a little too big, but they were perfect to him, and right now they offered a hesitant smile.

She pulled the door open. "Ranger?" She reached forward and brushed his cheek with her thumb. When she realized he was crying, her eyes turned wary. "Shane?"

He tried to speak. But the words wouldn't go past the huge burning knot in his throat.

"Ranger, you're scaring me. Talk to me." She cupped his face with both hands, pulling him closer as if she hoped to read his mind through proximity.

Ranger felt himself falling into her touch. God, he loved her.

Amy shook him, as if she could pull him from his stupor. "Ranger, dammit, what's wrong? Where is Shane?" Her words tumbled out, catching on her husband's name. Tears formed in her eyes, turning them almost gold.

Ranger pulled her tight, crushing her soft body to his, and buried his face in her hair. "Amy." Her soft scent wrapped around him, melting the ice block in his chest, pulling him back to the here and now. And then Ranger felt something hard between them and froze. Slowly, as if peeling off a bandage, Ranger pulled away and stared down at her stomach. Amy's robe parted and beneath she wore a tight black t-shirt and shorts, but that's wasn't what gut punched the breath from his body.

"Your pregnant?"

She waved a hand dismissively and demanded, "Tell me why you're here.."

His mouth moved but nothing came out except air. Shane hadn't told him...hadn't even mentioned..."Did Shane know?"

Her fierce expression wavered and Ranger knew her answer in an instant. He'd known Shane and Amy were having trouble before the deployment but hiding a baby from her husband? Ranger grabbed arms, anger fueling his movement. "You hid this from him?"

"Ranger, I've tried to call him, he won't answer. He won't call me back. He doesn't want me." Her voice trailed off on a harsh whisper, her eyes dark with hurt.

Shane was his best friend and even though

Ranger had secretly loved Amy for years, he still wanted them to be happy together. He loved them both.

But Shane is dead.

If only he could trade places with Shane. At that moment, he would gladly die if it would bring his best friend back and saved Amy this grief. She was too young to be a widow and he was too young to bury a best friend.

He had to tell her but his mouth wouldn't work. His tongue was thick and slow, his lips sluggish. "Shane..."

Amy shook her head. Her lips formed a 'no,' but she didn't make a sound. Ranger ignored the pain from her nails digging into his shoulders. "No. It's not true." There was that fire, that spark that lit her from the inside. Amy was a fighter.

Ranger dropped his head to hers and closed his eyes. "I'm sorry, honey." *Shane is dead.* He still couldn't say the words out loud, but now there was no need.

Her body jerked against him as she threw her arms around his neck and sobbed. Ranger cried right along with her. There was no shame. There was only pain.

"I'm sorry. I'm so sorry. It should have been me."

She squeezed him tight and cried harder, the only sound in the night.

"No, Ranger. No." Her words came out broken. She jerked and grabbed her stomach, gasping between sobs. "The baby. Something's wrong."

A storm of fear and adrenaline more furious than the storm raging around them exploded in him. He caught her right before he knees gave out. "Tell me what to do."

"Get me to the hospital. Please." Her last word came out sharp and shrill, and see clutched her belly.

"It's going to be okay, honey. It's going to be okay," Ranger's arms shook as he ran to his truck, his world collapsing into a black void. He couldn't lose Amy and Shane. He wouldn't survive.

Chapter Ten

Maxine Videl flipped off the bedroom light, leaving only the low glow of the lamps on the bedside tables to illuminate the man propped against the headboard. She crawled up the rustic wood bed and laid her head on Hank James chest. Her fingers wove through the smattering of blond and grey chest hair, enjoying the feel of its coarse yet soft texture. "Why didn't you tell me he was back."

Hank sighed and wrapped an arm around her shoulders. "They broke up almost five years ago. I think it's time that everyone just moved on, don't you?"

Maxine frowned, but bit back the sharp retort racing out of her mouth. Yes, it had been five years since Hank's adopted son, Hunter, had joined the military and left Evie, her daughter, in the dust. Five years Maxine had to watch Evie cringe and withdraw even more every time the man came home on leave. "I know. But you don't have to watch how much it hurts my daughter every time he shows up at our bar. And the damn fool always brings some girl with him too. Even though he watches Evie the whole time."

"You know how men are. Hardheaded.

Hunter isn't any different." Hank said.

"Stupid. You left that part out. It might've been five years, but those two still can't keep their eyes off one another. Problem is, your boy seems intent on hurting my girl any way he can. And I still don't know why."

Maxine secretly hoped Hank would just ask him, find out the truth of why Hunter and Evie had broken up all those years ago. And why he kept looking at Evie like she was his worst nightmare wrapped in a daydream. Something bad had happened, but everyone involved in the situation was being tightlipped as a damn mute.

"Now Maxi, he's a grown man. I'm not going to butt into his business." Hank squeezed her shoulders, his silent command for her to drop the subject. But Maxine had never been that good at holding her tongue. Or her temper.

She sat up, pulled out of his grasp and faced the man that held her own heart. After her husband's death a few years ago, Hank James was the only reason she hadn't turned into a hardened spinster. Her husband, Tom Videl, and Hank had been best friends for a long time, with Maxine completing the trio, but her relationship with the men had turned tumultuous. The inseparable days of their youth was destroyed by jealousy, and Maxine had been forced to choose between the two men of her dreams. She chose Tom, all the while knowing she crushed Hank's spirit, and a small part of her own right along with him.

Hank had retreated to try to revive Broken River Ranch, and become somewhat of a recluse. Tom and Maxine had had Evie and started a new life together. But deep in her heart Maxine always held a candle for Hank James, all the while loving her husband with her whole being. "Maybe it's time for you to say something. Those two belong together. You know it. I know it. And I'm sick and tired of watching them suffer."

Hank shifted, the light making his blond hair glow. Then his bright blue eyes met hers and stole her breath. But no matter if he released butterflies and bubbles in her belly, she was tired of sitting by as the helpless bystander.

"Don't look at me like that. I know that look. It's none of our business. Do you really think they would appreciate us sticking our nose where it doesn't belong?" Hank brushed a stray lock of her long brown hair behind her ear.

"They might not appreciate it at first, but dammit, you might get them to stop and think. And maybe even realize what they're missing before it's too late." Maxine, took his hand and threaded her fingers with his. Intertwining them.

"Did you ever think there might be a reason they're not together anymore? I know Hunter, and he's levelheaded. Almost cold in his calculations. He wouldn't be so angry with Evie without a reason." Maxine held in a snort. Hunter might act like a cool level headed commander, but she saw the fires banked in him. The pent up tension.

The only calm and collected James was the one sitting next to her right now.

Which did nothing to explain the huge gap between their children. Evie had never been flighty or cruel. She'd loved Hunter completely. And up until he hightailed it out of town, Maxie had thought Hunter felt the same way.

So what was so terrible that her daughter had ran into the arms of Marcus Carvant?

Maxine's anger wilted and she lay back against Hank, marveling at how hard his muscles were. Even in his fifties there wasn't a spare ounce of fat on the man. Mother Nature sure as hell hadn't been as kind to her, but she didn't hear Hank complaining. "I'm so tired of seeing her hurting. After Hunter, she'd been sad and depressed and lonely, but she still smiled some. After Marcus... I'm scared she's broken. And I'm scared Hunter is the only one that can fix it."

Marcus Carver, Mercy's slime bag mayor and all around asshole had taken advantage of Evie, but Maxine had been so excited her daughter was dating again she had ignored her instincts. Right up until the bastard nearly killed her daughter.

"I can't promise anything, but if the opportunity presents itself-" Hanks words were cut off by a loud crash in the house. "What the hell?"

Hank jumped from the bed, yanked open the nightstand drawer and pulled out his pistol. Maxine followed him, grabbing her robe and pulling it on in one swift movement. Hank stopped, turned and held up his hand. "Stay here."

"Like hell I will." Maxine grabbed her purse and pulled the small .38 revolver out, checked the safety, and cocked it.

"Dammit Maxi, this is no time to be hard headed." Hank stood tall, blocking her forward momentum.

She propped a hand on her all too generous hip and cocked her right eyebrow. "You really want to sit here and argue?"

"Fine. But if shit goes down you get out and call the sheriff." The square set to Hank's jaw spoke of his annoyance and made her smile. The man sure was sexy when he got riled. "Hard headed woman."

They eased from the bedroom and crept down the long hall, their bare feet silent as they crept down the polished hardwood floor of Hank's long ranch-style house. His rambler stretched out in almost two completely separate wings, with a few guest bedrooms and Hank's master bedroom on one end, the great room and kitchen in the middle and a couple more spare bedrooms on the other. Another crash echoed down the hall, followed by a peal of feminine laughter.

Maxine lowered her pistol, Hank glanced over his shoulder and then did the same. The muscles rippled across his taught back when he turned. Muscles honed by hard work. They rounded the corner into the kitchen. Hayden James, the only girl Hank adopted, lie sprawled on the kitchen floor behind an overturned chair. And a man, or boy depending how you looked at it, lying right beside her. That explained the two crashes.

Hank flipped on the lights. Maxine stepped around him and when she got a glimpse of his expression, she almost felt sorry for the girl. Hank was all cool and calm until you pushed him too far. Hayden had been pushing and pushing for the past year and Maxine had a feeling the girl just pushed her father over the edge of his own personal cliff.

"What the hell is going on? And who the hell is that?" Hank's voice snapped through the kitchen, the two kids, obviously drunk turned to stare in shock. The boy focused on the gun and the blood leeched from his face.

"Dad, let me explain." Hayden flopped over

onto an elbow, her words sluggish.

The boy paled even further, "Dad? How old are you?"

Hank answered, "Not old enough."

"Dad, stop. You're embarrassing me." Hayden attempted to get to her feet, somehow caught the edge of the kitchen table and righted herself.

"I'm fixing to embarrass you, right over my knee. You know the rules. No drinking. No boys in the house after midnight." His harsh tone would have sent grown men scudding, but not Hayden. Maxi had to give it to her, she didn't back down an inch.

"I'm twenty-one years old. I can drink and do whatever the hell I want!"

"Not while you live under my roof you can't. Now get your ass in bed before I do something I regret."

Hayden's long blonde hair hung wild and curly down to her waist. Her normally clear blue eyes were bloodshot, her cheeks flushed red from the effects of too much to drink. And the platforms on her feet didn't help her steadiness one bit. "You're not my father. You can't tell me what to do."

Maxi gasped and covered her mouth. Hank had taken Hayden in at a young age, saving her from an awful life. Hank's already tight jaw started to tick, but under that gruff exterior, she could see the hurt Hayden's words had caused. "I'm the only father you have. You better fucking count your blessings you're not with your real father. Because I'm the only one that gives a damn. Get your ass to bed. Now!"

Everyone in the room jumped at Hank's sharp tone, and Hayden, bless her heart, slammed her lips together and stumbled from the room. Probably the smartest thing the girl had done in a long while.

Hank turned on the boy before Maxine could intervene. He'd at least managed to get to his feet during the father daughter fight, and backed up to the front door, fumbling for the handle and an escape. When he saw Hank advance, he threw up his hands in surrender. "Hey man, I thought she was older. I'm sorry."

Maxi watched Hank lift his pistol and take aim at the boy's chin. Shit. A night she'd intended to use coaxing him over to her point of view was screwed by a couple of drunk kids. Not that she was worried he'd actually hurt the kid. Scare him – yes.

"Hey boy, because that's what you are." Hank stalked closer, shoving his pistol in the back of his jeans and grabbed the young man around the neck. "You're not a man. A man wouldn't get a girl drunk and bring her home hoping to get lucky. Which one of you drove? How much have you been drinking? Did you drive my daughter home drunk?"

"Please, sir. We were just goofing around, having some fun. I swear I didn't mean any harm by it." His words cut off when Hank squeezed, shutting off his oxygen supply for a second. Maxine would have been worried if it were anyone else, but not Hank James. The man made his life rescuing orphaned and abused kids. She seriously doubted he would suddenly start hurting them.

Plus, the less drunk drivers the better. Sometimes all these kids needed was to get the ever loving crap scared out of them to keep them from doing something so stupid again. She pulled out a stool and sat, carefully placing her pistol on the counter. Her movement caught the boy's attention. "Ma'am, please. Can't you talk to him?"

"Sorry, but you stepped in it. You're on your own."

He swallowed, his Adam's apple bobbing fast like a jig in the water with a catfish on the line.

"I have half a mind to shoot you and throw you out back in my pond. Let the gators eat you." Hank pressed forward.

"No. I swear, if you let me leave, you'll never see me again."

"Now you want to drive drunk again?" Hank ground out.

"I can call a friend. He can be here in five minutes to pick me up."

Maxine had a feeling that whatever alcohol the kid ingested earlier that night had evaporated, but no need to tell Hank. He was on a roll. "How about I call the sheriff, let him get you for a DWI."

The boy broke, blubbering and sobbing, "No, please. I'm trying to get into law school. If I get something on my record I'm screwed."

"What do you think Maxi? Should we use him as gator bait or call the sheriff?" Hank didn't look at her when he spoke, he pressed his entire body against the boy's, squishing him against the door.

"Dad. Get off him." Hayden flew back into the kitchen, still dressed in the same clothes. Hank spun around and the boy seized on his opportunity for an escape, fumbled with the doorknob and ran out of the house.

"You let a drunk drive you home?" If Hank was mad before, he was furious now.

"He only had one beer. Jeremy was the DD tonight, he drove us all home."

"And what, you were going to invite him to your bed to thank him?"

Hayden took a step back, staring at her father with eyes wide. "How could you say that to me?"

Hank gestured to her wildly, "Look at yourself. How you dress. Showing off your body, drinking with strange men, inviting them into my home. What do you think it looks like when you act like that? Do you really think a man will ever respect a girl like that?"

"Maybe it's just the real me. In my blood." Hayden screamed back. Tears ran down her face.

Hank grabbed her by the arms and Maxine stepped from the stool, ready to intervene if things got too heated. Hank would never physically harm his daughter, but he may say something he would regret.

"You listen to me, your mother might have been a slut. And you're worthless father a drunk piece of shit. But that's not you. You're smart. You're kind. You're better than this. And I love you too much to watch you throw your life away."

"No, I'm not. I'm not worth anything. You don't know anything. You don't know what I did."

Hank shook her, "I don't care what you did, or what you think you did. This is not the answer."

Hank's hands were shaking and Hayden was sobbing. Maxi couldn't hold off anymore. She stepped up and put her arm gently around the young girl. "I think everyone should just go to bed. Everything always looks better in the morning after a good nights sleep. Don't you agree Hank?"

Hank looked at her like she'd gone crazy, but Maxi didn't give in. She steered the girl down the hall to her bedroom, ignoring Hank following right behind. He waited in the hall while Maxine helped get Hayden into a nightdress and in bed. She passed out not one minute after her head hit the pillow. Maxine crept back into the hall, easing the door shut behind her and held a finger to her lips for Hank to stay quiet.

He closed his mouth. Maxi went to his bedroom and climbed back into bed, knowing this was the best place for the coming storm. Hank's expression was a mixture of anger and hurt and confusion. He slunk onto the edge of the bed and Maxi immediately hugged him from behind.

He grabbed her and held on tight, his body tense beneath hers. "I don't know what she's talking about, and honestly I'm scared to ask. Over this past year she's just gotten worse and worse. I thought maybe it was some delayed teenage rebellion thing, but I was wrong. She's hurting and I don't know why and I don't know what to do to fix it."

Maxine pulled him backwards and he let her until he was lying back on the bed and she was leaning over him, stroking his face with her fingers. "Whatever it is it can be solved. I'll be here to help. You know your boys will. But tonight is not the time."

She pressed her lips to his with a soft kiss and Hank groaned wrapping his arms around her and turning them until he was on top of her. "I need you."

Maxine smiled, "I'm right here. What are you waiting for?"

Chapter Eleven

Stupid. Stupid. Stupid.

Evie braced her hands on the pedestal porcelain sink, cursing the too-bright lights in her bathroom for highlighting the dark circles under her eyes. The hollowed out cheekbones. She was underweight. Overstressed. She could definitely pass for a Hollywood actress in drug rehab.

"Ugh." Even her groan came out weak. Sick of looking at herself, she flipped the light off and went into her bedroom. The window-unit air conditioner, circa 1980, sputtered and spit and shrieked, but at least it got her bedroom down below the hundred-degree heat.

Evie flopped onto the bed, her body as lifeless as a fish on a dock. The drone of the AC unit combined with the steady staccato of her warped ceiling fan would normally have been enough white noise to soothe her to sleep. But not tonight. She could've taken a horse tranquilizer without stirring.

She rolled over and grabbed her phone. Two o'clock. Crap. There was no way she was going to enjoy a visit to the sandman in this state of mind. For the last couple of years, her life had been on par with a Lifetime drama, but in these past two days it had shifted into Bruce Willis action. No point in lying here. Alone. In bed. She headed downstairs to the kitchen.

She snatched a beer and rubbed the cold bottle against her face before taking a drink. The chill eased some of her tension. Perhaps a good girl would have grabbed a glass of milk. Maybe opted for some comfort food. But that was all behind her, and the loss of her good-girl status could be dated back to the end of her second relationship.

And now here she stood, alone, twenty-seven years old, with a sum total of two exes under her belt. Two exes who had failed to leave her with a warm and fuzzy tonight.

She slammed the bottle down, cracking it loudly against her speckled countertop. The cheap Formica didn't even give up a scratch.

Her mind spun round and round, like a tetherball in the hand of an overzealous third-grader. Attempting to wrap her thoughts around tonight's events made her brain bounce out of control.

Being on Marcus Carvant's right side was downright dangerous, so she didn't even want to think about being on his wrong side. But Evie being on any side of Marcus was better than her mother being dead.

And she had no doubt Maxine would take it first.

She had to figure out a way to appease Marcus. Make the deal and push it through. Forget the fact she would be running marijuana. Jail time wouldn't even begin to cover her sentence if they were caught.

Better her than her family.

Evie took another swig of the cold brew, hoping to wash down some of her revulsion.

How could she work with that...monster? Help him, knowing he'd screw her in the end?

Evie picked her cell phone up from the counter. The empty screen glowed bright, glaring at her. Daring her to use it.

Before she realized her fingers were moving, she pulled up the number and hit the call button. Shaking, she lifted the phone to her ear. The phone rang three times before he answered. "Evangeline." Her stomach dropped with dread. "I knew it wouldn't take you long to see my reasoning."

Evie swallowed spasmodically, trying to get her throat to work, to push the words out of her mouth. Her body fought her, as if it knew she shouldn't be talking to him. "Marcus."

Disgust swept through her from merely voicing his name. Evie bent forward, clutched the counter for support.

"I've been looking forward to getting reacquainted. Why don't you come over so we can discuss this matter in person?" His tone was so reasonable, almost likeable. But Evie knew what that practiced Southern drawl hid.

"What do you want?" Evie straightened and grabbed her beer, needing whatever liquid courage she could garner.

Marcus *tsked*. "Manners. I thought we'd worked through all this." He sighed. Evie could picture the look of disappointment on his face. The resignation. Like she was a child caught coloring on daddy's walls.

A child afraid of a spanking. Only Marcus didn't give spankings. Evie shuddered again.

Flashes of dark closets and no food sparked in her mind. Her side throbbed and she fought the urge to rub her scar.

His brand. His mark of ownership.

No. No more. Her only hope of reclaiming her life lay in beating him. And if she had to do it alone, she would. Even if it was at the point of a gun. "What. Do. You. Want."

She would figure out how to get the drugs and turn him over to the authorities. Just not in Mercy. She would have to go big. Maybe the FBI?

"We will have to work on that tone, too. Do I need to remind you what happens to bad girls?" His soft words slithered down her spine.

"We aren't together any more. You don't own me. I can talk any damn way I please. Now tell me what the fuck you want me to do." Her voice boomed through the small kitchen.

He didn't respond.

Evie heard him breathing hard through the phone. Knew he was waiting. Figuring out a way to gain the upper hand. Her chest locked down, her ribcage seeming to fold in on itself and crush her lungs.

If he had been in this room with her, she knew she'd already be on the floor. By now, she'd have broken bones.

Another flash—Evie crawling across the floor, trying to escape him. The smell of her burning flesh singing her nose. Unimaginable pain radiating up her side. The feel of smooth, polished hardwood under her fingers as she pulled herself along the floor.

Marcus's voice yanked her back to the present. "Let's dispense with the pretense that you've grown a back bone. Because we both know you're only trying to put on a front for that pathetic little group of trash you call an organization. You *will* work for me. You will do exactly as I say. Or I will kill your white trash mother." Marcus paused and Evie stood frozen in place. "Just like I killed your father."

Bile blasted up her throat, threatening to erupt. A cold sweat broke across her neck.

"So you did set him up. You planted the drugs," Evie said.

"I delivered a message. A message you got loud and clear."

"You...you killed him to punish me?" Evie choked.

"Yes."

Guilt punched her stomach, knocking the wind from her lungs. Her knees buckled. Evie sank to the floor. She'd suspected this earlier, but he just confirmed her worst nightmare. It was her fault. Her fault her father was dead.

"I see I've gotten your attention. Now, let me be clear. You will deliver my shipment downriver. You will personally handle the process. Your boat. Alone. I'll take care of everything else."

"And if I don't?" Evie said.

"Then I'll deliver the same message to your mother."

* * *

Evie had made a deal with the devil.

She wished she could call upon an angel to blast the asshole straight back to hell.

Messages. Marcus dealt in messages. Subtle ones. Veiled threats. But not with the Videls. No, his message to her was as clear as the note he had nailed to her father's chest.

Evie had never found out what that note

said, but the day after her father's funeral, Grandpa C.W. moved his camper into Maxine's backyard. And that night, he called a family meeting. And that was when everything changed.

Bracing her elbows on the counter, she lowered her head into her hands. She'd safely skated below Marcus's radar for so long now, thinking she could carefully slide down the social ladder and out of sight.

Cold sweat trickled across her upper lip and bile rose up her throat again. Evie lifted the beer to her lips, trying to wash the burning back down.

Boom!

Her kitchen door rattled.

Evie jerked, slamming the bottle into her front teeth, the loud crack echoing through her bones. Pain shot straight up her nose and took root in her brain. "Ow!"

"Evie, it's me, Hunter. Saw your light on."

Evie rubbed her mouth and went to the door. "What are you doing here?" she asked, pulling the flowered curtain to the side.

"I was just out riding around. Saw your kitchen light on. Thought I'd see if you were still awake."

Evie leaned her head against the door and took a deep breath. Why couldn't he leave her alone? She was barely holding her sanity together as it was, and life with Hunter had never been calm and controlled. She knew she should just send him away for good, but her treacherous body didn't seem to agree, because it sure wasn't her common sense that reached forward and turned the knob.

Hunter stood under her porch light, dark shadows painting the planes of his face. His shoulders dropped and he let out a long breath. Her heart tugged at his lost look and the tightness inside her chest slipped.

"A little stalker-ish, don't you think?"

Hunter shrugged, his massive size suddenly reminding her of the grizzly bear in the bar. God, he was sexy. Definitely all male, none of that metro crap. Just pure, raw sensuality and control. The intensity of his dark brown eyes was enough to drown her on dry land.

"You do realize it's two o'clock in the morning, right?" she asked. And she was wearing an old nightgown three sizes too big. *Crap.* Cheri's comment about her clothes had resonated with her. First thing on her to-do list, shopping.

"I'm sorry. I didn't realize it was so late. Did you wait up for me?" he asked, his tone teasing and light.

Evie caught herself wanting to smile, wanting to let him in and get close. But no, she'd done that before, and it had landed her in a pile of cow shit.

"I've had a long night and would like to get to bed. So...do you mind?" Evie tightened her hold on the door knob, her heart kicking her sternum like a toddler having a temper tantrum.

As she started to shut the door, Hunter's arm shot out, preventing it from moving an inch. "Actually, I really could use a beer. And a friend."

Evie studied him. His eyes looked haunted. Sad. Just like that night all those years ago. They had been a few years out of high school, desperate for each other, but about as stable as a boat with holes. They fought loud and long and hard. And it was Hunter who walked away. He'd given her his back and climbed into his truck, sparing her one last look before gunning out of her driveway on squealing tires. His eyes had that same glint to them tonight. "What's wrong?"

Hunter shook his head, his expression changing into a mask of smooth forehead and barely-there smile. To anyone else, he would have looked relaxed. But his eyes darkened from their melt-me milk chocolate to despair-dark espresso. "Please, Evie."

Evie's breath caught. Hunter James didn't beg. Or apologize. A man like him didn't even have the word mistake in his vocabulary. A part of her crumbled inside and she stepped back, closing the door quietly behind him after he followed her into the house.

He went straight to the fridge and uncapped a beer, but instead of downing it, he placed his drink on the island and turned to face her. They were alone in her kitchen, no more than a few feet separating them. His arms crossed over his chest, the black T-shirt stretched tight over his bulging biceps. Veins popped on his forearms. Her mouth watered.

The quiet sounds of the kitchen—the hum of the refrigerator and water *pinging* from the leaky faucet—faded.

Hunter leaned back on the island. He was calm now. Lethally calm.

The skin across the back of her neck pulled tight and she rubbed at the tension there, needing to do something besides stand there under the concentrated light of his gaze.

But the need in his eyes and the pain in his soul pulled her toward him. She walked slowly across the room, not stopping until her toes touched his boots. "Please, tell me what's wrong."

His gaze focused on her lips for a mind-numbing moment before meeting her eyes. No matter how much he tried to hide it, Evie saw his pain. There was an unease in him that hadn't been there earlier.

She almost stepped forward and put her arms around him. Almost. Instead, she wrapped her arms about her own waist.

"We were sent on a mission. It was all going fine." He tapped a finger on his thigh, fast and strangely off beat. "We breached the compound looking for our target. But it was too easy. Of course, by then it was too late."

Evie's chest constricted. All this time she had pictured him jumping out of helicopters, doing the Rambo thing. He was as invincible in her dreams as he had been in real life. But Rambo didn't get taken down. Ever.

"I led my team to the building intel wanted us to check out. We might as well have followed the yellow-brick road. They were smart. They waited until we were in the center of the compound. We had no way out. We found our intel officer. He'd been dead for a while. Tortured."

Evie's hand flew to her mouth. The way Hunter said that... He could have been talking about fishing for all the emotion in his voice.

"I'm sorry." What else could she say?

"The gunfire started when we evacuated the building. I went first so I could distract the terrorists and my men could get out." Hunter's voice was still low and monotone, like he was giving a report on his truck transmission. Not life and death combat.

"Your leg?"

Hunter kept going, looking somewhere over

her head. "After I got hit, it slowed the whole group down, but somehow we managed to get out. We made it." He picked up his beer and took a drink, seemingly on autopilot.

Evie leaned forward and laid her hand on his arm. "I'm so glad you're safe. That the rest of you got out okay." She didn't know what she would have done if he'd been killed. Would she have even known?

The thought brought her up short.

His harsh laugh scraped across her nerves. "That's just it. The rest of us didn't make it out safe."

Her veins froze. *Who? Who didn't make it?*

"I saw Ranger. He's okay."

"Yeah, me and Ranger are fine." His lips twisted, but the expression on his face didn't even resemble a smile.

Who else? Evie wracked her mind. The problem was, the James brothers' role in the military was about as clear to her as black glass. She never got specifics, no one did. "Hunter." Her nails dug into his arm and she wanted to shake him until the words came out.

He turned back to her, his careful mask gone. In its place was a despair so dark it stole her breath. If she hadn't been holding on to him, she would have doubled over. Someone had died. Someone she knew. *Oh God.*

"Shane didn't make it. He stayed behind to cover our escape, because I was too weak from my injury to do it myself."

Evie's lungs twisted, leaving no room for air. "Amy... Does she know?" The words ripped up her throat and brought tears to her eyes. How would this affect her pregnancy?

Hunter scrubbed a hand down his face. "She knew he was missing in action. She kept quiet. But now, tonight, the condolences officer showed up at the bar tonight looking for me. He wanted to take me to her house, but I knew it would be better for Ranger to tell her the news."

"Oh no. I need to be with her." Evie had her purse in hand and was at the door before she even realized her feet had moved. She dug and fumbled through her bottomless purse, but it was impossible to see through the tears. Her chest heaved as a sob escaped, and she covered her eyes.

Hunter's arms surrounded her and she turned into him, needing his strength.

"I'm so sorry, Hunter."

He squeezed her tighter, his masculine scent filling her senses.

"As soon as we regrouped we tried to go back for him, but it was too late. He was gone." A shudder wracked his body and Evie wrapped her arms around his waist. Hunter buried his face in her hair, his hot breath caressing her ear. A shiver worked down her spine.

"Our commander was notified that Shane was dead two days ago. He had to verify. The DNA matched." Hunter's voice was quiet with anguish. He didn't cry, but quiet tears slipped down her cheeks.

"It's my fault. It should have been me."

His words hit her hard. Evie pulled back and grasped his face between her hands. "You were shot. Injured. There was no way it was your fault."

Hunter's hands surrounded hers, trying to pull them away, but she held on tight and forced him to look at her, to see the truth in her gaze.

"You said it yourself. You were ambushed. You're not responsible."

His gaze turned hot. "I will always be responsible for Shane's death."

Chapter Twelve

Pity and Pain. Not what Hunter wanted to see in Evie's gaze. Not when anger heated his veins and self-loathing filled his soul. Right now, he needed to forget all of that.

He needed Evie.

He focused on her soft lips. Small currents of lust shot from the points where her fingers touched his skin. He harnessed his desire, using it to drive away his dark thoughts.

When his lips touched hers, his unrest settled for a moment. He pressed harder, seeking more, and her lips parted for him.

He cupped her ass, palming those perfect cheeks, and nestled between her thighs. He forced her head back and caught her answering whimper in his mouth, swallowing it whole.

She fit against him perfectly. Sleek and smooth. Hot and curvy. Made for his hands alone.

Her fingers dug into his short hair, her nails scraping his scalp. He deepened the kiss, turned and pinned her against the refrigerator, and explored her with leisure.

She tasted so damn good. Too good. A mix of honey and sugar and spice. And damn if it wasn't the perfect distraction.

Hunter tilted his hips forward, pushing himself against her core, needing to get closer. Evie moaned, and the vibration of the soft sound massaged his insides. She bit down on his lower lip, tugging and licking. The sharp bite of pain followed by her soothing touch did all sorts of things to his restraint.

Hunter shoved his thoughts of failure away and locked them down tight. There wasn't room in his head for anything but the woman in his arms.

Hunter threaded his fingers through hers and lifted their hands overhead. Her satin skin caressed him. Her nipples hardened against his chest.

"God, I've missed this. I've missed you," Hunter whispered, grinding his cock against her harder, the thin strips of her nightgown the only thing separating them. He completely surrounded her, enclosed her in his body, his arms, his strength.

"You taste so fucking good." He growled against her lips and then buried his face against her chest. Too good. He should be slipping in questions, pumping her for information. Tracking down that missing weapons shipment he knew was meant for Al Seriq.

"Hunter." Evie pushed against his shoulders.

Her scent blocked his thoughts. She smelled so sweet. He wanted to eat her alive.

"This is too fast, I can't..."

"Yes, you can. You need this as much as I do." His words were harsh with desire. Hunter lifted Evie and sucked her nipple through her nightgown, wringing a gasp from her. Her legs clamped around his waist and she bucked against him. "That's it, baby. Let go." He tugged harder, longing to rip her nightgown off and get to the bare skin beneath. Her nails dug into his wrists, tiny pinpricks of pain and pleasure.

She was a goddamn drug and he was addicted.

"Hunter... We can't... We have to stop," she gasped out, her hips rolling in direct contradiction to her words.

"You don't want me to stop, baby." She needed to stop thinking and just feel. He couldn't form a thought except to get inside her and never leave. Fuck the mission.

"No, Hunter. Stop." She used force this time, pounding his shoulders, the impact breaking through the haze of lust.

His brain moved at the pace of a slug, barely able to process her command, but he forced himself to drop his head and take a deep breath and regain control. Of course, nothing less than a subzero shower could control his raging hard on.

"Shit, I'm sorry, Evie. I shouldn't have taken advantage of you like that. I just..." He grabbed her waist and put her on the floor, the small gap between them feeling like the Grand Canyon after how close they'd been moments ago.

Evie leaned back and held a hand to her lips. "I understand. We're both hurting."

Hunter nodded, trying to focus on something other than the raging need inside him. "It's been raining a shit-ton since I've been back." Jesus Christ, he might as well be talking to the grocery store clerk.

Evie burst out laughing.

"What's so funny?"

"Nothing. Just, you know. The weather?"

"Would you rather I talk about how bad I

want to fuck you right now?"

Her laughter cut off abruptly and she shook her head.

He smiled. "Do you have a better idea?"

Evie swallowed and looked around the room. "Ummm..."

His body tightened, ready to dive in for more if she changed her mind, but a ball of black fur sailed from out of nowhere and landed on his head. "What the hell?" Claws locked into his neck, sending little trickles of blood dripping down his shoulders.

"Rooster! No!" Evie lunged forward and pulled the furry missile from his head. Sharp claws held on tight, scraping his skin.

"What *is* that?" Hunter's voice boomed through the room and the cat hissed and leaped from Evie's arms, claws outstretched. Hunter ducked sideways, swiping an arm to protect himself, and stepped into a bowl of water on the floor.

The cat ran back to its mistress, smart enough to recognize danger. Evie cuddled the scrawny creature in her arms, soothing it with soft words and slow strokes.

"*That* is a he. And his name is Rooster." The feline had patches of orange and white mixed in with the black. A few bald spots. Its tail looked like it had been through a meat grater. But the mangy cat's most notable feature was its black eye patch.

Evie eased around the breakfast bar, like she knew Hunter was five seconds from making cat stew. Good idea.

"The eye patch?"

Rooster eyed him with one freakishly yellow

orb and hissed.

"He was almost dead when I found him. I finally got him eating and healthy. Now he's my little bodyguard. And he doesn't really like men. I'm guessing whoever blinded and skinned him was male."

Rooster hissed again.

"I can see that." Hunter kept a close watch on the mangy cat.

"You're bleeding." Evie put Rooster out the back door. She walked back to Hunter and dabbed his neck with a finger. The answering sting came soon enough. "He can be a bit territorial."

"Like Genghis Khan can be a bit aggressive." Shit. Cock blocked by a cat. Ranger would never let him live it down.

"You should clean that up. I've got some alcohol and bandages upstairs."

Evie led the way. Her full nightgown did little to conceal the sexy sway of her hips, and the memory of how her ass felt in his hands almost hurt.

She walked through the second door down the hall into a bedroom with the most God-awful wallpaper he'd ever seen. Pink. Purple. Blue. Flowers and stems. Ivory background. "Jesus." He'd stepped into his great-grandmother's bedroom.

"I'm renting. I wouldn't feel right about making any big changes to Ms. Buela's house."

"Ms. Buela moved? Nursing home?"

Evie dropped her head for a moment and wrapped a hand around one of the posts of the four-poster bed before answering, "No. She died in her sleep. Pastor Don said she went real peaceful."

His head swam. Bombs, he could do. Missing body parts, he could do. Shit, he'd sewn his sergeant's half-blown arm back on. But dead old ladies' bedrooms? Hell no.

"Are you okay?" Evie gave him a strange look.

Hunter took a step back, edging toward the door. "Did she die in here?"

Evie's smile was sinful and she seemed to revel in his alarm. "No, in the recliner downstairs. She was watching her favorite TV show."

"Let me guess—The Shining?" The wallpaper. It was the wallpaper. Any minute two little girls wearing white dresses were going to come walking out of the closet.

Evie choked off a laugh. "Wheel of Fortune."

He paused, almost in the hall. "You got a guest bathroom?"

"Only if you like purple better."

She was laughing at him. Damn if he was going to let a girl make fun of him. Even if it was for the mission.

"Okay. Let's do this." Hunter sucked in a breath and headed into the bathroom, only to be brought up short by Pepto Bismol-pink walls. He caught sight of Evie behind him in the mirror, her hand hovering over her mouth again.

"Did she ever have a husband?"

"Not as far as I know."

"I can tell."

"Lots of women like pink."

Hunter turned to face Evie. "Pink? I'm going to be lucky if I don't come out of here smelling like roses."

Evie chuckled and reached past him into a closet. She handed him a pink washcloth and a bottle of alcohol. He rolled his eyes.

"Holler if you need anything else. The bandages are right in the cabinet." She shut the door behind her.

Hunter turned and caught his reflection in the frilly vanity mirror. The grin on his face looked goofy and out of place, but it was his first real smile in who knew how long.

Chapter Thirteen

Evie stepped out on the back porch, thankful she'd thought to repair the ripped screen last week. If anyone doubted the ferocity of Mercy's insect life, her house would serve as ample proof. Or at least it would have if the doubters had swung by a week ago. She'd walked outside into a storm of mosquitos, beetles, and flies, her bug zapper shooting sparks in a futile attempt to keep the critters under control.

To get the situation under control, Evie had dropped a bomb, literally. She'd bought the repellant at the hardware store, set the timer, and run. All that was left after the explosion was three dustpans of dead insects and a layer of zapper-fried moths.

Cheri and Amy had come over to help clean up.

Now Evie would be going to Amy's house. But not for spring cleaning. *Dammit.*

Why Amy? Hadn't she been through enough?

And Hunter held himself responsible.

This night was going down in her book of records as one of the shittiest in her life.

She rolled her head side to side, forcing the small muscles down her spine to relax. She was wound up tight—still agitated by Marcus's dark promises. And Hunter's reappearance in her life wasn't helping.

Except for that nagging, you're-gonna-regret-it-later part of her brain that was doing a dance. No, it was doing the bump-and-grind.

Her body stirred with urges she hadn't felt in so long she almost didn't recognize them for what they were. Images of his dark head lowered to her chest floated through her vision, and her nipples tightened, eager for his mouth.

No. She had to stay in control. Keep it together. He couldn't walk in here and expect her to just jump into bed with him like he'd never left. Like nothing had changed. *Everything* had changed.

Evie's stomach grumbled, sending her back into the house to check the cheese dip she'd put on the stove and grab a whiskey. Tonight called for something a little stronger than beer.

She thought she heard something in the kitchen, but it was already a second too late. A hand wrapped around her throat and Sherriff Brown walked her backward onto the porch, leaving her kitchen door wide open. Evie screamed, but she couldn't get enough air to make a real sound.

He pushed her against the wall, her feet dangling off the floor. The smell of tequila assaulted her nose.

"My women know to have something better than cheese dip waiting." Brown leaned in and pressed a wet kiss to her cheek. Her stomach rolled and she would have gagged if she'd been able to suck in enough air. "Marcus let you get away with too much. If you were mine, I'd teach you how to be a real woman."

Evie choked, stars floating in her vision. Her heart started beating triple-time.

"Like right now. Silent. Your eyes begging. That's a perfect woman." Brown's voice rolled with enough menace to make Ted Bundy cringe.

His lips trailed across her cheek and his teeth bit down on her lower lip until she whimpered. Evie kicked him as hard as she could, but her attempts were futile and frail. Her vision blurred, the overhead light seemed to flicker. The porch started fading.

Brown's fingers finally released their hold and she collapsed to the floor, her knees slamming into the rough wooden planks. Pain shot up her legs, down her shins. She coughed and gagged, trying to suck in enough oxygen to keep herself conscious. Evie pushed up from the floor, but her arms were too weak.

"Now *this* is where you belong. At my feet." Brown squatted and grabbed her chin, yanking her face to his. He handled her like she was his property.

Anger finally slid past her fear and she slapped his hand away. She jumped up, looked around, and found a weapon. Her pruning shears stood propped in the corner. Ten feet.

She took a step, ready to lunge, but Brown's arm wrapped around her waist. His other hand yanked her hair and pain ripped through her scalp. This time she managed to scream, and she prayed Hunter would hear.

"I'm here to deliver a message." Brown licked her neck, sliding his slimy tongue from her collarbone up to her ear.

"I don't care what you're here for." She

jabbed an elbow into his stomach.

Brown grunted and pushed her. She stumbled but managed to catch her balance. Turning to face him, she started to slink backward, toward the stairs. Toward Hunter.

The sheriff's face turned dark red. A fanatical gleam shone bright in his gaze. "The little kitten grew some claws? Don't worry, I'll remove them."

Evie took another step back. Brown moved with her. She knew she wouldn't be able to take a trained law enforcement officer in hand-to-hand combat, not even with her diploma from self-defense class. She needed someone stronger, bigger, and more badass than the Hulk to help her. "Hunter!"

Brown roared and lunged. She got in one more step backward before he threw her to the ground. His elbow landed in her stomach and Evie's knees bowed up. Air leaked from her mouth in short gasps, as if he'd punctured a lung. She couldn't seem to get enough air. Stars danced overhead as she lay there, stunned.

Brown's slap snapped her head to the right, sending pain exploding across her face. Blood trickled out of the corner of her mouth. *This can't be happening. Not again.*

"Like I said before you opened your fucking mouth, I'm here to remind you to do as you're told."

"Apparently you missed the memo. I've already agreed to do what he wants." She squeezed the words past her clenched teeth. Brown's face paled and a flicker of indecision skated across his eyes. "Uh-oh, did the big bad sheriff get left out of the loop?"

Brown grabbed her jaw, forcing her to look at

him. "Marcus can't wipe his ass without me. Got it?"

"Really? Then why are you so surprised we've already made an arrangement? Didn't he tell you?" Brown's grip tightened. The pain was excruciating, but Evie refused to cow to him. She would never submit to Brown.

"You want to see what I can do? Want to see why you better do as I say?" Spit flew from Brown's lips and Evie cringed away. Brown pulled a phone from his pocket and shoved it in her face. "Marcus might sit in the big chair, but only because of the real men on the ground."

"Real men don't beat women. They don't put on a fake badge and pretend to be a cop. You are the furthest thing from a man." Evie punctuated each word. Rage seemed to roll out of her very pores.

Brown's lip pulled up sharply to the right. "Your dad said the same thing. Right before I blew his brains out."

Her heart stopped. Brown shoved his phone in her face. She tried to recoil from the video he pulled up, but the floor held her immobile. Trapped between a hard place and a sadist's hands.

Her father. On his knees, his hands bound behind him, a gun pressed to the side of his head.

She couldn't see who was holding the gun, but she saw the shoes. Cop shoes. Brown pants. "You coward."

"Watch, Evie. Watch and see what a real man can do." Brown squeezed her jaw until she thought it would break.

Her dad pressed his lips together into a tight line. His eyes were hard. Granite. Furious. He didn't beg, didn't so much as acknowledge the man holding the gun. Her dad, her hero. He'd never once caved to pressure. Never.

She heard the retort of fire. Saw the bright yellow blast explode from the end of the pistol. Saw her dad fall to the side in the dirt.

Her whole body went cold. Her mind shut down. Her lungs locked.

She heard screams, but she didn't realize they were coming from her own throat until Brown slapped her again.

"Shut up!"

A gun clicked and she sobbed. But the sound wasn't from the video. Hunter stood behind Brown, a pistol pressed to the back of the sheriff's skull.

"Get the fuck off her." Hunter's voice was dark. Deadly. Welcome.

Brown's eyes met hers. The rage ripping across his face was frightening.

Hunter pressed the gun harder against Brown's skull, lowering the bastard's head closer to hers. Revulsion rolled through Evie's body and she turned away. The sheriff's nails dug into her jaw, but she kept silent.

"Drop the phone and stand up. Keep your fucking hands where I can see them." Hunter punctuated each word. "Or I'll blow your goddamn head off those weak excuses for shoulders."

Brown put his phone on the floor and lifted his hands. His uniform wrinkled now, the strips of his rank almost as distorted as the man wearing them.

Evie wanted to squeeze her eyes shut. Block them out. Block out the memory of that terrible video. She started shaking. She didn't know if it was from rage or shock or terror.

But she grabbed the cell phone and got to her feet, her knees locked tight to keep from falling. It was evidence. She could use it against him.

"Get out. Now. Before I kill you." Hunter's jaw locked tight, and his eyes... His eyes were almost black. Hunter's pistol was still pressed to the sheriff's skull.

"You're going to regret this. You should have kept to your own, Hunter." Brown's voice shook with fear. Evie felt the first tinge of satisfaction and prayed Hunter would shoot the man.

"I am keeping to my own. You fuck with her, you fuck with me. Now get up."

Evie's eyes widened just as Brown's did. The sheriff turned to look at her but then whipped his attention back to the man holding the gun. He slowly rose to his feet.

Hunter held the pistol in his right hand, his left cupping the grip. He pressed the weapon to Brown's forehead.

"Out," Hunter bit out, his voice as deadly as the weapon in his hands.

Brown backed down the back porch steps. "Don't forget my message, Evie."

She grabbed the chair beside her before her knees buckled.

Hunter fired a round, and the bullet sent a plug of grass and dirt flying into the air next to Brown. The sheriff took off around the side of the house. A few seconds later his tires spun out of her driveway.

"You should have shot him." Evie trembled harder, her teeth chattering. The phone buzzed in her hand.

The video.

She threw the phone and ran for the trash can, no longer able to hold the bile inside.

Hunter followed her and grabbed her hair, holding it off her face and rubbing small circles on her back.

When she finished emptying her stomach, the tears started and Hunter pulled her into his arms, cocooning his body around hers. But nothing could protect her from what she'd seen.

"He—he killed my father," she choked out between sobs. "He had it on video...and he made me watch."

Chapter Fourteen

Evie doubled over, clutching her stomach, and would have fallen to her knees if he hadn't grabbed her.

Hunter lifted her in his arms. "Jesus Christ."

He buried his face in her hair, inhaled her sweet scent, and prayed it would cap his rage. But each one of her sobs ripped open a fresh pit of anger.

He carried her inside, sat on the couch, and held her there, unable to think of anything else he could do to ease her pain.

Hunter stroked her hair, her shoulders, her arms. Anything to soothe her. "Don't worry about him. That fucker is going to feed the gators in Red Fork Bayou."

Cows had been known to disappear down Red Fork Road and the only things to turn up would be horns and hoofs. Brown's bones were smaller and would be easier for their breed of gator to digest.

She sobbed harder, clutching him like she feared she would fall through the floor if she didn't hold on tight enough. Earlier tonight, his only thought had been to get her to trust him so he could use her. Now all he could think about was protecting her. Shielding her. Keeping her safe.

And killing the sheriff.

"Evie, you need to tell me what the hell is going on." Hunter needed to know. He had to find out if she was really working with Marcus.

Evie's sobs slowed to hiccups and her tremors reduced to an occasional shake. "I'm not ready to talk about...it."

Hunter grabbed her shoulders, making sure to be gentle, and eased her away so he could study her. She blinked, sniffled, and looked away.

"Evie, look at me." Hunter waited for her to turn back to him. "I came home to recover from being shot in combat. I expected to hang out with my family. Hopefully spend some time with you."

Evie trembled again and Hunter cupped her cheek. He needed her to buy his line of bullshit, no matter how bitter the words tasted in his mouth. At least they contained a grain of truth. "I missed you. I was really scared you wouldn't even look at me, let alone talk to me, but I hoped. I hoped every day for the past three months, while I was holed up in that hospital."

"Hunter..."

"Let me finish."

Evie leaned away from him. His tone had been drill-sergeant harsh and he realized he'd gotten way too used to talking to soldiers.

"I get to you, finally and the goddamn sheriff attacks you in your own home. Makes you watch a video of your dad's murder."

Tears filled her eyes and spilled down her pale cheeks.

It felt like metal in a tornado was ripping up his insides. Her tears had always sent his hero syndrome into overdrive. Going into this thing, he'd prepared himself to see her cry. To beg and plead for his mercy. But now, actually confronted with this flesh-and-blood Evie, he realized he'd wasted his time. There was no preparing for this.

"You need to tell me what the fuck is going on, honey. Because I feel like I just got stuck in a mud pit and the gators are circling." And if he didn't get her to admit the truth willingly, the CIA would take it from her. Either by coercion or force.

Evie hung in his grip, wrung out and pitiful. Her left eye was already swelling. "I don't want you to get involved. It's not safe." Her breathing hitched.

Hunter almost sighed. At least she hadn't told him it was none of his business or tried to kick him out of her house. She was scared. And she needed him. He knew it. She knew it.

"How about I pour us a drink? Got anything stronger than beer?"

"In the cabinet over the fridge. Jack Daniels."

His favorite. He and Evie used to sip the whiskey slow, savoring it as they watched flames leap in their bonfire. "I knew you thought about me."

She stiffened. "Whatever. I can't help it if you have good taste in whiskey."

Hunter couldn't hold back a small smile. He could tell the shock was fading. She would need someone to catch her when it disappeared entirely and reality set in. And he would be there.

Hunter eased her to the couch and went to the back porch, found the cell phone and placed it on the counter. He could get this to Hoyt later. Then Hunter would know everything about the sheriff. What he ate. What he drank. Where he pissed.

He went back to the kitchen and grabbed two shot glasses and a full bottle of Jack before returning to the living room.

Evie hunched on the faded blue couch, her shoulders slumped, her head cradled in her hands. Her posture screamed defeat.

"Here, take this." Hunter handed Evie a full shot glass, put the bottle on the floor, and sat beside her. There was wariness in her gaze again, but he intended to fix that fast. "Go on. Down it. It will help soothe your nerves."

She looked at him like he'd turned into a cockroach. "You think a drink will make me forget seeing my dad murdered?"

"Not one drink. More like ten. I'm going for past normal drunk and into permanent liver damage."

"Maybe death by liver would be preferable to death by sheriff." Evie downed the whole glass and Hunter hurried to refill it.

"Maybe if you talked to me, let me help you, you wouldn't have to contemplate death by anything." Hunter sat his shot glass on the end table behind him, knocking over a picture in the process.

He picked up the old frame and studied the photo, surprised to see his own father smiling back at him. It was a younger, blonder version of Hank James, but he still had intense blue eyes capable of piercing steel. Evie's dad, Tom Videl, stood on the other side. Both men had an arm wrapped around a very young and very attractive Maxine.

"Can you believe how young they were?" Evie said.

"I didn't know Hank hung out with your parents."

"Yeah, from what C.W. has told me, they all used to be real close."

"What happened?"

"I–I don't know. I tried to ask C.W. but he never answers my questions straight. Half the time I have no idea what he's talking about. I think he was one of those vets who should have been diagnosed with PTSD." Evie placed a hand on his shoulder and studied the picture.

Hunter stiffened, that small touch igniting his need for her. "I don't think they knew much about PTSD back then." Her fingers curled, sinking deeper into his skin, and his desire ratcheted up another hundred degrees. The image of her fingers wrapped around his cock took hostage of all other thoughts.

He carefully placed the photo back on the table. "Your grandpa is one tough man. I talked to him tonight."

"Why?"

Hunter met her gaze dead on. "I asked his permission to date you."

Evie paled and leaned away, but he caught her hand. He needed to touch her. He didn't know why.

He needed to be with her. But he had to remember why he was here. He had to get her trust.

So he could betray her.

Sourness coated his tongue at the thought. The idea that had seemed so easy just a month ago now made his body scream in revolt.

"You didn't."

"I did. And he didn't kill me." Hunter said.

"Jesus."

"I'm asking you to fill me in. I know some bad shit is going down and I think you may be caught in the middle." Hunter watched the expressions flicker across her face. Knew she wanted to run. He wasn't going to let her.

"I don't know what you think is happening, but you're wrong. C.W. is crazy, I told you that. Things are just business as usual." She was hedging, her smile fake and brittle.

"I'll tell you what I think. I think that sheriff is dirty and I think he's trying to get you to do something you don't want to do. I think you need my help. I think your dad would want you to ask for it."

Her smile cracked. "That's low."

Hunter refilled her shot glass and tilted it toward her lips. "Here, this will help. Swallowing the truth is harder than believing the lies."

Evie kept her gaze glued to his and tilted the glass back. Number three. She couldn't weigh over a buck ten at most. Her tolerance should top out after shot number five. Lesson number one from Mr. J- get your enemy wasted and pump them for information. Except Evie sure as shit didn't feel like an enemy.

Hunter poured another and passed the glass back to her. Evie tucked a strand of long blonde hair behind her ear before accepting the glass. Then she bit her lip and Hunter groaned. She had the sexiest mouth he'd ever seen. Ever imagined. And right now, he wanted to do things to those lips that would make the devil blush.

Evie dropped her brows. "You okay?"

Hunter nodded and downed his first shot. The liquid fire seared a path down to his stomach, but it did nothing to tame the heat in his dick. "Yeah, just remembered something." Like how sweet her mouth looked wrapped around his cock.

She didn't say anything, but her look clearly said she didn't believe him.

"Evie, I can help you. I take out scum every day. Usually in other countries, sure, but assholes are assholes, no matter what their nationality."

Evie touched her neck, flinched, and downed the liquor in her glass. Shot number four.

She tilted her head to the side, giving him an eyeful of the swelling on her face. The small bit of dried blood at the corner of her mouth. The cold control he'd managed to maintain for so long vanished.

Then he saw her neck.

Brown's fingerprints stood out against her golden skin. The need to kill rose sharp and fast. Hunter accepted it. He let the beast loose from its cage. He didn't yell or roar. He didn't jump up and pace. He harnessed the killer inside him, letting him sink into his pores. Familiar. Comfortable. Necessary.

Evie refilled her own glass this time. Hunter couldn't move. Couldn't think past peeling Brown's fingernails back with his hunting knife.

"Can you stop staring at me, please?" Evie said.

"Are you going to tell me about Brown?"

Evie cleared her throat and leaned back against the couch cushions. Her nightgown pulled high, exposing her thighs. Her knees parted, just a couple of inches.

Hunter had to sit on his free hand to hold it down. The last thing he needed was to sink into her hot flesh and totally forget the mission. No matter how much the thought drove him insane.

"It's not really Brown. I mean, he's involved. But Marcus is the one. Brown is his lackey."

Hunter ripped his focus from daydreams about her panties to her confession.

Evie blushed and pulled her gown down. He might as well be sixteen and horny, not a covert killer on a mission, because damn if her rosy cheeks didn't make him think about how rosy her ass would look after a spanking. He downed his whiskey, but the burn didn't take the edge off. His cock was so swollen he was sure his zipper would leave an imprint on it.

Evie downed shot number five.

This consumption countdown better yield rewards bigger than a freaking NASA launch, 'cause he was about to explode. He grabbed her arm. *Marcus. Brown.* Evie was the only connection. He needed more information from her. "So what did he want?"

Evie lurched up from the couch and tilted sideways, and Hunter grabbed her just in time to keep her from falling into the coffee table. He hooked an arm around her small waist and dove backward, landing in a heap on the couch.

Her on the bottom.

Him on top.

He ground his hips between her legs, unable to resist the temptation spread before him.

"Hunter..." Evie arched into him. Once again, only the thin layer of her nightgown separated their skin. Damn nightgown.

"Evie, be still." Her reaction to him was obliterating his control.

Evie froze.

Point one for Team Hunter. Now he needed to get her to hold still so he could interrogate her without screwing her brains out. Or his.

He grabbed her wrists and lifted them over her head, pinning them to the couch cushion. He couldn't help the little grind forward. Fuck she was so perfect. Just right for him.

No. No. No. He couldn't let himself forget what was going on. She was far from perfect. She was suspected of being involved in international terrorism. And he was here to take her down and find out all she knew.

"Better. Now as long as you stay there you will be safe. If you move, I can't make any promises..."

Evie wriggled her hips away, her cheeks flushed, her blue eyes dark.

"I've been thinking about you for a long time. Holding you. Touching you like this. I don't know how much longer I can keep myself in check."

"What do you want?" He enjoyed the desperation in her voice. She wanted him too.

"I want the truth. I want to know why your father was murdered. I want to know why that asshat who calls himself sheriff was here assaulting you." He tried to keep calm but his rage boiled too close to the surface.

"You're only home a little while. You don't need to get involved in my messed up life. I can handle it."

"Really, Evie? Is this how you handle things? By letting some asshole beat you in your own home?" Hunter's voice went quiet. Dark. Deadly, but he didn't blow up, didn't get lost in the haze of rage. He was calm. Cold. As cold as the blade he'd use to slice Brown's neck.

"Stop it, Hunter. Just stop." Evie's voice shook. Her body shook. She bucked and he stood, nowhere near monster enough to hold down a terrified woman.

"Stop what, Evie? Trying to put together this crazy puzzle? How about I tell you what I think?" Hunter snatched the bottle from the floor and took a swig straight from it.

"I think Marcus ordered Brown to kill your father to cover his operation. And now, whatever he was covering up is coming out of hiding and he needs help to move it. Probably guns. Could be drugs. And he's planning on making you his pawn to do the dirty work so he can keep his hands clean."

Evie fumbled behind her and clutched the window frame. "How did you figure that out?"

"I guess you've been in it so long you can't see the forest for the trees. But I can see the trees. See 'em real good. And I see you either standing next to Marcus or crushed under him."

Chapter Fifteen

"So what is it, Evie? You a drug runner or a weapons dealer?"

"A what?" What was he saying? Her? She could hardly wrap her head around it. All she could think about was that video. It would haunt her in her sleep, she knew that.

"You heard me. Drugs or guns? I can smell shit when I step in it."

Guns. Downriver. Mexico. How long would Marcus give her?

As if he'd heard her thoughts, her phone pinged in the kitchen. Evie ran to read the message. *Tomorrow. Five p.m. Coldwater Paper Mill dock. Bring your boat.*

She didn't recognize the number, but she recognized an order for what it was. He'd already made his threat.

C.W. had gifted her with his remade Vietnam-era Mark II gun ship to evade taxes. He'd sold it to her for a dollar and each year she paid her six cents to the government.

"Was that Brown?"

Evie jumped. Hunter stood right behind her, but she hadn't heard him move from the couch.

"No." Not a lie. Not exactly. God, the desire to

tell Hunter everything, to plead for his help, filled her. After everything he'd been through, his injury, losing his friend...how could she ask him to risk his life for her?

She couldn't. She would take care of her problem, and she would do it alone.

"Who was it then?"

"Who the hell are you to interrogate me? It's none of your business who sends me texts." Evie managed to pull off the affronted act even though she was quaking like a terrified little girl inside.

"I'm the guy who saved your life. And it's looking like this won't be the only time I'll need to step in." Hunter turned her around, his hands heavy on her shoulders.

Evie yanked free of his grip. "Aren't you forgetting one teeny tiny fact? You left me. And you show up expecting me to just bow down before you?"

"Is your second job moving illegal weapons?"

His question came so fast and blunt it caught her off guard.

"The closest I've come to a gun was the one my ex-fiancé pointed at my head." Hunter jerked back, and she relished the shock on his face. "I'm not moving anything. I own a bar. I sell alcohol. That's it." She needed to keep it close to the truth, at least until she figured out what the freaking hell she could do to get out of this mess. No need to tell him about their little money laundering operation.

"Yeah, and I've been traveling across the world to serve as a tour guide for missionaries," Hunter said.

Evie wanted to punch him. Then she wanted to wrap her hands around his neck and kiss that smart-ass expression right off his face. But no way would she give him a second chance to stomp on her heart.

"Sounds like you also do a little extra on the side."

"Sounds like you have quite an imagination."

"Evie, after tonight, my imagination couldn't come close. Why won't you let me help you?"

Because if she let him in he would only break her heart. Destroy her. Completely. If she'd learned one thing lately, it was this: She could only depend on herself. "I don't need your help. I told you. I can handle it."

She wanted to tell him she'd fallen for Marcus's good-boy pretense. Got engaged to him without thought. Without reservation. But that wasn't true. Evie had used Marcus to get over Hunter.

It was her fault. She'd ignored her parents. Her instincts. Her father. Instead of testing the waters, she'd jumped in headfirst and pulled her family down with her.

* * *

"Show me then. Show me how you can handle a real man," Hunter dared her. Got in her face.

"Forget it. Forget everything and go home, Hunter."

"You want me to forget what he just did to you?"

"Yes, I do." Evie punctuated each word. "Yes, I want you to forget. It shouldn't be too hard. You've done it before. And it seemed real easy for you back then."

"Forget? You think I forgot about you? I

couldn't get you out of my head."

Evie's could feel her eyes going from saucer-wide to paper thin in a split second. "Really? You thought about me all the time, but you never called? Never tried to contact me?" She made a sound, some distorted version of laughter.

"I wasn't going to beg. You know that. I tried to forgive you, but I sure as shit wasn't going to be the first one to come crawling back." Hunter's muscles tensed. Swelled. He tightened his hands into fists at his sides.

"Forgive *me*?" Evie's voice rose higher, almost shrieking. "You're the one who left. You're the one who walked out. Not me."

"Goddammit! What did you expect me to do?" He grabbed her and lifted her up before he realized what he was doing. Her feet dangled in the air, her eyes level with his.

He could see the fright in her gaze and regretted his outburst, but then she kicked him. Hard. In the knee, right below his gunshot wound.

"I expected you to stay."

Hunter let go, his fingers opening on reflex to grab his injured leg. He'd been wrong. She wasn't some fearful little girl. She should work for fucking ISA as their director of torture.

Her feet hit the floor and her hands landed on her hips in a perfect representation of an angry female in charge. All she needed was a bullwhip and a pair of metal clamps for electrocution.

Hunter rubbed his wound, trying to get the fresh agony down to a dull throb.

Where was the guilt he'd expected to see in her eyes? She had the audacity to yell at him when she was the one who had cheated?

"You expected me to stay after you kissed

Marcus? That's right. I followed you that night. I wanted to make up. But you ran straight to that bastard."

The guilt he'd been expecting filled her gaze, for a second, and then her expression hardened. "You think I kissed him? You idiot. He kissed me. If you'd stayed around long enough, you would have seen me slap his face."

"Sure, okay. If that's true, why were you with him in the first place?" He wasn't stupid. She would say anything to cover her ass.

"I wasn't. I went to our spot to calm down. I knew you needed some space. He was waiting. Like he knew I would be there," Evie said.

"I am not an idiot. I know you wanted him. Or his money. You got engaged to him right after I left." He was yelling at her. Acting like a crazy, jealous, love-sick boyfriend. It was like all those years had just melted away.

"You are an idiot, Hunter James. I never wanted him. I wanted you. But you left." Tears threatened her eyes.

Fuck. This whole night had gone wrong.

Hunter threw up his hands and stormed out the front door. Her voice taunted him.

"Go ahead. Run away. That's all you're good at anyway." Evie's voice followed him outside.

Hunter raced down the drive, across the gravel road, down a dock as old as her house, and stopped at the water's edge. He was breathing hard, his chest expanding and contracting with all the force of an air compressor.

The rain had stopped, but the moon was still hidden by clouds. Darkness surrounded him, except for the dim yellow light on the electric pole in her front yard. He crouched and sunk his fingertips into the Mississippi. As if her waters could somehow wash away the emotions tearing up his insides.

But the river kept rushing past, her current strong, unbroken and nearly to the top of the dock. All that planning overseas. The cold calculation to systematically break down Evie's barriers, destroy her resistance, and infiltrate her organization. All of it was disintegrating.

He hadn't planned on the heat in her gaze. He hadn't planned on the electric current from her touch. He hadn't planned on the niggle of doubt about her guilt eating at his resolve.

The recon and reports just weren't adding up with what was really happening. If Evie was in Marcus' pocket, why would he have her beaten?

Hunter stood and wiped his hand on his jeans, his dog tags rattling against his chest. To win this battle, he needed to forget what the intel said. The Evie he'd thought he expected to find here didn't exist. He was no longer sure of anything. But he knew he wanted her no matter what.

And this need, this longing wouldn't change until he figured it out. Until he gained her trust.

Chapter Sixteen

Evie dabbed a wet washcloth on the dried blood trailing down her chin, careful not to press too hard on her swollen lip. Experience had taught her the wonders of a little bit of peroxide to clean up blood. And the power of frozen peas to shrink a swelling eye.

The woman staring at her in the mirror had gone from drug-rehab actress to black-and-blue housewife. Not someone she didn't recognize, just a familiar face from her past she'd hoped never to see again.

The sight sobered her.

She rinsed the cloth in the sink and watched the water turn from clear to pink. Her dad's blood had looked almost black in the video.

And here she stood, alone, wiping blood off her face, wishing Hunter were still there. Something she'd done a lot of in the past.

Then, as if she'd summoned him with her thoughts, *there he was.* Brown eyes. Bare chest. Beyond-sexy face.

Evie spun around so fast she had to grab onto the bathroom counter to keep from falling. "I thought you left."

His expression looked different. Fine lines

seemed to have cropped up around his eyes and mouth. Her fingers tingled with awareness.

"I almost did."

The words hung between them, heavier than the humidity.

"I almost got in my truck and left. But then I walked out to the river. And I thought about what you said. And I realized you were right. I should have stayed. I should have trusted you enough to talk to you about it."

Her thoughts faltered. Hunter, a man who never apologized, who never screwed up, was admitting he'd been wrong.

She'd been prepared to yell at him. To argue and tell him what an asshole he'd been. But she hadn't been prepared for this. He'd yanked her anger out from beneath her feet, leaving her on shaky ground.

Hunter took the washcloth from her hand and dabbed at her cheek. And Evie let him.

He rinsed the cloth and pressed it to her lip again, so gently, his touch nourishing some empty part inside her.

"I want another chance, Evie. I know I don't deserve it, but I want it."

She flinched and he pulled back, concern written across his gaze. "Did I press too hard?"

Not on her bruise. On her heart. He'd left her raw and aching. Aching for something she didn't believe she could ever have again.

But by God, she wanted it. Wanted him at that moment more than she wanted to breathe.

Could she risk it? If he hurt her again, she'd never be able to patch her heart back together, not even with gorilla glue.

"You hurt me." The words tumbled out with

the force of an avalanche.

Hunter's gaze turned fierce, eating her up with its intensity. She expected him to take her into his arms and devour her mouth, as he'd wanted to do all night.

But he kept smoothing the washcloth down her face and neck. Like he was contemplating some life or death decision. "I know. I was stupid. We were both young and stupid."

And then the cloth was gone and his palm was in its place, cupping her cheek. Evie leaned into his touch.

Hunter closed his eyes and took a deep breath. She saw his hunger. His need. But she saw something else too. Control.

"I will never hurt you like that again. Never," Hunter said. But was he really being honest with her? Why did she feel like he was holding something back?

"Thinking about causing you pain rips me apart."

His words broke past her defenses. She was left with an undisguised hunger. "Hunter."

He snagged her hand and twined their fingers together. Then he rested his forehead against hers.

Evie melted. That small, binding touch warmed her from her fingertips to her toes. "Come on, let's get you some aspirin and something for that shiner."

She followed him down the stairs and into the kitchen.

As he rummaged in the freezer, the smell of burnt food hit her. Oh no, the cheese. She raced to the stove, only to find the pot in the sink to her right, filled with water.

"When I pulled my head out of my ass, I realized what the burning smell was coming from." Hunter directed her to sit and draped a bag of peas over her eye.

"Thank you. I'd completely forgotten."

She sat down at the breakfast bar and he took the seat next to her, pulling it close so he could press the frozen bag to her eye. She took it from him. "You're welcome."

Heat stole up her cheeks and she was grateful for the bag covering half her face. His deep voice did all kinds of strange things to her insides.

He traced a figure eight on her knee—a motion that mesmerized her. Chills spread up her thigh and moisture formed between her legs. She swallowed but didn't pull away. His touch felt too good.

"So, why the muumuu? You that hard up for money?" Hunter's voice came as if from a distance.

She was still under the trance of his fingers, but she managed to croak out a few words. "Just haven't bought clothes in a while."

"What made you buy it to begin with?" His face scrunched up.

"It's comfortable." Weak response. She knew it. He knew it.

"Keep the peas on your face." Hunter disappeared outside and returned, with a green duffel bag draped over his shoulder. She'd almost forgotten how tall he was. He had to duck his head to get through the door. And when he stood up straight, she got a good look at his rippling chest, narrow waist and broad shoulders. Muscles outlined even better under his rain soaked shirt.

His skin was sinfully tan, and those jeans fit him just right.

And here she was. Bruised. Bloody. In a muumuu. She wanted to cry.

Hunter plopped his duffel on the floor and rummaged through it. "Sorry if I get your floor wet. The rain started back up. I'm assuming this type of nightgown is all you own?"

He looked up and Evie nodded.

"Well, as a token of our renewed friendship, I'm going to make one request. Burn it. Burn every last nightgown you own." Hunter held out a bundled up piece of green material and Evie took it.

It unfurled into a T-shirt. Hunter's T-shirt.

"You can sleep in that. I'll take you shopping for something new tomorrow."

Evie swallowed. He wanted her to sleep in his T-shirt, surrounded by his scent. The small amount of moisture between her thighs doubled.

"Okay." Jesus. She was going to have to get control over her mouth.

Chapter Seventeen

Hunter woke to filtered sunlight streaming across his face and warmth no blanket could ever provide cuddled against him. He lay on his side, Evie spooned into the curve of his body, her bottom snuggled against his dick.

She scooted backward in her sleep, wiggling her too-tempting behind against him. His hand covered her hip and pulled her closer. Her T-shirt—rather, his T-shirt—rode up to her waist, revealing white cotton panties and long lean legs. Raw need slid down his spine.

Hunter's hand trailed from her waist down her thigh, then back up again, marveling at her quiet beauty. She was the most naturally sexy woman he'd ever met.

Hunter propped himself up on his elbow and studied her peaceful expression. The graceful curve of her nose. Her lush, parted lips. Perfect golden skin. Her hair mussed from sleep, spread around her in wild tangles. She took his breath away.

Hunter eased her shirt to her ribcage, stopping when she rolled onto her back and stretched, arching into his touch. His fingers splayed wide and he marveled at how his hand spanned her flat belly and small waist. Her toes didn't even come close to the end of the bed. His hung off the edge.

The river rushed outside, but he ignored the sound. It had probably risen more last night.

He checked his watch. It was pushing one p.m. They'd slept all day. He hadn't slept past six a.m. since joining the military. Evie was getting to him in ways he couldn't even understand.

She opened her eyes.

"Good afternoon, sleepyhead," Hunter said.

Evie froze in mid-stretch and turned her head in slow motion in his direction. He smiled.

She stuttered. "What are you doing in my bed?"

He'd gone to sleep on the couch, but her screams had awakened him soon after. It had taken him a full ten minutes to calm her down and a full ten seconds to decide to slide into bed beside her.

It only reinforced his decision when she immediately quieted and draped her body over his. He considered the torture of his painful arousal a worthy sacrifice.

Especially since he got to hold her. All night.

"You had a nightmare. Holding you was the only way I could get you to calm down." The truth. Mostly.

Evie wiggled and froze. Her hip had come into contact with his hardness. Damn if she wasn't hot when she got all flustered.

"You slept in that? In my bed?" Hunter glanced down. He had on his underwear. So did she. What was the big deal?

"Yep."

"But...but..."

Hunter took pity. "This is more than I usually sleep in, so count yourself lucky. I could have gone commando."

Her already pink cheeks turning bright red, she jumped from the bed and tugged her shirt down in one motion.

He frowned at the loss of her lovely ass.

"Did we...*do* anything?"

The beast in him enjoyed her worry. "Honey, I don't take advantage of sleeping beauties. Believe me, you'll know when we do something. That's a promise."

She seemed to settle down some, but she didn't quit tugging down on her shirt. Which was pointless. His T-shirt practically touched her knees, completely protecting her from his gaze. But something about seeing Evie in his clothes made him want to beat on his chest caveman-style and shout, "Mine!"

"Did I say anything? Last night? In my sleep?" She was looking at the floor, but she kept making covert glances at him through her thick black lashes.

"No." Unable to stand the distance between them, Hunter tossed the covers back and got out of bed. He tipped her chin up. "And if you don't quit looking at me like that, I'm going to make good on that promise."

She bit her lip and he groaned. "What if I want you to make good on that promise?"

Every muscle in his body went taut. She wanted him too?

"Make sure of that, Evie," he forced himself to say. "Because when I start, I don't think I'll be able to stop."

Hunter held himself back, clenching his

hands at his sides to keep from touching her.

Evie stared at him, her gaze swallowing him whole, and stepped forward, placing her hands on his bare chest. She rose up on her toes, eyes wide open. Hunter met her halfway. Their lips melded together, her hands circled his neck, and he carried her back to the bed.

He broke contact with her mouth for as long as it took to rip his T-shirt from her body. They fell to the bed and Hunter braced his weight on his elbows to hold himself over her. Her legs spread for him and his hips nestled between her thighs. Her breasts were pressed to his chest.

Need like he'd never dreamed of filled his blood. His veins. His pores. Until he was nothing but lust.

Evie moaned into his mouth and he deepened the kiss, slanting his mouth over hers. He needed to get deeper. To take all of her.

One hand drifted down to cup the heavy weight of her breast. He teased her nipple, rolling the dusky tip between his fingers. When she arched, he lowered his mouth to replace his hand and took her in between his lips, sliding his hand beneath her back and lifting her for his enjoyment.

Her taste was intoxicating. Crazy. His blood licked through his body, burning his skin from the inside out. All other thoughts, sounds, and plans vanished.

There was only Evie.

"Hunter." His name was a plea on her lips. Rich and wild. Her hands wound behind his head, holding him to her. His lips closed on her other breast, licking and nipping until she begged him once more.

Then he trailed down her navel, stopping to plant a small kiss. Then he went lower. She sucked in a breath, her stomach hollowed out between her hipbones. His chin hit the top of her panties.

Her innocent white cotton panties. Fuck.

It took all his control not to rip them right off her body and plunge into her.

Instead, he rose and took her mouth once more. Wanting to drive her wild, he slid his fingers up her thigh, pushed her panties to the side, and found her soaking wet.

For him.

His woman.

She wanted him.

Her hips bucked, seeking pleasure, and he grazed a finger over her clit. She gasped. He repeated the motion with light flicks until she was rocking her hips to his rhythm.

She tore her mouth from his. "Hunter, please." She was panting, her gaze pleading.

And he was running low on control.

She didn't protest when he ripped off her panties and pushed her legs wide. Or when he stared at the prettiest sight he'd ever seen.

Unable to resist for another second, he lowered his head and tasted her. He was lost.

* * *

Evie's head dropped back on the mattress, her body bending under the onslaught of Hunter's tongue. He flicked with light, short strokes. Teasing. Taunting. Torturing.

Then his lips closed over that centermost part of her and sucked her between his lips. The air left her body. She couldn't breathe. Couldn't move. Couldn't do anything but tangle her fingers in the sheets and hold on.

He launched her higher. Past the clouds. Into the ozone.

She shouldn't want this. Shouldn't crave his touch. But what she felt right now was beyond wanting. Beyond needing. His finger slid inside her and stroked her like a master musician.

"You taste like heaven." His low growl had her panting harder, riding his finger.

"Hunter, please. I need..." She didn't know what she needed, only that he—and only he—could provide it.

He withdrew from her, the loss leaving her empty and desperate. He rose over her, his face coming even with hers. His lips took hers then, possessing her mouth with force. His tongue plunged inside and she parted for the invasion.

He pushed her thighs farther apart and she felt him nudging against her core. She let her legs fall open, ready. Waiting.

"Shit. I don't have a condom." Hunter paused.

"It's okay. I'm on the pill."

"Thank God." Hunter eased into her, teasing her by stopping when he was barely in and pulling out. She wrapped her legs around his waist, ready to pull him back to her, but there was no need. He slid forward again. Thrusting deeper this time. Stretching her. Pushing her limits. Deeper. Harder. Until he bottomed out and stole her breath.

He filled her completely, reaching places she hadn't even known existed. She'd never felt so good. So complete.

She locked her heels together, holding him

tight. He grabbed her arms and pinned them above her head, holding her gaze. He didn't speak, but she understood. He was in control. He would take what he wanted.

And she would love every minute.

Hunter pulled back and slammed into her, and the force of his thrust pushed her up the bed. Evie cried out, the pleasure bordering on pain as he pounded into her until she didn't know where she stopped and he started. He knocked down that wall she'd built inside her soul until she let loose and embraced Hunter with every fiber of her body.

He thrust hard. Fast. Deep. "Don't stop, Hunter. Please, don't stop," Evie sobbed, so close to climaxing.

"I won't, baby. I promise." Hunter took her until she screamed her release. He stiffened over her. "You feel so good. Better than I remember," he gritted out. And then his muscles pulled taut, and he shouted his release.

They collapsed onto her bed in a tangled mass of sweat and sex and satisfaction.

He fell on top of her, supporting his weight enough to be comforting instead of suffocating. Evie kept her legs locked around him, unwilling to break their bond.

He released her wrists and threaded his fingers through hers. The inferno simmered down to a more languid heat.

Evie became aware of the tenderness between her legs, feeling the fact that she had gone over two years without sex.

Hunter lifted his head, the lazy smile stretching his lips that of a tiger that had just finished eating its prey. Only Evie was the one who had been devoured.

And she'd liked it.

"Wow," she said, unable to resist returning his grin.

"You're welcome."

She laughed and punched him in the arm. The movement pulled her body to the side and she felt him shift inside her. Still hard. She gasped and grabbed his shoulders.

"You keep wiggling around like that and we're gonna be here all afternoon."

She *wanted* to be here all afternoon. All night. But she had a bar to run. And a mother to protect. Evie's brow dipped as she felt the harsh realities of her life pulling her from the warm cocoon of Hunter James.

As if he sensed her pulling back, Hunter thrust forward, fusing them together. "How about we stay here." He thrust again. "All afternoon." Hunter repeated the movement and Evie grabbed his arms. "All night." Again he pushed inside.

He didn't stop. And Evie didn't want him to.

Chapter Eighteen

Evie lay in bed, satisfied and replete. She'd forgotten how wonderfully relaxed good sex made her. Hell, she'd forgotten about sex completely. But the soreness between her legs and the man's arm pillowing her head brought that fact into sharp focus.

She rolled over, stretching, and her gaze fell on Hunter's black Seiko watch. Sixteen thirty-five. "Hunter, why doesn't your watch tell time?"

Hunter curled his body around hers, and she snuggled back into him, not surprised to find him hard and ready. Little zaps of electricity shot through her body, not the intense voltage from earlier, but still enough to make her wriggle her behind.

"It does tell time, honey. It's military time."

"Oh, well, what time is it?" The damn sun had stayed hidden for so long it was hard to gauge how much time had passed. The river was rushing by so loud it sounded like it was in her front yard instead of across the road.

"Sixteen-thirty." She could almost feel his smile against her neck.

"I know." Evie threw an elbow back. Soft but with enough force to make her point. "Normal-people time please."

"Four-thirty." Hunter nuzzled her neck.

Evie shot up, her head slamming into his chin. She ignored his sharp protest of pain and launched from the bed. "You let me sleep all day?"

Hunter rose up on his elbow, his gaze focused on her body. Evie realized she was still butt-naked and grabbed his discarded shirt from the floor. When she stood, semi-clothed, her hands immediately went to her hips.

"If you call that sleeping, we need to start over. I didn't do my job right. Come here." Hunter held out a hand and her traitorous body longed to jump back between the sheets with her own personal sex god.

"Hunter. I have to be at work in thirty minutes." And the meeting. God, the meeting. She was supposed to be at Coldwater in thirty minutes. How could she have forgotten? She had to shower, change, and ditch Hunter. Fast.

"No. I have work. I need you to leave so I can get ready." Evie lifted her chin and crossed her arms, steeling herself for an argument.

"Work? Call in. You and your mom own the bar. Right?"

Evie spoke slowly, enunciating her words. "Yes. But we're short-handed. Why do you think I had to help break up that fight last night?"

Hunter's smooth forehead wrinkled and his brows dropped. "I don't know. I just thought you did that sort of thing now. You know, the new Evie."

"Well, the new Evie doesn't like to break up fights. Just like she doesn't like for people to ignore her when she tells them to leave her house."

Hunter's face darkened and he started to rise. "I don't follow orders." He sat now, the sheet draped over his hips barely hiding his hardness. His feet hit the floor, the sheet fell away, and Evie swallowed.

"Now come here." Hunter took a step forward and Evie bolted out of the bedroom door. "Evie," Hunter called after her, but she knew she had to get some distance. Now.

So she ran. She ran before her stupid mouth got the better of her and admitted the truth. Then Hunter would never let her go.

Her footsteps sounded like a herd of cows thumping on the hardwood floor. She'd always run flat-footed. Her dad said she couldn't sneak up on a deaf man shooting a cannon. Evie looked back over her shoulder, caught a heart-stopping glimpse of spectacular abs, and missed the first step of the stairs.

She grabbed for the banister and put on the breaks, sliding her palm down the smooth surface. But she had too much momentum and her shoulder slammed into the wall, rattling the old pictures and sending one of them to the floor. She felt a brief moment of gratitude that all her home decor came from the dollar store.

"Evie!" Hunter's voice was loud enough to shake the pictures almost as much as her football ram had done. Or maybe that was his heavy footsteps as he chased after her.

She knew she was a goner if he caught her. All her remaining resistance would fall away and she'd tell him everything.

She flew halfway down the stairs and looked back over her shoulder. Having been up and down these steps a million times, she took them for granted, knowing her feet would find the way. But her feet tangled and she fell forward again, face first. Her arms stretched overhead like she was diving for a winning catch and slapped the water with the force of a charging bull.

Warm wet enveloped her. She opened her eyes, but the liquid was dark. Dirty. So she slammed them shut again.

Evie flailed her arms like a preteen in an awkward stage. Her head broke the surface and she gulped in air.

She'd been underwater for maybe two seconds, maybe twenty— her concept of time was skewed by the rapid-fire heartbeat pounding in her chest.

She treaded water and spun around. Her entire living room was submerged, and only the top halves of her walls were visible. Muddy water swirled around her, obscuring anything below its surface. Her couch, gone. Recliner, gone. House, gone.

Evie continued circling, and it took a couple of passes before reality sank in. The torrential rain had finally pushed the Mississippi past her limits. And the river had pushed past the limits of her house.

By the time she completed her fourth turn, she started to get dizzy. Problem was, she didn't have anything solid to grab to stop the spinning. She stuck her arms out, scissored her legs, slowed her progress.

Finally, the room stopped and she stopped, but water kept swirling around her. She maneuvered herself around to face the kitchen. Her heart stopped. Again.

"What the hell?" Hunter's thundering

footsteps came to a stop. Evie turned to him, completely dumbfounded.

"The river." Those two words were enough.

The kitchen was clearly visible through the submerged half of the wide-arched opening. It was all destroyed. Her beautiful black and white tile floor. Her refrigerator. Her...everything.

What would she do? All of her belongings were under water.

"Evie, don't move."

She ignored him, busy scanning her surroundings, her thoughts swirling as out of control as the river in her house. It was all gone. "The cell phone." Her video. Her proof. She'd left it on the back porch.

How could she ever hope to take them down now? She'd planned to bring the phone to the meeting and use it as leverage against Marcus. The one bit of evidence that would have proved her father's murder was gone. The Mississippi had swallowed up her hope.

"Dammit, Evie. Freeze." Hunter's voice finally penetrated the fog of surrealism that had taken over her mind. She turned to him in shock and her mind snapped straight when she saw the pistol in his hand. Her mind snapped in two.

"You too? Why is everyone trying to freaking kill me?" Her entire world had been blown to pieces. First Marcus. Then Brown. Then Hunter. Now Mother-freaking-Nature.

What was next? A tornado? No, that would be too predictable. It would have to be a snowstorm. A blizzard maybe. "Go ahead. Shoot me. If you think I'm going to beg, you've got another thing coming. My life could not possibly get any worse than it is right now."

"Shut up, Evie. I'm not aiming at you."

A picture frame floated in front of her on its way to the kitchen. Mrs. Buela smiled up at her from her perch in a 1940s Ford.

A shot blasted through the house. Water sprayed the right side of Evie's face and she clasped her hands over her ears, trying to block out the explosion. The shot had deafened her. She turned, as if she could track the bullet into the water, and froze.

A black-and-tan mass floated past her shoulder. A water moccasin—its body as big around as her arm, minus a head. Her ears started ringing. Her chest squeezed tight.

Before she even saw him move, Hunter was down there with her. His hand shot past her and grabbed the snake and he tossed it toward her living room window. The damn thing was longer than her couch.

Hunter scooped her into his arms then and carried her to the top of her staircase. She knew her mouth was hanging open like a fish, but she couldn't help it. It was too much. She gave into that mental crack and fell apart. And let Hunter catch her.

Chapter Nineteen

Hunter's heart was still pounding when he pulled Evie into his lap at the top of the staircase and wrapped his arms around her. It would take him a good year to get over the shock of seeing that water moccasin rear up behind her. The damn thing had been over six feet long.

Hunter had been so distracted by her body he'd failed to notice the entire Mississippi River had been making its way inside the house.

Evie's whole body trembled and shook. He recognized the signs of shock. He'd seen it plenty of times in soldiers in battle. But he'd never felt the need to offer comfort.

Until today.

"Listen, it's going to be okay. You're going to be okay. This house is just a house. A rental, no less. You can get another one. Hell, I'll build you another one." His voice was raw. He'd almost lost her. Twice. The sheriff had been easy to ward off. After all, he was familiar with his kind of evil. But the water flooding her house...he was no match for Mother Nature.

Hunter held her at arms length and peered into her eyes. Her pupils were slightly dilated. Her mouth slack. "Evie, I need you to focus. We have to get moving."

She didn't even blink. "Snap out of it, honey. If I have to, I'll throw you over my shoulder, but we gotta leave now." The river kept moving, still rising, and if it got much higher, her house would tear from its foundation. Whether they were inside or not.

Evie's bright blue eyes were dull and vacant. He needed to snap her out of it. He shook her, but her head flopped back and forth on her shoulder, disjointed. The way you wrested a soldier from shock was to slap him. But he couldn't do that to her, particularly not when the swelling bruise on her cheek reminded him of another man who'd hit her.

Hunter gritted his teeth. Now wasn't the time to think about taking revenge. He had to get them to safety first.

Not knowing what else to do, he sealed his lips over hers. He put every bit of longing, of worry, of need into that kiss. He hadn't lied to her today. He couldn't get enough of her. Knew now he never would.

Evie's lips remained slack at first. Unresponsive. Hunter wrapped his hand in her drenched hair and brought her closer. Finally, he felt the tentative touch of her tongue to his and groaned in relief. But he didn't pull back. Didn't stop. His need for her surpassed everything else. His world had narrowed to the woman in his arms. His woman.

The possible terrorist.

Hunter pulled back and Evie touched her lips.

"You okay now?"

"I...I think so." Her voice was still shaky.

"Can you stand?"

"Yes," Evie said.

Hunter helped her to her feet and tugged her down the hall to her bedroom. He pulled the wet T-shirt over her head, ran to the bathroom, and returned with a towel. Evie collapsed onto the bed, her body deflating like a flat tire. Her hair hung in long, wet strings down her back. Some of the color had returned to her cheeks, but they were still nowhere near normal.

Even so, they had to move. Now. Hunter knelt before her, his wet jeans constricting. "I need you to get dressed. Then we're going to gather up a few things and look for a way out. Can you do that?"

Evie nodded but didn't move. Hunter pulled her hands from the edge of the towel. "Can you do that?" he repeated.

She blew out a sigh. "Okay. I can do that."

She stood, her legs unstable at first, and then crossed to her dresser. Once Hunter was satisfied she could complete the simple task without falling over, he went to the bathroom to dry himself off.

When he returned, Evie had pulled on a pair of low-slung jeans and a white tank top. Her wet hair was in a ponytail. But most importantly, she seemed to have overcome the worst of her shock. "What do we need to do?"

Pride swelled in him. She wasn't hysterical or breaking down and sobbing. He knew grown men who wouldn't have handled the situation with this much strength.

"Do you have a backpack or bag of anything up here?"

Evie disappeared into her closet and emerged

with a yellow and blue backpack. Hunter cringed, but at least it wasn't pink. He checked his watch. Five-thirty. A whole hour had passed in what seemed like a minute. Dark would hit sometime in the next hour and a half, which meant they would be camping outside tonight.

"You got a lighter?"

"I've got matches. And a lantern."

"How about a flashlight?" Hunter said.

Evie opened the top drawer on her nightstand and pulled out a flashlight. Hunter reached past her and pulled out her pistol. "You have a license for this?"

Evie gave him a pointed look, her annoyance clear. "Actually I do. It just happens to be in my purse. Downstairs. In the kitchen. You're welcome to go check."

"I like it when you get angry. Your cheeks get all flushed and sexy." Hunter tucked her pistol into his waistband at his back. Evie scowled, her face turning even redder. Before he could check himself, he placed a quick kiss on her lips and was rewarded by the disappearance of her frown.

They gathered more items, gathering anything useful they could find upstairs. Unfortunately, her house wasn't military stocked, but they were able to scrounge up matches, some old rope and tarp from the attic, and extra socks. Hunter rolled Evie's quilt up with the rope and affixed it to the top of the backpack. She grabbed a nearly full bottle of water off her nightstand. Hunter risked swimming back to the kitchen for a knife, can opener, and some canned goods. It wasn't going to be a gourmet supper, but it would be a hell of a lot better than nothing.

He was satisfied they could get by for at least

one night in the woods. His wallet and phone were sunk, right along with Evie's. There would be no calling for help.

He opened the upstairs hall window over the front porch, and looked out, hardly able to process his surroundings.

Her entire property was underwater. The only things visible were treetops, raging water, and debris. The sky was grey, and it looked like the clouds were ready to deliver another deluge of rain. Thunder rumbled downriver. The shit storm wasn't over.

The closest house had to be a few miles away, so running into someone else was unlikely.

A loud clank echoed across the water, drawing Hunter's attention. He almost fell over in relief. An old aluminum fishing boat had gotten tangled in a small patch of cypress trees to his left. If he could swim to it, he could literally dock at Evie's front porch and pick her up.

"What do you see?" Evie crowded his side and slipped in between him and the window. Hunter wrapped his arms around her, unable to resist the temptation.

"I'm going to swim out to that boat." Hunter pointed over her shoulder and leaned down, using the opportunity to nuzzle her neck.

"Can you carry the backpack overhead so it doesn't get wet?"

"No." Hunter lifted his hands to the underside of her breasts, his eyes locked on the nipples hardening under her shirt. "I'm going to leave it here with you. I'll get the boat and bring it back."

Evie stiffened and pushed his hands down. "I'm coming with you."

She turned and he braced for a fight, but what he saw in her eyes wasn't anger. It was fear.

Hunter's hands covered her shoulders. "Listen, there are some really strong currents out there. It's too dangerous. I can go faster if I don't have to worry about a rip current pulling you under."

Evie bit her lip before nodding her head.

"Okay. You're right."

Hunter placed a quick kiss on her lips. "Thank you. I'll be right back."

He folded his body through the open window and stood for a moment on the back porch roof. The water flowed by a few feet below him. Sticks, trees, and other debris were carried by the swift river current. The boat was about fifty yards downriver. Perfect.

He dove into the water and swam, not breaking the surface again until he needed oxygen. Hunter did a quick assessment of his immediate area and kept swimming, careful to keep an eye out for debris.

He was halfway to the boat when Evie called out. "Hunter, watch out!"

He turned and saw the end of a log racing toward his head. He ducked down and dodged left, kicking the water with all his strength. Something sharp scraped his calf and knocked his legs back, but when Hunter broke the surface again, the log was past him. Evie stood on the porch roof, hands pressed to her lips. He ignored the pain and waved at her before continuing on toward the boat. Of course, the damn log had hit his bad leg.

Hunter closed the distance quickly and heaved himself over the edge of the aluminum boat. The old POS was definitely not Bass Pro quality, but damn if it wasn't a gift from God. One paddle lay in the bottom. Hunter grabbed it and quickly rowed back to the house and grabbed hold of the porch roof. Evie tossed the backpack into the boat and he held it steady for her so she could climb aboard.

"Are we going to take the boat all the way to the Wharf?" Evie settled on the front bench, facing him.

"No. We don't know how much more water is coming or if the dam has busted. We need to get to the levee and hike back to town." Hunter pushed off, keeping a careful eye out for stray trees.

"That will take forever." Evie stared at him like he'd lost his mind.

Hunter tamped down his frustration. "Would you rather risk dying in a flood? Look at the clouds, honey. What if it starts raining again and we're stuck in the middle of the river?"

He could see she still didn't believe him. "Can't you just row to the edge if we see more water coming?"

Hunter shook his head, rowing toward the levee with long, sure strokes. "I'm not Superman. We'd get about halfway before being swallowed alive."

Evie gripped the sides of the boat, her knuckles white. "But it's a ten mile hike back to town..."

He picked up her thought and finished it. "We'll have to spend the night outside."

Chapter Twenty

Evie would be stuck overnight with Hunter. Again.

In the past twelve hours she'd not only slept with her ex, she'd had sex with him. Multiple times. And thinking about being in close quarters with him again got her all hot and bothered. Shit, she was acting worse than a horny teenager.

"You're looking at me like you're going to vomit."

Evie focused on him. He'd taken off his wet shirt, revealing his bare chest, and his pecs popped out each time he rowed, their already large mass growing even bigger. His abs rippled, his biceps flexed, and her thighs clenched. His dog tags jangled, the long silver chain shifting with his movements, and she found herself jealous of its proximity to him. Jealous and guilty. Why wasn't she more afraid of what would happen now that she'd missed her five o'clock appointment with Marcus? What if something happened to her mother?

She flushed and quickly glanced at the water, afraid Hunter would be able to read her thoughts. "Sorry. I'm just not fond of sleeping outside."

"Who said anything about sleeping?"

Evie's gaze bounced back to his and their stares locked. She recognized the look as the one he used to give her right before he kissed her. Oh god, he hadn't forgotten that heavy-lidded look. If anything, he'd gotten better at it. Her insides turned to goo and little shots of pleasure pulsed through her core.

"You want to walk all night?" She knew that wasn't what he meant. Not even close. But she couldn't help baiting him.

"If that's what you call sex, then yes, I want to walk all night long." Hunter's lips stretched into a slow, lazy grin, one that would have made her knees buckle if she hadn't already been sitting. Thank the Lord they were stuck in this boat, otherwise she might have just attacked him.

She gave him her best scowl and averted her gaze. The bottom of the fishing boat had rusted and looked like one hard kick would knock a hole clear through the bottom. She pulled the backpack off the floor and hugged it to her.

After several minutes of tense silence passed, the boat rocked and slammed to a stop. Hunter rowed them onto a small ledge, covered in grass, on the slope of the levee. He hopped out and held the boat. "Your destination."

Destination, her ass. More like a never-ending nightmare that stretched out for miles and miles. She loved the levee. Loved cruising down the long gravel road at the top. But right now all she could see were the hours and hours of uninterrupted time with a shirtless Hunter James. And nowhere to take advantage of him.

"Leave the backpack. I'll get it. You get to the top."

Hunter held out a hand and she took it, using the leverage to hop from the front of the boat onto the slope of the levee.

As she climbed to the top, Hunter held the backpack overhead and got off the boat, then pushed it away.

"Hey. Why did you do that? What if we need the boat?" Evie's heart climbed into her throat as Hunter clambered up the side of the levee.

"We won't need it. Besides, that bucket of tin wouldn't have made it much farther." Hunter talked so matter-of-factly. As if they hadn't almost drowned in a ramshackle deathtrap.

Evie swallowed as Hunter put on the backpack and started walking, quickly outstripping her. She only stared after him. Dammit. She was starting to remember just how frustrating he could be. Evie took off behind him, gravel crunching beneath her boots, but Hunter didn't slow down to wait. Which gave her ample opportunity to gaze at his wide shoulders.

A pair of black scorpion tattoos wrapped over his traps, their claws open and pointed toward his spine. Their sharp tails curved up his shoulders, poisonous tips level with his neck. The savage beasts seemed to embody the man. The thought nudged at her conscious. Telling her to keep her distance. He was a predator.

And she was in danger of being paralyzed by his venom.

She shook away the dark thought. "Nice tattoos."

"Thanks."

Evie picked up her pace, determined not to let him leave her behind. "What do they stand for?" As if to mock her, he flexed his back. The scorpions shifted and damn if butterflies didn't tickle her insides.

He gave no response, just kept walking.

"Most people who get tattoos do it for a reason. Even if it is just to show off their muscles." Bitterness crept into her voice, and she embraced the emotion—anything to camouflage the depth of her attraction to him.

Hunter stopped so fast she slammed into his back. He turned and she had to back up a step. "You talk more than I remember."

"Why are you evading my question?"

"Why are you so curious?" Hunter countered.

Because she couldn't stop thinking about him. She wanted to fill in all the gaps of lost time that stood between them.

"I'm just making conversation." And wondering how many other women had seen those tats.

"Are you having second thoughts? About earlier?" Hunter's voice went as quiet as still water.

Evie swallowed at the sight of the storm clouds in his gaze. "No. I'm not. I just wish I could erase the past and start over."

Hunter wrapped his hands around her arms and pulled her close that she could feel the heat radiating off his skin. "I wish a lot of things. I *remember* a lot of things. Like how soft your hair is. How sweet your skin smells right here." Hunter lifted her and inhaled deep from the area right below her ear.

Evie closed her eyes against her will as goosebumps skimmed down her spine.

"How your skin is softer than pure Egyptian cotton." His voice dropped low and his breath was hot against her flesh. He yanked her to his chest and her nipples hardened at the contact.

"That you have the most gorgeous mouth God ever created."

Lust simmered in her, pushing her past warm to hot. She should be running to Mercy, trying to save her club. Her family. Trying to figure out what to do about Marcus. Instead her eyes slid shut and she let him take her mouth in a soul-obliterating kiss.

"That night should have never happened." Hunter trailed kisses down her neck, her collarbone. Evie dug her fingers into his shoulders, holding on tight as tendrils of pleasure climbed her body like vines.

"When I saw you with him, I couldn't handle it. I thought we were turning into my parents all over again."

His words stabbed her in the chest, twisted the knife, and sucked the breath right out of her body. Shock gave way to the dawning realization that he had thought she might be like his mother. His cheating, lying mother.

"How could you think that?" Evie gasped out, struggling to find her breath under the onslaught of his lips.

Hunter nipped her neck, the small bit of pain sending a rush of desire through her body. "I just saw you two and I couldn't think."

"So you left rather than do to me what your father did to your mother?" Her words warped under the weight of her misery. The heartache from five years ago exploded in her chest. Hunter's father had murdered his mother right in front of him and Ranger. And all because she'd had an affair.

Then he had taken a pistol to his own head.

It had almost ruined Hunter.

"I was scared I would turn into my dad. I knew I would die if I ever hurt you, but I couldn't take the chance I'd do something I'd regret. His blood runs in my veins." Hunter pulled back and held her away. The pain in his gaze was heartbreaking.

Evie reached up and cupped his cheek. "You are not your father. That man might have been your biological father, but Hank is your real dad. He raised you. He taught you to be a man. You would never hurt me. I know that."

Hunter's teeth clenched so tight the muscles in his jaw expanded an inch. His hands fisted at his sides.

Compassion ripped more bricks from the part of her self-protective wall that still stood. "You are not him. Do you hear me?"

Hunter got quiet. Distant. His shoulders drooped and she saw the fight leaving his body. Saw, for the first time, the fatigue.

"Hunter." Evie placed her hand on his chest. "I hated you for abandoning me, but..." All the pain and anger and fear balled up inside her chest. Evie took a deep breath, resolving to release it and to put the past in the past. "I don't blame you now that I know the truth."

She held her breath, trying to hold back from breaking down. Hunter stared down at her hand, but she refused to move it. He needed to see her. Needed to feel her support. She almost buckled when his hand covered hers.

Chapter Twenty-one

Evie's hand burned through his chest right into his heart. He wanted to believe her. Wanted it more than he had wanted anything in a long time. But could he risk turning into a sap who believed whatever line of bull anyone fed him?

"Hunter?"

Her eyes were so vulnerable, so open. He was having a hell of a time trying to convince himself this small beautiful creature staring up at him was evil.

His friends had said she was evil.

The CIA had said she was evil.

Hunter had said she was evil. But now-he didn't believe it.

"I believe you."

She offered up a trembling smile and he accepted, warmth filling some empty part inside of him. Hunter capped it off. He still had a mission to complete. Just because he believed she hadn't cheated on him five years ago didn't mean she hadn't gotten involved with criminals.

It was his job to find out the truth. Regardless of his feelings. He suspected more and more that she'd gotten involved against her will and he had every intention of finding the real threat. And squashing it before Evie got hurt. "Let's get moving. The sun is about to set and I would feel better if we made it at least a couple of miles before making camp."

"Okay." They headed toward town, Hunter behind Evie now. He needed more time to think, to process, and to plan.

The river rushed by, ripping and rolling no more than six feet away. He'd been close to the river before—that was nothing new. He'd swam in her waters every summer after Hank adopted him. But he'd never been this close while on top of a forty-foot high levee. He'd never seen the Mississippi crest the tops of trees or sweep houses away from their foundations.

Even the birds didn't know what to do. They circled and occasionally swooped for fish in the water, only to come up, wings flapping and squawking, apparently thrown off by the unexpected rise in the water.

Evie's house had been one of the few left on the river side of the levee. After the last big flood in 1977, most folks rebuilt on the town side, protected by the levee from flood waters. And as long as the levee held, the rest of Mercy was safe.

Thank god he had Evie's gun. It wasn't his Glock, but it was still protection. The rising water could only benefit certain things, and half of them weren't a friend to humans. The fish were no big deal. He'd already killed a water moccasin today, and the alligators? He wasn't going there.

But then again, the flood had benefitted him too. After all, Evie was walking in front of him and they were in this thing together. And damn if she wasn't wearing those jeans that had glitter on the back pockets. Each step, each unconsciously graceful roll of her hips caught the light and twinkled. Taunting him. Drawing his gaze like a fucking bull's-eye target.

She'd pulled her hair up into one of those loose sloppy buns on top of her head. On someone else it might have looked trashy, but it emphasized the curve of Evie's neck and the soft skin leading down her spine. Hunter cleared his throat and looked away, his mind sinking into his pants. The last thing he needed was a walking hard-on.

"I should thank you, for saving my life," Evie said.

Hunter's body tightened and he almost stopped walking. The image of the moccasin poised to strike her lovely neck filled him with fear. With rage. If it had struck, she would have died. They had been fifteen miles from town with no phones. No transportation. No help.

And he was thinking about how nice it would be to cup her ass, rip her shirt off, and palm those lovely breasts. What was wrong with him?

"No thanks needed. It was just a gut reaction."

Hunter cringed, thankful she didn't turn around. His ability to smooth talk women had never been stellar, but it seemed to disappear altogether around Evie. "I mean yeah, when I saw the snake there, I..."

Evie turned then, her eyes wide and surprised. "You mean you were concerned for my safety?"

If he didn't stop grinding his teeth, he wouldn't have any left. "Hard to imagine right?"

She softened, as if she could read his mind. "No, not so hard."

Hunter opted to keep his mouth shut this time. Why his CO had thought he would be good at seducing her into confiding in him was beyond his comprehension. The only thing he was good at coaxing was a bullet from the chamber.

She started walking again and he hurried to catch up. "I'm sorry about your house."

He was proud of how she'd sucked it up and helped him after her initial shock, but when he stopped to think about it, she hadn't given him much information since last night—heck, there had been too many distractions for him to even ask any questions. He needed to know more. Especially if he was going to shield her from her enemies. "So you and your mom bought a bar?"

"Yeah." She kept walking.

"How did you end up with a dump like that?"

"Are you talking trash about my bar?"

"Well, sorry to say, but it is a shit hole."

Evie stopped then and her expression could have fried him like an egg on boiling pavement. "A shit hole was all we could afford when the county refused to pay Dad's pension."

Something was definitely off. The situation didn't add up. The girl he had known had her toes and fingers painted matching shades of pink every week. She wore dresses. Fuzzy sweaters. Cute sandals.

But the woman walking beside him wore boots and ripped up jeans and hard-ass muscle shirts. And had a chip on her shoulder.

"Sorry, I guess that came out wrong." Hunter had never put his foot in his mouth this many times in consecutive order. "It just surprises me that you own a bar like that. I thought you couldn't stand those sorts of places."

Evie kept her blue eyes fixed forward and Hunter didn't like the hard lines around her eyes. "Like I said. Things got hard. We had to make do."

But did she have to make do running weapons for a terrorist?

"I'm sorry about your dad. He was a good man. Mercy is a worse place without him."

Evie snorted. "You don't have to tell me that. You got to meet the new sheriff up close and personal last night. I'd say worse is an understatement."

The desire for revenge rose inside him again—hot and quick. Brown wasn't a big man, but he was bigger than Evie. And when he remembered the sight of his hands wrapped around Evie's neck... "I promise you, Evie, that fucker is going to pay. I'll take care of it as soon as we get back to Mercy."

Evie spun and slammed her hands into his chest. "No." She cleared her throat. "No. You'll just make it harder for us."

Her words just confirmed his suspicion she was being coerced. The worried expression on her face made him hold his tongue. He knew exactly what he would do to Brown once he got his hands on him. No need to make her panic. "Okay. I'll leave him alone. For now."

Probably not exactly what she was looking for from him, but it was the best he could do. He would just have to hope the sheriff stayed out of his field of vision.

Besides, there were other challenges for him to face. And what had just walked into his line of vision was infinitely more dangerous than Sheriff Brown.

Chapter Twenty-two

Her father had always told her not to poke a bear. But after he shot a mountain lion in front of her, right after repeating that hackneyed piece of wisdom, she decided to dismiss his words.

Maybe that was why, when her tangled mind registered that she'd slapped Hunter on his big, hard, sexy chest, she didn't pull back. Why her fingers itched to trace the ridges of his pecs.

Or maybe it was the simple fact that Hunter wanted to defend her. And it had been so long since any man had lifted a fist in her defense instead of to attack her.

Desire slammed into her palms first, rolled up her arms, and slid down her spine. She didn't want to poke the bear. She wanted to stroke his fur.

She lifted up on her toes, grabbed his shoulders, and leaned in to kiss him. But Hunter was distracted, his gaze focused on something over her shoulder. He tensed and she felt his heart accelerate. "Don't move," he whispered.

Shock slapped her hormones all the way down to the unyielding levee of packed dirt and gravel. His arm wrapped around her and formed a band of iron around her waist that locked her in place.

Hunter eased her to his side and she folded around his body like ClingWrap. When he turned, she moved with him. When he lifted his free arm, she froze at the sight of the 9mm in his hand. When she saw what he was aiming at, her heart sputtered like a tapped-out coffee maker.

Alligator.

Huge. Ugly. Big teeth that extended down past his closed jaw.

"Evie." Hunter lowered his mouth to her ear. "I want you to very carefully get behind me."

Evie nodded, and slid her left foot sideways until she was straddling his thigh. The alligator shifted, moving less than an inch, but with a reptilian speed that stunned her. She froze. Her heart drummed so fast in her chest it turned into a straight dull roar instead of a thump, thump, thump.

"It's okay. Just get behind me." His free hand caressed her back, the caress brief and barely there, but enough to give her the strength to continue her journey behind him. Finally, after jerking from every little snap and crackle of the gravel behind her, Evie pressed her chest to Hunter's back.

"What are you going to do?"

"Try and distract him." Hunter eased down into a crouch, his pistol still raised, and grabbed a rock. It took every teeny tiny bit of her will power not to take off running.

Hunter's hand shot forward and the rock plopped in the river. The gator's tail whipped into a C and he disappeared into the water with the speed of the devil himself. Evie swallowed and grabbed Hunter's shoulders. Three close calls.

Three. *When it rains it pours.*

"You must have really pissed Mother Nature off." Hunter stood and holstered the gun at his back.

Evie cleared her throat and said, "Must have been all the paper plates."

Hunter smiled, his tan skin breaking into lines crafted from hours in the sun. She tilted her head back and wrapped her arms around him again. His narrow waist and solid chest were too inviting for words, especially after this latest brush with death.

"I guess you can thank me for saving your life. Again."

"I have to agree, a little thanking is definitely in order." Evie pulled him down, relishing his surprise. This time, *she* kissed *him*.

When they pulled apart a moment later, they were both panting. This afternoon's bout of mind-numbing sex had been like the aftermath of eating that small tenth of an ounce of dark chocolate recommended by her doctor. She craved more. And more. And more. Until she was so full she thought she might die. But she still wanted more.

"If you don't stop looking at me like that, I'm going to take you right here, in the middle of the road," Hunter said.

"If I remember correctly, we did that here before. Only we were in the front seat of your truck." The windows had fogged up in two seconds. Hunter had left her streaked palm prints on them all week.

He tilted his head back and scrubbed his head, the tension thick enough to cut through the humidity. And Evie enjoyed his discomfort with a lighthearted pleasure she hadn't felt since high school.

Unable to resist teasing him a little more, she leaned up on her toes and whispered, "You know, I doubt anyone will be driving down the levee today. Flood and all, you know? And it's getting dark."

Hunter's gaze dropped and her satisfied smile turned rigid. His dark brown eyes had gone black with lust.

She swallowed, her throat suddenly too tight.

She had poked the bear.

Evie spun and took off, the gravel crunching under her boots. She made it a few steps and then her feet left the ground. Hunter threw her over his shoulder, caveman style. And her face became very acquainted with his very sexy, very round backside.

"I remember fogging up the windows in my truck. But I don't remember doing it against a tree."

A tree. Was he serious? The thought of having sex out in the open, where they could get caught, was...incredibly hot.

But also incredibly scary.

Evie pounded on his back. "Put me down this instant. We can't do it out here. I was just playing."

Hunter smacked her butt and she yelped.

"That's just a taste, babe." He kept walking and started humming. And if she wasn't mistaken, she thought she recognized Justin Timberlake's "What Goes Around Comes Around." Bastard.

She needed to regain the upper hand. Desperate times called for desperate measures. She sank her teeth into his ass. Hunter howled and pulled her over his shoulder so fast her head swam.

"You little wild cat. I'm going to tan your ass for that." Hunter rubbed his behind, but his eyes glowed with carnal promise.

"Nice song. I didn't know you listened to JT."

"I've found I have a taste for songs about revenge."

"Really? Or just boy bands?" Where had that come from? Where had any of this come from? Her first reaction with Hunter had been to poke and tease, not cower and run.

Realization dawned. It was *because* of Hunter. Because, despite everything, she still trusted him.

And deep down, she still loved him.

Her stomach shook with the realization, and she had the feeling of standing at the edge of an open airplane, getting ready to skydive without a parachute. The intensity of the sensation pushed outward into her arms and legs, sending her thoughts tumbling out of control. Then Hunter's arms surrounded her and yanked the parachute cord. And suddenly she was floating, her body light and fuzzy and kissed by the sun.

She met him halfway in a wild crash of lips and tongue. A combination of fuel and fire, ready to combust. The trembling in her body returned, but it wasn't from fear this time. It was a Richter scale nine-point-five earthquake.

Hunter lifted her and she locked her legs around his waist. This was it. What she had been missing since he left. For the past few years, she'd fallen into the sinkhole of anxiety and panic attacks, unable to save herself before she sank. But Hunter had thrown her a rope.

They broke apart, gasping for air, and Evie grabbed his face between her palms. She needed to see his strength. To feel it. Her sun wasn't a bright yellow ball of fire. It was dark and steady and made of titanium.

A flat ball of rain spattered her forehead and she looked up. "It's raining. Again." A huge fissure inside her was separating her common sense from her heart, but each time he kissed her, the gap spread wider. And she didn't have any hope of keeping one foot on each side. She had to choose.

Common sense. A dull, dreary, lonely life. No risk to her heart. No risk of unimaginable pleasure.

Or Hunter.

Evie took a deep breath and jumped.

Chapter Twenty-three

Evie had that RPG-about-to-explode-on-his-ass look and Hunter wondered if it was due to his caveman act.

But then his little kitten morphed into a tiger and attacked him. She sucked his bottom lip between her teeth and he groaned, his hands drawn to her butt like magnetic opposites. He'd been dreaming of how sweet her lip would taste between his own teeth before she turned the tables on him. And he fucking loved it.

If he'd been a bear, he would have growled. Instead he had to settle for the deep rumble of pleasure in his chest. Her mouth explored his, tentatively at first, but quickly growing more aggressive. His little firecracker needed to be in control this time. He could feel the change in her. He knew she'd made a decision. One that was vitally important to her.

Evie nipped and licked her way down his jaw, his neck, his shoulder. She bit down, hard, and Hunter pulled her to him, forcing her center to rub up and down his jeans-covered cock. Gravel road or not, he was going to be inside that tight little body soon, and if her actions spoke true, she wanted the same thing.

"Hold on." Hunter slipped the backpack off one of his arms and fought to disentangle the other one. The sun had set and there was only a dim grey glow just over the horizon. Darkness hit fast, the thick cover of clouds hiding the moonlight.

Hunter ran down the dry side of the levee, into the woods at the bottom. A few minutes later he returned with his prize, a bundle of sticks and an old beer box.

"What are you doing?"

"I'm building a fire. We can sleep here. The sunlight will be gone soon." He grabbed the backpack and dug for a match. He'd been lucky to spy the edge of white and blue cardboard sticking out from a pile of trash that had protected it from the rain. Perfect for kindling.

"Perfect." Evie grabbed the quilt and spread it next to the pile of sticks.

He had a small fire going in less than five minutes. By the time he stood to survey his work, Evie was on her knees, tank top off and bare breasts swinging free. The glow from the old-time lantern danced across her skin and turned it to pure gold. Hunter paused in the process of undressing himself, transfixed by the most sensual creature he'd ever beheld. Time slowed. Evie knelt and undid the top button of her jeans. That small event set off a chain reaction in Hunter. He ripped off his own clothes and stood before her. Naked.

Evie cupped him, her small hand circling beneath his balls, and lifted. He spread his legs wider. She stroked him until he couldn't hold back the grunts and groans. Her lips looked swollen and moist and her mouth was situated perfectly to take his cock. Hunter's control slipped and he wrapped a hand in her hair and guided her to him. Evie pulled back and Hunter thrust forward, seeking her lips.

"My turn," Evie said. He let go of her hair and just rested his hands, sweat beading his back at the torturous wait. A second later he was rewarded when her hot little mouth surrounded him.

Fuck, he'd been dreaming about her mouth on him for too long. But the reality was so much sweeter than any dream.

* * *

Evie moved in a dream-like trance, locked into pleasure and lust and desire. Hunter's cock stretched her lips wide and tight. His salty taste was like heaven.

She didn't know what creature had taken over her body, but she fed off the heady power of knowing she was the only one who could make Hunter James lose control. Evie sucked hard and flicked her tongue on the underside of his tip. Hunter jerked and gasped, his fingers yanking her hair. "Witch."

Evie smiled around him and continued to explore. She wrapped her hand around the base of his shaft, taking up the space her mouth couldn't touch. Then she started sucking him in deeper, harder, tighter, feeling him pulse and throb in her mouth. Hunter groaned, hoarse with need.

Her other hand drifted back to his sac, cupping and teasing the heavy, silken weight of it in her palm. Hunter's hands pulled tighter in her hair, and his thrusts came harder. Faster.

Evie moaned around his hot flesh, the feeling of sensual power rising higher in her body. Her breasts were heavy with need, her core wet and ready. Sucking him like this, taking the control from him, aroused her. The sensation of him stretching her lips taut, filling her so completely that she tasted, smelled, and felt only Hunter, drove her wild.

"Jesus Christ." Hunter thrust deep and held her still, his cock buried in her throat. Evie fought the urge to choke and forced herself to relax. She wanted to take all of him, so she let Hunter take over, pulling out and thrusting forward while she sucked hard. Wanting to make him lose control completely, she pulled her lips back and scraped her teeth lightly down his length. Hunter roared and a drop of his salty essence spilled onto her tongue before he pulled out.

It felt like less than a second had passed before his hands encircled her waist. Hunter turned her quickly onto her hands and knees and slammed inside her before she could speak. Evie arched, a gasp escaping her lips as he spread her wet folds wide, thrusting into her with a power that left her weak.

He latched on to her hips and drilled into her, hard and fast, her whole body jerking forward with each thrust. His finger found her clit and rubbed it in small circles in time with his movements. Evie's head dropped between her shoulders, his touch sapping all the strength from her muscles. The ball of heat building in her core expanded until it was ready to explode.

Each time he filled her, he stroked her clit. Sending her higher. She burned. Ached. He stretched her until she couldn't take any more, then he thrust deeper. Took more. Took her control. She shattered, the scream sliding out of her open mouth, drifting across the water. Down the road. The woods. Everywhere. But she didn't care. Couldn't think.

Evie convulsed around him and her fingers dug into the blanket as Hunter continued to plunge into her, stretching her orgasm out into one long roller coaster ride of pleasure. Hunter slammed in one more time and roared his release.

Evie collapsed onto her chest, Hunter still holding her hips high. Her body shook, quivered. Small aftershocks of electricity zinged through her. He'd taken her control and lost his.

The fire had dwindled to a glowing pile of embers and smoke. Its hazy glow illuminated the gravel right around it and nothing else. Hunter pulled out of her a few moments later. Evie was distantly aware of his movements, but she was overwhelmingly aware of the emptiness she felt after his retreat. Hunter had filled those missing parts inside her, parts of which she had only recently become aware. And she knew she could never go back to being without him. To being alone. She needed him.

He added more limbs to the fire and then fell onto the blanket beside her and she snuggled into his arms, loving the feel of his body completely surrounding hers.

He had told her she was the reason he'd come home. Up until tonight, she hadn't believed him. Hadn't dared to let herself fall for him again, but she had realized something tonight.

Hunter might have been the reason she fell apart the first time, but he had also put her back together. Made her whole.

Chapter Twenty-four

Evie had gone from timid to torrential in a split second. Despite the loss of his ability to speak coherently around her, he'd met his first objective. They'd reestablished their trust in each other. But instead of cold detachment and calm confidence he usually tried to project, he felt incredible heat and the need to protect.

She'd been on her knees, staring up at him with something close to worship and he had reveled in her gaze as much as the heavenly feel of her lips around his cock. She wasn't just a mission. No matter how much he tried to lie to himself, he knew she had slipped into his heart. Maybe she'd never left.

And he wanted her to love him.

The thought came out of left field, slammed into his chest, and nearly knocked him on his ass.

Hunter swallowed, his throat tight and dry. Dammit. Evie had dumped his mission on its head and now he needed to find a compass to point him back in the right direction.

Theft. Guns. Murder.

Then he looked at Evie, cuddled in his arms, and saw the angry bruises around her neck. She needed protection from Marcus and his man. She needed him. And he vowed right then and there he would do everything in his power to save her.

"Listen, Evie. I've been trying to talk to you since last night. About the reason I came home."

She rolled over in his arms and lifted her fingers up to graze his cheek, leaving small spikes of electricity in their wake. "It's okay, Hunter. You don't have to say anything else. Let's just enjoy our time together and when you have to leave again it will be okay. No hurt feelings. No expectations."

"But that's not what I want." It was true. He needed her to love him. To want him no matter where he was stationed. He needed someone to come home to.

Shit. Waxing poetic? He had to get it together. She thought he'd come home just for her. And he was starting to believe it himself. All he could think about was how much he wanted to hold her, to sink into her again. When he should be thinking about using her and discarding her.

Goddamn mission was killing him.

But Hunter James didn't fail or quit. He got the job done. He had to compartmentalize. Figure out a way to tuck his emotions back into the steel vault in his mind and finish.

Evie wasn't his target anymore. She wasn't totally innocent either, even if her blue eyes stayed fixed on him with a naive yearning. Even if she kissed him like she was years out of practice. Even if all he could think about was how sweet her moans sounded when he slid into her.

"Hunter, I really am happy you're home. And I want to be with you. More. Like this. But I'm scared." Her voice wavered with barely hidden indecision. She tottered back-and-forth and he had to tip the weight fully in his favor.

He took a deep breath and ignored the burning ache in his chest. Think. Plan a strategy for infiltration.

"Look, last night, when I saw him on top of you...last night something snapped inside me. It was stupid of me to stay away for so long. I've thought about you. All the time. No matter where I was." He paused and grabbed her hand, turning it palm up. "In the middle of the desert." He kissed her palm and inhaled deep, filling his senses with her sweet scent.

"I would think about you late at night, when I stood outside the tent and looked up at the stars. Remember how we used to lie on the sandbar? Remember how many stars we'd see spread out over the river? Remember *our* star?" Hunter kissed each of her fingertips, taking his time, savoring each one. Each time she gasped and those small breathy sounds chinked away a piece of his armor. Blood flooded his cock, those little sounds driving him crazy. He let go of her hand and pulled her chest flush with his, savoring the feel of her hard nipples digging into his skin.

"No matter where I was, I found our star." Hunter kept his voice low. He kissed the tip of her nose. Her cheeks. Her head. Evie's fingers dug into his arms.

Her breathing increased, and every time she inhaled, her nipples pushed harder against him. He didn't know how much longer he could hold back. Fire licked his skin wherever they touched.

He wanted her with a savage need that took control of his body. Took control of everything. Hunter flipped her onto her back, nudged her legs apart, and rammed inside. He didn't need to see if she was still wet. Her gaze, her body told him how much she wanted him. Evie arched and her mouth opened, but no sound came out.

Hunter watched her expression, watched her tilt her head back and close her eyes as he thrust slow and deep inside her. "And I always wondered..." He pulled out and thrust forward, not stopping until he hit her core. "If you were staring at our star with me," he said gently, invading the warm cocoon of her body each time he spoke. She spasmed against him and her eyes flew open. "If you were thinking about me..." He slammed in again, his strokes long and sure. "...like I was thinking about you." Hunter ignored the vise in his chest and took her mouth in a brutal and possessive kiss. He felt the visceral need to mark her. To make sure she understood she was his. Always had been. Always would be. And he knew it had nothing to do with his mission.

Evie's heels dug into his thighs and urged him on. She moaned into his mouth and arched into his touch. Hunter couldn't get deep enough; he needed more. He tore his mouth from hers and leaned back enough to pull her legs over his shoulders. He drilled into her, using her hips to yank her closer and bring their contact deeper, until her body went rigid and she screamed his name into the night. She clenched around him so tight he could no longer hold back. He let go, his release bursting inside her moist warmth. Marking her from the inside out. His.

Hunter fell forward, barely catching himself on his elbows, his orgasm draining every last bit of energy from his body. Evie's eyes closed, her breath coming deep and fast, just like his. Being inside Evie, being a part of her, had opened up the emotions he'd kept carefully hidden for so long. He took her lips. She opened for him and sucked his tongue into her mouth, then wrapped her arms around his neck and pulled him down to her.

Everything he'd said had been the truth. Not an act. But what he wanted didn't matter to his CO. He had to find a way to get the real bad guy and protect Evie.

* * *

Evie lay limp and replete in Hunter's arms. All of her fight, all of her willpower, every single ounce of common sense, lay in the dirt beneath them.

He had literally pounded her defenses to dust. She smiled. And she'd enjoyed every minute. He might have to leave again for work, but he was here now. He'd proven himself to her over and over. He had opened up and let her know exactly how he felt. He wanted her. The *real* her. Not just her body. Not just for a few days. He wanted her to be his home.

Warmth slid into her, filling her as much as Hunter's body had a few minutes earlier. Her heart seemed to swell past the confines of her rib cage. She didn't recognize the emotion at first. It had been too long. Hope.

Hope for a future. For a life she could share with someone. A family. Kids.

Whoa. She needed to keep these thoughts under lock and key. Kids were definitely way down the road and she didn't want to scare Hunter off right after she'd gotten him back.

"We're gonna have to move soon. We need to make camp." Hunter's chest rumbled under her ear as he spoke.

"Just one more minute." Life could change in an instant, so she wanted to savor this moment. Remember it.

She still couldn't believe he'd left because of Marcus. Chills covered her body, despite the raging heat of the air and Hunter's body against hers. Everything made sense now. His abrupt departure. His mom.

Fierce protectiveness welled up inside her and she embraced the emotion. Hunter was the size of a giant and more than capable of defending himself, but that didn't mean he didn't need someone to watch out for him.

He squeezed her tightly and she snuggled deeper into his embrace. Despite the wounds of his past, he hadn't stopped wanting her even though he'd thought she was a cheater.

Something inside her splintered open. "I can't believe you still wanted me after you thought I cheated on you."

Hunter pulled her up and lifted her on top of his chest. His eyes had deepened from black to obsidian. She had no idea what he was thinking. But she still hurt. For him. He caught her first tear on his cheek.

"Honey, don't cry. That was a long time ago. Let's live in the present. I don't want to think about it anymore. I just want you." His hands cradled her head to pull her down so he could kiss her forehead.

"I want you too. I missed you so much. I could barely get out of bed after you first left." The words spilled out as fast as her tears, and Hunter caught every one.

"Shhh. Let's not talk about the past. It's over.

We're here together. Now. And I intend to enjoy every second." His gentle words and touch were like a safety blanket.

"Okay. Let's live in the now." Her stomach grumbled at that exact moment and she smiled down at the man who had managed to make her feel again. "Too bad we don't have food."

Hunter's answering grin filled his entire face. "Actually, while you were packing, I swam back down to the kitchen and grabbed some canned food."

Evie clutched his face and planted a big kiss on his lips. "I knew I loved you, Hunter James."

Chapter Twenty-five

Hunter looked right into her eyes and forced himself to say, "I love you too."

Evie's smile disappeared. The golden light flickering from the fire highlighted the paleness his words caused. He'd done worse things in his life, but none of those things had felt this bad.

"Hunter...I was just playing... I don't think we're ready for that yet." She tried to stand, but he held her tight. He'd been dealt his cards, played his hand, and now he had to stick to his bluff.

"You weren't playing any more than I was. Admit it, Evie. You love me too," Hunter whispered, the harsh sound of his voice grating across his own skin.

"I...need to think." Evie pushed against his chest again, and this time he let her stand.

He followed her up, fighting—and failing—to tear his gaze from her perfect breasts. She presented him with her back, taking his choice away. With the light from the fire, he finally got a chance to look at her. Really look at her. He didn't know at what point his dick had become his brain, but his gaze fell south, straight to her incomparable ass.

It screeched to a halt at her hip. The light illuminated a red puckered scar, just above her right butt cheek.

Hunter took a step forward, focusing on the scar. When he realized what he was seeing, he started to shake with anger. "What the fuck is that?"

M.C. The initials were branding-iron clear.

Pain nearly bent him forward. Nearly took him to his knees. "He did that to you?" Hunter pointed at her hip. "That goddamn son of a bitch fucking *branded* you?"

Fury engulfed him, demolishing any fixation on her naked flesh. Destroying any thoughts about lying and love and loss.

His ability to maintain any myth of detachment went up in smoke. There would be no nonchalant assassination for Marcus Carvant. No smooth knife to the neck. That motherfucker was as good as butchered meat.

Evie spun around, her eyes wide with confusion. "What? Another gator?"

Hunter grabbed her shoulder, spun her, and pointed at her scar. "That, Evie. How did you get that scar?"

Evie turned to face him again, her eyes wide with fear. She held up her hands, palms flat, as if she could keep him back. "It's nothing. I swear. Just an accident. I fell." She took a few steps away, but Hunter stalked toward her, ignoring the gravel digging into his bare feet. Her face lost all color, and tension filled the air between them like the buzz of insects. He'd seen that kind of fear before. But not in Evie's eyes.

His mother used to say the same thing to the cops whenever a neighbor called to report his father for domestic abuse.

Suddenly everything made sense. The baggy clothes. The distance. "He's dead."

Any doubt he'd harbored of Evie's willing involvement with Marcus ceased to exist.

Evie's entire body jerked. "Hunter, this is crazy. Let's get dressed, find somewhere to make camp. We can talk then."

Every word she said might as well have been a knife thrown into his chest. Her entire stance screamed escape. She kept backing up, her body tight. Defensive.

He didn't see her nudity anymore. He couldn't tear his gaze from her blue eyes and the dark knowledge she was trying to hide behind them.

"You can keep running from me, Evie, but I'm not going to give up. I've seen scars like those before. I've got my own." Hunter kicked his leg around and pointed to his calf, where a smaller version of the scorpions on his back resided.

He couldn't get a tattoo of the initials TF-S. No one on their team could, on the off-chance someone would recognize the initials. But the person who'd branded Evie hadn't cared about recognition. He clearly thought he was above punishment.

Hunter knew he was making a mistake, but he grabbed her arm and spun her around. He held her to him, traced the initials with his fingers. Evie sobbed and jerked away, her anguish a living, breathing thing between them.

This time she didn't back away. She didn't hold her hands up to ward him off.

She ran.

"Evie. Wait." Hunter took off after her. The

night, the clouds, the levee, it all disappeared. She was the only thing that mattered. Hunter ran with every ounce of willpower he possessed.

He caught up to her and grabbed her arm, but Evie screamed and kicked like a madwoman.

"Evie, stop. Stop fighting me." Hunter carried her back to their blanket. Stood her in front of him and didn't let go. Her hysterical sobbing wrenched his heart, and her harsh breathing and flushed cheeks painted a clear picture of terror.

"Evie, I'm sorry." Hunter fought to keep his voice cool. Calm. Gentle. When all he could do was think about killing Marcus.

"Please, honey. I shouldn't have yelled. I know that. Please don't be mad. I just need you to talk to me. Tell me the truth. Tell me what happened."

Evie's gaze dropped to his hands and Hunter realized he'd squeezed harder with each word. He forced his fingers to loosen their grip, but he didn't let go. He knew she would run if he did.

"I told you. It's nothing." She kept her gaze down, avoiding him.

"Evie..." A light appeared in his peripheral vision and he yanked his gaze to the right. Headlights. With a set of four-bar lights across the top.

Shit.

"Evie, get dressed. Someone's coming." Hunter dropped her arms and grabbed his jeans.

Evie hurriedly yanked on her shirt and grabbed her jeans. "Oh my God. That's Brown."

The truck was coming in fast. He must have come back, saw her flooded house, and kept going. A large trail of dust was visible even in the dark.

Hunter pulled on his boots. "Are you sure?"

The truck moved at high speed, the tires spinning around the last curve before the straight stretch leading to where he and Evie stood. In not much time at all, the vehicle would be right on top of them.

"Yes. That's his truck." Evie buttoned her jeans and yanked on her boots.

Hunter grabbed the backpack and Evie's hand and took off down the side of the levee, away from the river. Their fire and blanket might as well be a beacon; there was no way Brown hadn't seen them.

Tall grass slapped Hunter's jeans and a flock of moths exploded out of the weeds as Evie and Hunter ran through them. The truck squalled to a stop and gravel flew. Crunched. Hunter and Evie broke into the tree line paralleling the levee.

A door slammed. Then another one. "Evangeline Videl, you'd better get back here."

Hunter ignored Brown's shout and continued to run. The trees grew thick, the vines and underbrush thicker. Razor vines slashed at his chest and jeans.

"Look here, Sheriff. The lady left us her underwear. Think she's trying to tell us something?" Another voice Hunter didn't recognize, but he would bet money it was one of the shithead deputies he'd seen at the bar.

"Oh no," Evie gasped behind him.

"Ignore them. Keep moving," Hunter commanded, and then cut left, making sure to vary their trail. He knew these woods. This levee. He was pretty sure they were only about a mile from Silo Farm.

"I saw 'em run down here. Look, here are

their tracks," the strange voice said.

"Good," Brown said, his voice pitched low. "Hunter, I know you're out there too. Surrender yourself and we won't hurt the girl."

Hunter pulled Evie to a stop, positioned her against a wide tree trunk, and listened. Leaves crunched about a hundred yards behind them. He indicated for Evie to keep still and leaned to the side, scanning the woods. He didn't have to look hard. Two flashlight beams stood out clearly through the trees.

"Last chance, James. I know you're out there. I know you have our girl. You should know we have guns. And spotlights. And we *will* find you." Brown continued his forward progress, walking blind, headed in the opposite direction.

They needed to move, now, if they wanted to elude the sheriff and his deputy.

* * *

Evie's breath sawed in and out of her chest, feeling like shards of glass ripping up and down her throat. Was she really this out of shape? Geez, perhaps a workout regimen would be worth getting up early for after all. Searing pain shot through her left side and she slapped her hand over the area. "Cramp."

Hunter grabbed her arm and yanked her forward. "Move it."

As much as she wanted to fall to the ground and curl into a ball, she complied. The one thing stronger than the pain was her need to survive.

"I'd like to keep my arm in its socket," she snapped. Great. Sarcasm. She needed Hunter to live. After all, it wasn't like she'd taken Survival 101. The closest she ever got to real hiking was a long walk up the stairs to the Wharf. And even then she had a freaking rail for support.

Now all she had was two-hundred pounds of raw strength and determination pulling her forward like the little engine that could—on steroids.

"Then you should keep your mouth shut and keep your attention focused on running." Hunter pulled harder.

Evie leaped to keep up. The heat stole what little oxygen supply she had available. Mud sucked her boots down and caked on an extra ten pounds, easy. Whatever water she'd managed to consume earlier had sweated out hours ago. If it weren't for the ninety percent humidity, she would have shriveled up like a dried cornhusk.

A branch slapped her in the face and she sucked in a breath at the sting. Tree, one. Evie, zero.

They kept up a steady run, weaving in and out of the tall pines and ash trees. Evie ducked and dodged, trying to mimic Hunter's moves, but the lack of light combined with their fast pace ensured she hit every possible limb. Thorns and rough foliage snagged her skin and jeans. The moon peeked out every few minutes, casting a spare amount of light on the densely packed leaves and mud beneath their feet.

A sharp retort sounded from behind them and Evie heard a shrill whine buzz past her ear.

"Shit." Hunter yanked her to the ground and threw his massive body over hers.

"Was that what I think it was?" Evie struggled for calm, but her tone was sharp.

"Hush." Hunter covered her mouth with his hand, inadvertently shoving dirt between her lips.

She tried to give him her go-to-hell face, but

her heart was too busy trying to pound its way out of her chest. Her blood thumped in her ears so loudly she was surprised the entire forest didn't echo with the force of it.

Hunter shoved her backpack under a thicket and flattened even more on top of her, shifting so that his chest was smashing her into the soft earth and his hips nestled between her spread legs. He was crushing her. And instead of getting angry, she could only focus on how well he fit between her thighs.

She'd lost it. She needed to get with it. She was running for her life, through the woods in the dark, and yet she was busy panting after Hunter. No wonder the dumb blondes always ended up dead in movies.

A limb snapped and Hunter's head jerked up. Her heart stopped. That's when she heard it. Two men, breathing hard, no more than ten feet away.

"I swear they went this way. Can't miss that blonde hair out here."

Evie's eyes widened and she tried to cover her hair. There was no mistaking that back woods voice. Roger Clemens, Brown's top deputy, a man known for his tracking skills. Hunter kept her arms pinned and shook his head for her to be still.

Stupid. Stupid. Stupid. Why hadn't she covered her hair? Put mud in it or something?

"Shut up, dumb ass. You wanna let them know where we are?" Brown's harsh whisper grated across her skin.

The pair stopped a few feet away. Evie held her breath. She could see their boots beneath the thicket separating them. Fear crawled through her veins. She should be at home. Curled up on the couch with Rooster and a movie.

Not here. Not in this horror show.

"You hear anything?" Roger said.

Brown gave no response. The night bugs went silent, no longer providing the small camouflage of sound.

Her lungs burned. She couldn't hold her breath much longer. Something crashed through the woods in the distance.

"Marcus wants Evie alive. Don't shoot unless you're sure it's not her. Got it?"

"Got it," Roger said. The men took off left, perpendicular to their previous direction. And, more importantly, away from Hunter and Evie.

Once they were too far to hear, Evie expelled her breath and choked for air. Hunter stood and pulled her to her feet. "We have to run. It's our only chance. I want you to stay right behind me. If we can get to Silo Farms, we can wire a truck and get to town."

"Silo Farms shut down years ago," Evie said.

Hunter gave her a dark look. "Our other option is to hide in the woods and pray my brother miraculously figures out we're being chased, then finds us in the middle of nowhere before Brown and Roger do."

Well when he put it so sweetly. "I just wanted you to know."

"Got it. Now are you going to trust me to get us out of here alive or do you have a better plan?"

"Did a stick wedge in your ass or something?" After everything she'd been through in the last twenty-four hours, the last thing she needed was his attitude.

Hunter's jaw clenched. "The only thing wedged in my ass is you. Believe me."

"I thought you military guys were supposed to have that whole knight-in-shining-armor thing going for you. You know, rescuing damsels in distress, and all that." Evie looked up at him through her mud-encrusted lashes. Temptress she was not. Hillbilly queen—definitely.

Hunter grabbed her arms and yanked her to him. Electricity sizzled between them. "Damsels in distress don't smell like stale dirt. And they also don't sass their heroes."

"Yeah, what else, Lancelot?"

"They reward their heroes with a kiss." Hunter's words shocked her into silence a second before he crushed his lips to hers. Evie fought to hold on to her logic. Fought hard. Then his tongue slipped between her lips and her logic went on a trip to wonderland.

Her nipples tightened against his chest and she wrapped her arms around his neck, pulling him down for more. Just a little taste. That's all she needed. Just a taste.

* * *

The fear he'd seen in Evie's eyes while they were lying silent on the ground, inches from discovery and death, had once again awakened his need to protect her. To shelter her. To rescue her. He was freaking Lancelot reincarnated.

Now he felt her lips and the moist heat of her tongue and he wanted to strip her down and back her up to the nearest tree. But he couldn't.

Hunter broke the kiss even though his dick was waging a battle to bust through the zipper of his pants. He took a step back. He had to get them to safety. If it were just him, he would circle back and take out the bad guys. But Evie was vulnerable. And she was the target.

"I know you can't keep your hands off me, but we gotta get out of here," Hunter said.

Evie punched his arm and he couldn't hold back a grin. "You kissed me," she said.

"Your come-fuck-me look was calling my name, sweetheart."

"You...you..."

"Angel?" Hunter supplied, enjoying the angry flush spreading across her cheeks.

"Devil."

"Yours to command."

Evie rolled her eyes. "You have any idea which direction we need to go?"

"I can track a man though the desert without a compass. I'm pretty sure I can navigate us through these woods."

"Prove it." Evie turned and took a step. A stick snapped and Hunter grabbed her around the waist before she could move again. Her shoulder had caught a small tree limb. No big deal. Unless you were being tracked. Animals broke tree limbs all the time, but much lower to the ground. The branch Evie had snapped was chest level.

The flashlights arched in their direction and they dropped to the ground again. Evie's breathing was coming quick and harsh. He needed to calm her down. He wrapped his arms around her and rubbed her back in soothing circles.

His hand brushed her scar. He stiffened but forced himself to relax. The anger he'd felt earlier rose again, faster than the flooded river. Only now, he had an outlet.

He kept his gaze locked on the lights. They had stopped moving and were pointed at the ground now. Evie trembled but quieted.

The lights flickered off and plunged them into total darkness. No one made a sound. No animals. No insects. The night creatures stayed away from the new predators.

He and Evie lay in the mud behind three hardwoods growing close together. The trees' slightly raised trunks and close proximity provided cover. For now.

Hunter had to stash Evie somewhere safe. Then maybe it was time to go hunting.

He leaned in close to her ear. Her sweet and spicy scent filled his senses. "Listen, I need you to hide. I don't think we have much of a chance at getting away on foot now. The only option is for me to get them before they can get us."

Evie shook her head immediately, bumping the underside of his chin in the process. "Shh. It'll be okay. I know what I'm doing." Hunter rolled and studied their surroundings. Other than the clump of trees, an empty space extended behind them for at least ten feet. Then more trees. No bushes. They had inadvertently landed in the best spot to hide.

Hunter rose, keeping his body in line with the middle tree. Careful not to make a sound, he shrugged off the backpack and passed it down to Evie. Using hand gestures, he indicated for her to follow his lead and began scooping up dirt and mud and rubbing it on the backpack. The bright yellow pack might as well have been a beacon. Once they were done camouflaging the pack, his gaze drew to her white tank top. If the backpack had been a beacon, then her shirt might as well have been a flashing neon sign.

He scooped up more dirt and scrubbed it on her shirt, stopping to savor the weight of her breasts in his palms. Evie scowled. He shrugged and offered no excuse.

When he was satisfied she had sufficient camouflage, he pushed her back into the cover of the trees. Her vulnerable, scared gaze tugged at him, but he knew the best way of protecting her was to go on the offense.

Staying in a crouch, Hunter crept forward through the woods. His gun was tucked safely in his jeans; his hands were free and at the ready.

Once he'd gotten far enough, he stopped and listened. The absence of sound in front of him was as telling as if his prey had started dancing a jig. Hunter closed his eyes and listened. The wind shuffled through the trees, rattling leaves softly in the night. Bullfrogs croaked and cicadas chirped.

Then he heard it. The unmistakable sound of a watch alarm, followed by a barely discernible curse. Forest survival lesson number one: turn off all watch and cell phone alarms. Hunter smiled in the darkness. He set free the beast that had been pacing within him since Brown's visit last night, the one that was frothing at the mouth after seeing the brand on Evie's hip.

It was time for one of the government's top assassins to get to work.

Chapter Twenty-six

Hunter had left her alone. In the dark. With a mad man bent on his very own killing spree.

Evie squatted in the darkness and clutched the backpack to her chest. Her legs were like spaghetti noodles. They wouldn't support her if she tried to stand, but the rest of her body was tense to the point of shattering.

Her palms started to sweat. She gripped the backpack tighter.

The silence and darkness were weighing on her.

She tried to tune her ear in to every minute sound within range, straining so hard she nearly jumped out of her skin when Brown shouted again.

"Evie, remember that old family video we watched together last night? The one with your dad? If you don't get your ass out here right now, we're going to do the same thing to your mother."

Fear jackhammered her heart. She squeezed her eyes shut, slammed her teeth together, and fought back a sob. A low groan fought its way up her throat, but she clamped her lips together.

Not her mother. Maxine might have gone behind her back to try and wrest control of the

MRG, but she and C.W. were all the family Evie had left.

"Come on, girl. I ain't got all night. You got about ten seconds to show yourself or I'm leaving." Brown's voice bounced off the trees around her, making it sound creepier and deadlier than usual.

She wanted so desperately to defend herself against this maniac, but she didn't have a weapon. Hunter. She needed to trust Hunter to take care of this.

"Tell you what, you give up now, and I won't even kill your new boy toy."

Did they have Hunter? Fear threatened to engulf her. If they had captured him, there was no hope left. They would kill him and Maxine and everyone who was important to her.

Her heart pumped furiously and her palms turned cold despite the thousand-degree heat. Maybe it was time to turn herself in. Marcus wanted her alive.

Evie's muscles bunched as she eased a trembling hand to the ground to push herself up. Her fingers squished in mud. She commanded her body to move, to rise. But she might as well have sprouted roots from the soles of her boots and taken anchor in the ground. Her body was paralyzed with fear.

Her senses went into overdrive, as if to compensate for her body's failure to move, and her hearing suddenly turned sharp and acute. But the main thing she picked up on was silence. No one spoke. No whippoorwills sang. No bullfrogs croaked. Nothing.

A breeze ruffled the leaves around her, but to her sensitive ears, it sounded more like glass shattering than a gentle rustle.

She looked left and right, too scared to break cover to look behind her. Her eyes slowly adjusted to the darkness and she could make out certain shapes. Distinguish the difference between trees and leaves.

Something tall and skinny directly to her right shifted sideways. Her heart jumped and she jerked back, slamming her head into the tree. The wind died down.

The logical part of her brain made a timid step forward and informed her the moving object was a sapling bending in the wind. But her heart continued its marathon race anyway.

Her mouth went as dry as the desert sand. And despite the fact she'd prayed for weeks for the rain to stop, she fervently wished for water.

A limb snapped near her and her entire body went cold. Her heart skidded to a stop so fast pain slammed into her ribcage and she clutched desperately at the backpack.

Another limb snapped and her heart jumpstarted. Blood flooded to her neck and face, taking any remaining heat from her hands and feet with it. Evie scrunched smaller. Too bad she didn't have a shrinking potion like Alice in Wonderland.

She heard a strange swoosh followed by a gurgling sound. Then the once silent night filled with violence. More leaves crackled, followed by what sounded like a whole herd of deer galloping through the forest. A man screamed. There was a grunt. A crash. Cursing.

Evie shuddered, fighting the urge to scream. Was Hunter dead? Was she alone, unarmed, in the woods with Brown?

Evie swallowed and cringed. She knew she should find somewhere better to hide, something to defend herself with, but she couldn't move.

Everything around her seemed to grow too big. The trees towered above her, their shadows reaching out with sinister claws. The wind picked up, masking all other sounds.

The backpack. Her chest expanded. What if Hunter had tucked a knife or something in there? Evie yanked the zipper and immediately cringed from the noise it made. But then she dove in and began a frantic search.

A man crouched next to her.

Her brain kicked on. The muscles in her throat constricted and released and she finally let out the scream that had been building inside her.

"Evie. It's me, Hunter. It's okay."

Evie blinked fast, tried to reconcile the fact that this man of shadows was on her side. "Hunter?" He nodded. She threw down the bag and grabbed his arms, reassured by the feel of his rock-hard biceps beneath her fingers. "Are you okay? Who screamed? Where is Brown?"

A door slammed and tires spun out in the distance. She held Hunter's gaze, needing an answer. Needing to know if her cowardice had signed her mother's death sentence.

"I got the deputy. Brown saw me and ran. I tried to get him, but he was already halfway up the levee." Had she thought the night was dark? Hunter's gaze was darker. And his expression was so cold she almost got chills.

She suddenly noticed the blood-soaked knife clutched in his right hand. There was a dead look in his eyes that terrified her. It was as if the Hunter she knew—the one who had saved her, held her, loved her—was gone and a ruthless mercenary was in his place.

Was this the Hunter the rest of the world saw? Concern for him overwhelmed her fright. She cupped his cheek, but he didn't move, didn't blink. He looked like the god of death frozen in stone.

"Are you okay?" Evie tried to draw him back to her.

"Yes." His curt one-word answer didn't reassure her.

Evie slid a hand down to his and slipped her fingers around the knife handle. He let it fall into her grasp. She carefully placed the killing object on the ground, making sure to keep her distance from the blood.

Then she caressed his jaw. Held his gaze.

"I failed."

"What?" Evie asked.

"I let Brown get away."

"I don't think you let him get away. He used his own man to distract you."

The only sign of anger he allowed himself was to clench his jaw. Evie eased closer, almost afraid to startle him, and put one knee into the wet mud. She trembled, but not from fear.

His dark gaze did something to her. Drove her past logic. Past desperation. She burned. She craved. Yearned for his kiss. His touch. The heat of his flesh against hers.

She needed to connect with him. Evie kept her eyes wide open and kissed him. She didn't let go, didn't relax until he closed his eyes. She forged forward, sought his tongue, and explored the moist depths of his mouth.

Hunter groaned and went to his knees,

wrapping his arms around her. Evie held on to his face, needing an anchor.

Fire licked her limbs.

Fire and something else. Something deeper. Something that went beyond lust and desire and approached tenderness. Passion. Love.

When they broke apart, she didn't pay attention to her soaked jeans or to the spray of blood on his handsome face. All Evie saw were his soulful eyes and how much she loved him.

She sucked in a shaky breath. "Are you okay?"

Hunter smiled, the expression small and barely there, but his eyes weren't the embodiment of the Grim Reaper anymore. "I'm supposed to ask you that. Not the other way around."

"True, you did leave me alone in a dark forest with a mad man." Evie tapped her chin, pretending to ponder whether she would forgive him.

"How did I know you would look at it that way?" Hunter said, his smile growing right along with the warmth in her heart.

"I thought that was the girlfriend's job. You know, to nag and point out all the bad stuff."

"Girlfriend?" Hunter said.

"Too much?"

"Not enough," he growled, yanking her forward and taking a kiss from her all-too-eager lips.

She had finally accepted the truth: she had never really stopped loving him and the only way to fill her empty shell of a soul was through Hunter James.

"Are you really okay?" Hunter asked.

Evie thought for a minute. The past few days

had surpassed the ninth gate of Hell, all but inventing a whole new tenth gate just to torture her. But she hadn't had to trudge through the horror alone.

Hunter would help her save her mother. And after they secured Maxine, she had every intention of asking for his help with Marcus and his weapons.

The Evie that had practically pissed in her pants at the first sign of trouble had ceased to exist. Now she was just pissed.

And she had a warrior by her side.

"Let's go." Evie retrieved his knife, wiped it clean on her jeans, and offered it to him.

He tucked it in his boot, checked his gun, and yanked a flashlight from the backpack. "I think Silo Farm is about a half-mile east of here. Can you run?"

"I can run circles around you."

Hunter lifted her chin with a crooked finger. "I don't know where all this spunk is coming from, but I like it. Let's see if you can back up that challenge." Hunter turned and took off, the flashlight bouncing off trees and brush in a smooth straight pattern. Evie sucked in a breath and followed, already knowing she didn't have a shot at keeping up with him. Even while running, he moved so silently she could barely hear him.

Tree limbs rushed by in a dark haze. Sharp thorns snagged her skin and hair, but she kept moving. She had a goal. A purpose. And Hunter.

Evie kept as close to him as she could, his flashlight the only illumination in the pitch-black night. They ran at the pace of a brisk jog and it wasn't long before Evie was out of breath.

Then the ground seemed to dip into a deep

ravine. She tripped forward and grabbed Hunter's shoulder for support.

"You doing okay?" he asked, pausing at the bottom.

Evie had managed to remain upright, barely, so she nodded, too out of breath to answer.

"The incline is steep. I want you to hold on to my jeans until we reach the top."

She nodded again. When Hunter turned she hooked two fingers into his center belt loop. Then he started up. Slow. He grabbed small trees as they climbed and Evie stayed latched onto him the whole while. Her very own mercenary.

Razor vines cut burning paths across her arms. Her feet slipped on the wet leaves and muddy ground and her lungs burned from the effort, but she kept going.

They reached the top, after what seemed like forever, and she couldn't stand up straight anymore. Her hands hit her knees and she sucked in big gulps of air.

"What happened to running circles?" Hunter said.

There still wasn't enough air in her lungs to fuel words, so Evie held up a finger.

"I see a field. We're at the edge of the woods."

"Okay." Another gasp. "Let's go." She stood and started past him, but he caught up with her in two strides.

They walked out of the woods. A dirt road cut perpendicular in front of them. A huge cotton field lay past that.

The bushy green plants grew so thick she couldn't discern one row from another, and they were at least a few inches taller than her own five-foot-two frame.

"Just stay close and watch out for snakes."

Great. Snakes. "I've had enough of those to last me two lifetimes," Evie said.

"Yeah, me too." Hunter started into the field and Evie tucked up close behind him. After they pushed past the first few plants, she couldn't see anything but leaves.

"This is worse than the woods." Leaves slapped her face, the plants at the perfect height.

"Just stay close, I can see over the top." Hunter kept going.

Their boots slushed and mucked through the mud underfoot, and Evie found herself cursing the rain again. Damn deluge had turned everything to mud.

Something stung her neck and she slapped hard. She came up with a small splatter of blood on her palm. Mosquito. All the water attracted the blood-sucking insects like flies to rotting food.

Hunter increased their pace and they finally emerged from the cotton. Of course, her sense of relief was short lived—as soon as they crossed another dirt road, they went into a cornfield. The damn corn stalks were twice as tall as the cotton and, without any moon, scary as hell. Fear tried to slip a toehold into her conscious, but she slapped it back. She wasn't going to let that scared little bitch take over. Not again.

By the time they emerged from the last field, Evie had been bitten more times than she could count and she'd acquired at least another five pounds of mud on her boots. But she didn't pay attention to that.

All she saw was Silo Farm.

Chapter Twenty-seven

Cal Silo's old white farmhouse sat off to the left, tucked against the levee, away from the main workshops. It looked so much like the house Evie rented, except hers was underwater. On the other side of the levee.

Dingy yellow light from atop an electric pole cast a glow on a driveway that spread wide and connected the house to the main workshop to their right. Behind that was another open shop with trailers and combines. Behind that, the grain bins.

"Come on, I'll start checking the shop for a truck. You check behind the house." Hunter prayed the old man had left something they could use for transportation. Anything. Shit. Evie was pale and out of breath, but he could tell she was terrified for her mom. All because he hadn't managed to keep his goddamn cool out in the field. He'd seen the deputy, and instead of checking his surroundings, he'd moved in for the kill.

Brown could have attacked him, but instead the bastard had run. Which was worse. Hunter could have easily overtaken the guy in hand-to-hand combat.

Now he had no one to fight but distance.

Evie nodded and took off toward the farmhouse. Hunter jogged around the first shop. It was a huge metal building with an opening down the right side that was used to shelter farm equipment. Silo Farm was the oldest in the area. And though Silo had moved most of his farming operations closer to town, he still used the old farm. Or he had. Before Hunter left.

Shit.

He passed a combine. Old. Flat tire.

A tractor. 1980's model at best and rusted across the whole engine. Shit.

Another combine. Fuck. Might as well be put in a museum. Apparently Silo kept everything, antiques included.

Hunter rounded the back. Three grain bins stood sentry, clumped together, with weeds growing waist high. It didn't look like it'd been mowed in a year.

Silo must have shut the whole farm down in Hunter's absence. Which meant anything of any value, anything that worked, would be at the new headquarters.

He stopped at the back corner of the shop and hung his head. A pile of trash rotted about a foot away. He'd never failed at a task in his entire career. Not one. But he'd failed twice tonight.

Worse: he'd failed Evie.

He punched the wall and metal rattled like wild thunder across the yard. Dammit. Then he punched it again. And again.

"Hunter." Her scream hit his ears. Could Brown have figured out where they were headed and circled back?

His heart stopped. He turned and ran,

destroying the distance between them, fear for
Evie eating up his defeat and spitting it out. He
didn't stop until he spotted her. Bent over. Hands
on knees. Gulping in air. His pistol was in his
hands in a second, but there was no sign of the
sheriff—or anyone—around them. "Evie? What's
wrong? Are you okay?"

She walked her hands up her legs, panting
and pale. "Yeah. I heard a bang and it scared me.
I thought maybe..."

Damn. His own anger and loss of control had
made her think Brown was back. "I'm sorry. I
accidentally hit something."

Evie nodded, short and quick. "I didn't find
anything at the house, and I got scared. But Silo
hasn't used this place in years. He wouldn't park
a truck here. I was coming to get you when I
heard the bangs."

Hunter lowered his gun and tucked it back
behind him. He wanted to tell her good news, but
there was no point in lying. "The shop is a bust.
Nothing."

Evie's hands hit her knees again and she
gasped for breath. The sound of her ragged
inhalations tore up his insides.

"Not even a freaking four-wheeler?" she
managed to choke out.

He could only shake his head. God, this
sucked even worse than his last mission. This was
his hometown, and it had gone FUBAR while he
was away.

She took a deep breath. Blew it out. Then
another. Held it in. He knew she was mentally
counting in threes. Trying to relax.

"Evie, I swear I'll figure something out."
Hunter touched her shoulders, her arms, needing

to calm her. The truth was he didn't know what he could do other than turn into Superman and fly them back to Mercy. It was fifteen miles away.

She gulped again and coughed. Hunter pounded on her back and nearly knocked her over. "Breathe, dammit. Come on. We will get to Mercy. I promise you."

"I can't... I should have just gone with him. With Brown."

He wanted to hold her close and kill that bastard at the same time. "Are you kidding me? The man nearly kills you one day and the next you would walk right into his trap?"

"I'd do it if it would save Mom." She stayed bent at the waist, her posture defeated.

Hell. No. He wasn't giving up and neither was she. Hunter scanned the farm again, searching for anything that might help. His gaze fell on the hangar. A sign, rusted and scratched but still legible, read, 'Silo's Flying Service.'

Hope struck like lightening. He could do it. He could fly them back to Mercy. And probably beat Brown back to town.

"Evie. Look." Hunter kept his gaze on the hangar and pointed. Evie straightened and turned. She grabbed his outstretched arm.

"Silo's Flying Service? A crop duster?" Her voice edged up a notch or two in pitch.

"We can get back to Mercy before Brown gets off the levee." Hunter couldn't contain his excitement. He hadn't failed. Not as long as there was an airplane in the hangar. He took off, not stopping until he stood right in front of the nondescript white metal door on the side of the building.

He raised a booted foot, pulled back, and

kicked as hard as he could right below the door handle. Pain shot up his leg and into his hip, but the damn door didn't move.

"Hunter! What are you doing? Are you crazy?"

"I'm getting you to your mom. Get back." Hunter pulled his good leg back again, ready to land another kick if he broke his foot.

"Are you crazy? That's a metal door. On a metal frame." Evie's tone kept rising higher with each word.

"Yeah. But we gotta get in there."

He raised his foot again and Evie stepped right in front of him.

"Evie, move." Hunter ground out, bracing for the next jar of pain.

Ignoring him, she bent over and lifted the door mat.

"Now *you're* crazy. You really think someone would leave a key..." Hunter's words trailed off and he lowered his foot. Evie stood proudly before him, a bronze key held in her fingers.

"You were saying?" she said, a hint of teasing in her voice.

"Nothing. Absolutely nothing." The damn woman was making him lose his mind. That was his only excuse. Her quick wit and bravery were making him fall in love with her. Again.

She winked and then turned to unlock the door. It swung open on rusty hinges, and she stepped back. The interior was pitch black.

Hunter clicked on his flashlight again and shone it through the opening. The first thing he noticed was the small yellow aircraft. "We found it."

Evie followed the light. She stayed silent.

Then she turned to him, her eyes wide. "When did you learn to fly?"

"I learned all sorts of things in the military." He'd learned to fly helicopters in warrant officer school. And he'd needed to land a fixed wing aircraft on at least two occasions. Like when his team's pilot had been shot through the windshield while waiting for TF-S to return. And that time in Sudan. Both times had been FUBAR. But he'd survived.

Evie backed up a step, away from the shop. "Since when does the military use crop dusters?"

"Not crop dusters. But other aircraft. Plus, I used to work at Smith's Flying Service when I was a kid. I learned a lot then too." He stepped inside and flicked on the light switch. Nothing happened. No buzzing fluorescent lights. Great.

Evie stood outside the door. "You're telling me you want me to ride in an airplane with you because you used to put fuel in a crop duster when you were ten years old."

"You're forgetting the whole military part."

"This is a bad idea. I saw a combine at the shop. We can take that." Evie started walking back down the drive.

Hunter grabbed her arm and pulled her to him. "That combine is at least twenty years old and the back tire is rotted. Even if I could get it to start, we couldn't drive it. This is our only option."

Evie shook her head frantically. "No. We missed something. We should go back and look some more."

"Evie. Listen. This is our only option if you want to get back to town in time to stop the sheriff." His only chance to redeem himself.

She pulled against him for a minute. Seemed

to come to some conclusion and let him pull her inside. "You're right. What do you need me to do?" He heard the fear in her voice. Saw it in her drooping stance. She needed a distraction.

"Let's get the hangar door open and let in some moonlight so I can check out the plane."

He waited until she started walking before he approached the aircraft. The crop duster was small and old.

He pulled open the cab. It had one freaking chair.

Where the hell would Evie sit? He quickly surveyed the interior, but found no extra space. The entire plane had been designed with one thing in mind: make as much room as possible for pesticides and as little room as possible for the single human who would fly the stick of gum.

Hunter grabbed the handle by the door and hefted himself into the seat. A single black stick protruded for steering. Way too few analog dials for reading on the dashboard. He grabbed beneath the seat and found the instruction manual, flipped the small booklet open. First page. Copyright 1965.

Holy mother of shit.

"You find what you need?" Evie leaned his way and Hunter quickly stuffed the book back under the seat.

"Everything but the key. There should be a box somewhere. Can you help look for it?

Evie stopped and started scanning the shop. Hunter took a deep breath. He was about to fly something he had no business flying. He jumped down to check the fuel. Half full. Perfect.

"Found some keys." Evie ran to him.

"Perfect." He couldn't resist dragging her to

him and claiming her mouth. She called to him. Everything about her filled him. Made him need her. Want her. Evie immediately opened her mouth to him and Hunter took what she offered and more. God, he couldn't get enough of her. Her soft skin. Her determination. Her love.

Get it together. What was wrong with him? He'd been on hundreds of missions. And he'd never let his emotions affect him this way. Never.

Evie stood there, fingers pressed to her mouth, staring up at him with her heart in her eyes. And he felt shame.

This was what he wanted, wasn't it? He'd wanted her to trust him, and she did. He'd wanted her to need him, and she did. Instead of elation, he felt like the trash he'd seen in the yard. Rotting and disgusting.

"Let's see if I can get her going."

Chapter Twenty-eight

Evie wobbled back a step and grabbed the side of the plane. Hunter had just smacked her with a hotter than hell kiss and left her hanging. Her insides were basically goo at this point.

He had broken their kiss, his gaze impossible to read. But his naked chest definitely distracted her. Big, thick, and packed with muscle. She wanted to kiss every single square inch.

She wanted to kiss other things as well.

Evie shook her head. What was wrong with her? She should be freaking out right now. Airplanes were not her thing. In fact, just the sight of one flying overhead sometimes caused her heart to stutter.

And now she was about to climb into this yellow LEGO-sized plane with Hunter?

The fact that he was willing to do this for her and her family...well, it only made her feel better about her decision to ask for his help with Marcus after they saved Maxine. She wasn't stupid. She knew she couldn't handle a snake like him alone.

He started the engine and her heart stopped. Maybe this wasn't such a good idea. People weren't meant to fly. The very concept didn't make sense. Her boots were made for walkin', not soaring through the air.

"Hunter, maybe we should talk about this some more." She edged back a step.

Hunter's gaze remained fixed on the airplane's dashboard, and Evie realized he couldn't hear her over the engine roar.

Her chest started to lock up. Then her stomach. Then her arms and legs. The panic attack hit hard and so fast she didn't have a prayer of stopping it. Yes, the burning pain that mimicked a heart attack was familiar, and yes, she had learned to talk herself down from it. Sometimes. But that was before the panic reached about an eight on her fear scale. Zero being a spider on the wall. Ten being, well, a quick visit to the emergency room for an anti-anxiety cocktail delivered straight to the vein.

This was definitely an eight. She'd shot up from two in the time it took for the engine to turn over.

Evie's feet kept moving her backward until she bumped the shelf lining the wall and jostled the stacks of discarded papers. *Breathe. Just breathe.* People flew all the time. Every day.

Wasn't flying supposed to be safer than driving? But no way was it safer than walking.

"Evie?" Hunter appeared not a foot away. She hadn't realized he'd followed her. Hadn't had room for anything but her panic.

"Evie," Hunter said again. She tried to get her jaw to open, her vocal cords to work. But all she managed was a brief lip flap and no sound.

"Have you ever flown?" Hunter asked.

Evie shook her head no. She never wanted to either.

"Listen. I promise you'll be okay. And we're

so close to Mercy that we'll be landing the minute after we take off. I swear." He grabbed her shoulders gently.

"I - I'm kind of afraid of flying."

"I can see that. Is there a reason?"

He was being so logical, she was almost ashamed of her illogical answer. "I don't have one. I'm just scared." She barely managed to get the words past her lips.

"Listen, I know you don't care that flying is safe. I've never had a phobia, but I understand it's not rational. So maybe this will help you." He grabbed her shoulders, caught her gaze and held it. "If we don't fly this plane back to Mercy, Brown will definitely get to Maxine first."

It was like an ice bucket had been upended over her head. She'd been so wrapped up in fear she had all but forgotten about her mom. About Brown.

Blood started pumping in her veins, building pressure slow and steady. She had no choice. It was her fear. Or her mom.

"Let's do it."

* * *

Hunter taxied the plane out of the hangar. Evie sat right behind his seat, squished in the small compartment, her knees to her chest. The airplane moved slowly as he maneuvered onto the dirt runway. It had headlights, thank God. She wasn't sure she could have handled complete darkness.

"You ready?" Hunter asked over his shoulder.

Was she ready to take off in an airplane smaller than her car and trust a sort-of pilot to fly it? "Yes."

Hunter pushed the throttle forward and they

took off, steadily building speed. Dirt and mud flew up and spattered on the sides of the aircraft, and each ping against the metal made her flinch.

Evie grabbed on to the chair and pulled herself level with Hunter's ear. "You sure you know what you're doing?" She almost yelled to be heard over the noise of the engine.

"I told you—trust me." Hunter pushed the throttle all the way forward and Evie gulped. She kept her eyes glued to the runway, feeling each bump they hit all the way down to her bones.

The headlights picked up the muddy road and the tall, overgrown grass lining the sides. The insects splattered on the windshield were also illuminated.

This was like a bad dream. If only she could wake up. Safe. Secure. In her comfortable bed.

Dark and light images took shape at the end of the runway. Cows.

Her lungs stopped all together. "Cows! Hunter, cows!"

"I see them. We gotta get more speed." He floored the gas and yanked back on the steering stick. The plane caught air and then bounced back onto the ground. Evie could make out distinct color patterns of brown and white on the big animals.

"Hunter, hurry!" She couldn't breathe, couldn't think past the possibility of their imminent death.

Hunter yanked back on the stick again and they caught air a second time. Evie's stomach dropped into her knees. The plane hit the ground again, restoring her stomach to its original position.

Her nails dug into the vinyl seat. She ducked

her head behind Hunter and closed her eyes, unable to watch.

She was going to die in this airplane. On the ground. Sometimes karma was a real bitch.

Then she felt the plane rise again, only this time they didn't touch back down. They rose high and fast and Evie's stomach plummeted back to the earth below. The plane jolted and a small scream escaped her lips.

"Cow," Hunter said over the roar of the engine.

Jesus. H. Christ. How was she here? Now? The plane glided through the air, smooth and easy. They dipped and rose over the trees and Hunter pulled them up higher. When they leveled out, he turned to look at her.

It was the same look her mother had given her after she'd finally overcome her fear enough to get on her first horse. She'd loved it. Now Hunter had that same expression, the one that said I-told-you-so.

And she would give it to him. They were in the air and he was flying. He turned back around.

The plane dipped and her stomach felt queasy again. This was why she avoided roller coasters. Of course, their frames were made of steel; the up and down movements of this plane were supported by absolutely nothing.

"We'll be there in a few minutes. I'm gonna try to land on Hank's driveway. It's long enough and it should be clear at this time of night," Hunter informed her and Evie latched on to the fact this whole ordeal would be over in a few minutes.

She chanced a peek out the side window. The moon had emerged from the clouds again and light spilled onto the earth. Evie sucked in a breath as she took in the sight below them. They were flying over a patchwork of fields of different shades of green. A canal ran up the center, Red Fork Bayou, and the moon reflected directly up at her from its depths. Evie realized that if she could just unclench her muscles for long enough, she would enjoy the ride.

But her muscles were on permanent lockdown. Her throat was so tight she could barely get in enough air to support brain function.

"You know you have to face your phobia to get over it," Hunter said. It was as if he could read her thoughts.

"Yeah, well, I have a phobia of jumping off bridges, should I give that a try?" Evie couldn't keep the sarcasm out of her voice. She couldn't give a crap about facing her fears. She would be out of the airplane as soon as the wheels stopped rolling.

"I guess if you're one of those people."

What kind of answer was that? "What people?"

"Stupid." His yelled response was so unexpected she burst out laughing. She wasn't stupid. Just smart. Smart people knew to keep their feet on the ground.

"There's Dad's house. I'm going to land. Hold on." Hunter turned the plane to the left, and they swooped through the air.

Evie tightened her grip on Hunter's chair. No. She was definitely not made for this whole air thing.

He swooped back right and they started to descend. "Oh god, oh god, oh god." The chant helped. Anything helped.

"You should be saying, 'Oh Hunter." Hunter yelled. They dipped some more.

"Oh god, oh god, oh god." Her chanting increased in volume.

The plane touched the ground. Then bounced back up into the air and Evie's heart followed the same rhythm, bouncing from her stomach into her throat and then back again. She kept her eyelids clenched shut.

The plane touched down again and stayed on the ground. She could hear the gravel pinging hard against the metal frame of the airplane. She could feel each and every pothole and bump down Hank's driveway.

"Hold on!" The plane skated sideways, sending mud and gravel and dirt flying. Evie's eyes skidded open just in time to see it sliding straight toward Hank's house. The plane slammed to a stop not twenty feet from the front door.

Hunter killed the airplane. The roar of the engine died, only to be replaced with the loud roaring in her ears. Her breath sawed in and out of her chest. When she got in enough air to think, she realized Hunter was breathing raggedly too. Then he slammed his hands onto the dashboard and gave a loud yell of triumph. "I did it. I told you I could do it."

The joy in his voice told her he had doubted himself.

"I'm glad at least one of us had some confidence," she said. "Now if you don't mind I'd like to get the hell out of this thing right now. Before I puke."

Hunter had the door open in less than five seconds flat. Once they were safe on the ground, he grabbed her hair and helped her onto her knees as she gulped for air.

"What the hell is going on here?"

Evie lifted her head to see Hank, and two other men she didn't recognize running toward them. All three men had guns and expressions that said they wouldn't hesitate to use them.

"Sorry, Dad. Didn't mean to wake you up in the middle of the night," Hunter said. Evie managed to straighten, but she didn't let go of his arm.

"Son, is that an airplane in my driveway?" Hank said. He approached Hunter, slow and cautious. Probably afraid his son had lost his mind.

The dark haired man let out a low whistle. "Since when did you learn to fly a crop duster?"

"Tonight."

Chapter Twenty-nine

"Tonight? What was all that crap about learning to fly for the military?" Evie locked her claws into his arm and pulled him toward her, ready to slice his jugular.

"I did learn, but a lot of it was through emergencies like tonight. I knew if I told you the truth you would be a lot more scared. And I also knew no matter how scared you were, you were going to get into the airplane. So I made an executive decision."

Evie wanted to smack that small sideways grin right off his handsome face. The man was looking at her like she should be thankful. Perhaps she would feel more gratitude after she punched him in the stomach. "So you lied to me? You could've killed me!"

Hunter leaned down, so close she could feel the bristle of his cheek against hers. "But I didn't." He kissed her before she could gasp out a response, and then straightened and turned to face the others.

Evangeline could not help but notice all three men were shirtless. Make that four, since technically Hunter hadn't been wearing a shirt for the past twenty-four hours. And all of them were handsome.

"I think you two need to come inside and tell us what's going on," Jared said, his black hair gleaming in the porch light, mussed from sleep.

"I can't wait to hear this story," Hoyt said.

"And I'd especially like to know why you're flying someone's crop duster down my driveway," Hank said. The man was still in good shape and he generated an air of authority. Evie could see why her mother would be attracted to him.

A sense of urgency slammed into her. Her mom. "Hunter, we don't have time to talk." Evie pulled on his arm.

Hunter turned to face her. "Let me give them a brief run down. They can help, Evie. Think about it. Won't we have a better chance of saving her with their help?"

Evie bit her lip, indecision sawing her in half. If they came, it would mean a lot more ammo on their side. But it would also cost them precious time.

Hunter grabbed her arms and caught her gaze, adding, "Don't you think Hank has a right to know about Maxine? Don't you think he would want to help to?"

"Hank has a right to know what?" Hank was heading toward them, apparently ready to be in the loop.

"You want to tell him?" Hunter asked.

Evie bit her lip and shook her head, no. They all went into the house and Hunter shut the door behind her. They walked through Hank's small entry and turned right into the living room. Two men, one blond, one dark, took up most of the couch along the wall.

"Evie, meet Hoyt and Jared Crow. They are

the best scout snipers in the entire force," Hunter said.

"Pleased to meet you," Evie said.

Hank stood, hands crossed over his chest, in front of the stone fireplace. Tension crackled in the room. They all seemed to be shooting off sparks of electricity.

It was too much. Everything was happening too fast. She needed to get out of this room. "Hunter, I need the restroom. Can you handle this?"

She tried not to let her fatigue show, but his hand cupped her cheek. He knew. He pressed a small kiss to her forehead and Evie leaned into his embrace, needing his strength. "Take your time. I'll share the news."

"Bathroom's down the hall on the left." Hank's voice broke into their brief moment of peace.

Evie left without looking back. A cellphone on the entry table caught her attention. She made a split-second decision and swiped it. Hunter could fill his dad and his friends in on the story. But Evie had to take care of her family.

She eased the bathroom door shut behind her and turned on the sink. Once the noise filled the bathroom, she plopped down on the toilet and dialed Marcus.

"I had a set back. I'm on my way. Do not hurt my mom." Evie got it all out before he could say a word.

"I thought we had an understanding. You missed your deadline," Marcus said.

Evie wanted to hyperventilate, but she forced herself to stay calm. "What have you done?"

"Nothing yet. Maxine is just my guest for

now. What happens to her depends on what you do next."

"Tell me what to do." If she could just get a clear plan out of him, she could tell Hunter everything. She trusted him. She knew he would help.

Marcus didn't respond. She could feel the satisfaction through the phone. If she was going to get Hunter and his men to help save her mom, she had to know exactly what Marcus planned. She could play the sad broken little woman any day of the freaking week.

"Please, tell me."

"Good girl. I knew you remembered. Now, listen and do exactly as I say."

* * *

Hunter waited until he heard the bathroom door shut before he began talking. "I went to her house last night and Sheriff Brown showed up."

Hoyt bit out a curse and jumped up from the couch. "So that wasn't just dirt on her face and neck?" He started pacing the living room.

Hunter shook his head slowly, trying to keep the rage from taking over. "No, I heard her scream from upstairs. He had her on the ground."

"That son of a bitch." Jared sat up from his sprawled back position on the couch. His relaxed stance turning deadly.

"What exactly does this have to do with Maxine?" Hank ground out. Hank had to be one of the most levelheaded men Hunter knew, but right now he looked like he was about to explode.

"Brown is threatening to kill Maxine if Evie doesn't do what he tells her to."

"And what exactly is it he's asking Evie to do?" Hank asked.

"Run an illegal weapons shipment downriver and launder the money through her bar." Hunter let the words hang in the air. Hoyt and Jared already knew what was going on, though not the power dynamics that were at play. Hank had no clue.

"So Brown is some kind of weapons dealer? That bastard doesn't have the pull for that kind of power," Hank said.

"No, but the mayor does," Hunter said.

"I'm not stupid. I know you didn't come home on R&R. Who the hell comes home for rest but brings his team with him? And sets up shop in my building? I've tried to keep my distance, keep my mouth shut, but dammit it's time you told me what the hell is going on." Hank didn't pull his punches. And Hunter might be bigger than his old man but Hank could hold his own.

"Dad, I..."

"Look, son. I know when you're gonna lie to me. I've been able to tell since you were a kid. If you won't tell me, don't waste your breath talking." Hank's steel-blue eyes flashed with anger and Hunter felt the pull of guilt.

"Shit." Hunter rubbed a hand over his jaw, frustration destroying his last nerve. He hadn't really wanted to involve Hank, but Brown had all but guaranteed it with his threat.

"Might as well go on and tell him." Hoyt quit pacing and resumed his seat on the couch. Elbows to knees, hands gripped together. Jared sat forward and nodded.

He knew he needed to get this out before Evie returned. Hunter held up a hand, and peeked around the corner. The bathroom door was shut and he could hear the sink running. His girl was flat worn out. He'd seen the battle-weary expression on her face. He knew why she'd left the room.

She would have broken down the minute they started talking about Maxine.

"Okay. You're right. There's a lot going on. I'm gonna hit the highlights and fill you in on the details later."

Hunter waited on Hank to nod before beginning.

"Me and my men," Hunter gestured to his teammates on the couch, "are on assignment. The terrorist we've been tracking in Pakistan has contacts in the U.S."

Hank bit out a curse and paced the room. "You mean in Mercy. My home."

"Yes. That's why I asked you to keep our presence quiet. Not for R&R, but so we could gather intel."

"Intel on who?"

"Marcus Carvant." Hunter sucked in a breath, knowing his next words were going to light a fire in his dad. "And the Videls."

Hank cursed, long and loud, and Hunter held up a hand to quiet his father. He needed Evie to stay in the bathroom.

"Is that what all the fuss is about over Maxine? Because you think she's a terrorist?"

Hoyt interrupted, "Not just Maxine." Hunter shot him a death stare and he lifted his hands in surrender. "What? He needs the whole story."

Hank stopped pacing and squared off with Hunter. "You think Evie is involved too? You've lost your mind."

"There is solid intel that Marcus's been in contact with the MRG." Hunter held up a hand to stop Hank from interrupting. "Marcus is definitely the one in charge, but we think he's tapped the MRG to move the weapons downriver to Mexico. And from there, the terrorists have arranged transportation to Pakistan."

"I'm gonna kill that son of a bitch," Hank bit out. They all stared. He'd never cursed like that before. Never.

"You're going to have to get in line." Hunter had every intention of taking the bastard out. Permanently.

"So you're trying to seduce Evie to get the intel on Marcus?" Hank all but spat the words. Hank was a vet. He believed in boots on the ground. Honor and duty. Not covert affairs.

Hunter's chest burned. He'd planned exactly that. That had been his plan at first, but now, hearing his dad say it out loud, he wanted to vomit.

"They sent us all home to infiltrate the group and find the weapons. They sent me specifically after Evie because of our history," Hunter glanced over his shoulder. He didn't want Evie to hear any of this. He would tell her later, when he could explain what happened. Even if she *were* directly involved, and he knew she wasn't, he was going to do everything in his power to make sure she didn't catch one ounce of blame.

"So you're using that girl to get to Marcus?"

Hunter heard a gasp and then a door slam. Evie. "Shit." She must have come out of the bathroom just in time to hear him. He took off after her, but his pursuit was more like a snail's pace than an all-out sprint.

Hank was right behind him. "My 12-gauge is missing from the wall." He pointed to the rack right beside the back door.

The sound of a truck cranking ripped his attention from the wall. Hunter ran outside, his father right behind him. Hank's truck sped by, throwing gravel like shrapnel. Hunter threw his arm over his face to protect himself from the volley of rocks. But not before he caught a glimpse of Evie at the steering wheel. The tears tracking down her cheeks were like acid on his soul.

Gravel pinged off the crop duster parked in the front yard.

"Dammit, I've only had that truck a week." Hank slammed a palm into the side of the house.

"I think she heard you." Hoyt came outside and stared down the drive. The cloud of dust she'd left behind hung in the air almost as heavy as her hurt.

"What gave you that idea?"

Hoyt shrugged and backed up. "Nothing."

"Maybe we should go after her." Jared stood in the doorway, his indolent expression pushing Hunter past his last scrap of control.

"Pack up. We're leaving right now. Need to get to headquarters, grab our gear and follow her."

"Where's Ranger?" Hank asked. Hoyt and Jared turned to Hunter.

The reminder of Shane's death cut sharp and deep. His unit had a right to know. They'd be just as devastated by TF-S's loss as he and Ranger were, but right now, Hunter just needed to get to Evie. "Ranger is with Amy," Hunter bit out.

Hoyt's expression morphed into disbelief. "He wouldn't do that." *Not with Shane's wife.* The unspoken words filled the kitchen, the pressure building outward.

"Why?" Jared said.

There was no choice but to tell them. "Shane's dead. We got confirmation." Hunter lifted his chin, fighting the pain clawing at his gut.

"Dammit!" Jared exploded and punched the kitchen wall, his fist driving through the sheet rock like paper. "It's my fault. I should have taken them out."

Guilt, heavy as a Humvee, settled on Hunter's shoulders. But the weight didn't belong on Jared, who'd done his job. "No, it's my fault. If I hadn't gotten shot, he wouldn't have had to drag ass behind me."

"You're blaming yourself because you were shot?" Hoyt shook his head. "Shane knew the risk of joining our team. We don't get the easy missions. It wasn't anyone's fault but the motherfuckers who shot him."

Hank's hand fell on Hunter's shoulder. "Look at me." He turned Hunter around to face him. "The curse of being leader is always feeling responsible. Even when you're not. What separates the great leaders is their ability to feel that responsibility but to also realize that when you're at war your men will die. And sometimes there's not a damn thing you can do to stop it."

Chapter Thirty

Evie could barely make out the road through her tears. She gripped the steering wheel tighter, grinding her hands back and forth on the leather. She'd been so stupid.

Again.

Hunter didn't love her. He hadn't come back for her. He was only using her. She was his...enemy.

She gagged on a sob. Bent forward under the weight. Her whole body ached with grief. Why? Why did these things always happen to her?

Evie fought to straighten her spine and get her emotions under control. She'd fallen for Hunter. Just like she had in the past. Only this time instead of breaking her heart, he'd shattered it.

God. She had to forget him. Forget men in general. She had her own mission. *Come on, get it together.* She needed to focus on what was important.

Saving her mom.

And she sure as shit didn't need a man to do that. Evie floored the gas pedal in her stolen truck, rolled the window down, and let the tears dry on her cheeks. The sweet smell of fresh soil filled the cab and she took a cleansing breath.

This was the last time she would let any man hurt her.

Fury ripped through her veins and she took Dead Man's curve going seventy miles an hour. She didn't know whose truck she'd stolen, but its back tires skated sideways. She had a brief flash of fear that she would flip, but she yanked the wheel back and the truck straightened out.

She hit the straight-away a mile from The Wharf and floored it. Bugs slapped the windshield so fast, she had to turn on her wipers.

Fuck Hunter James. Fuck Marcus Carvant. And fuck Sheriff Brown. Evie caressed the shotgun on the seat beside her, thankful she'd had enough sense to grab the weapon off the wall before sneaking out of Hank's house.

The 12-gauge would kill a bear, but she only needed it to kill Marcus.

The turn-off to the bar appeared on the left. She braked, barely making the drive, ready to gun it again. The river rose in front of her. Too close. Evie slammed on the brakes, coming to a stop a mere foot from the water.

Her heart beat fast and furious in her chest. The river had risen all the way up River Road, cutting off all access to her bar.

Her bar stood out of the water, barely, its stilts still keeping it high enough to avoid the flood. The Wharf was safe, but she had no way to get to it.

She was about a hundred yards from her destination. A hundred yards full of snakes, gators, and a rip current that could suck her under and send her downriver.

And no boat.

Swimming was the last resort. Every house downriver had a dock—or used to. And there was a boat at each of those docks. Evie took off running down the edge of the water, frantically searching for anything that would provide her with transportation.

A small river shack floated within fifteen feet of her and she paused, the sight of the old wood building drifting in the water just too weird. Too shocking. This flood had literally swept away a house—*many* houses.

Her furious heartbeat sped up. If it could take a house, it could take a bar. She had to hurry.

Her feet pounded down the water's edge. She searched everywhere. Looking in trees, on the shore, anywhere she could physically see.

There was no boat.

By the time she got back to the shore across from her bar, she was panting. Out of breath and running out of hope. Marcus had given her a specific time limit. Her mom could be safe and sound. Or scared and suffering.

Swimming was fast turning into her only option. Evie took stock of her clothing. Jeans, shirt, boots. All of it filthy. The boots had to go.

She ran back to the truck. She needed something that would float. If she got sucked under, she wouldn't be able to help her mom. The big gray four-by-four's leather interior was spotless and completely useless to her. She jumped into the back and pried open the chrome toolbox mounted beneath the back window.

A life vest. Orange. She snatched it out, her hands shaking with adrenaline, or fear, or both, and yanked it on. Evie ran back toward the water, kicked off her boots, and grabbed the shotgun. Holding it high, she waded in. Warm water surrounded her in an instant. The moon peeked out again, highlighted the water for a second, and then disappeared. Freaking Mother Nature couldn't spare a beam of moonlight to make her life a little easier. Now she wouldn't even be able to see any debris—or living things—in the water before swimming into them. But she kept right on swimming, one arm lifted overhead to keep her weapon dry. Her arms burned and her legs wanted to stop kicking. Something swam past on her right. Something alive and long and skinny.

Evie went rigid. The life vest was keeping her face out of the water, but it wouldn't do a damn thing to stop a snake bite. Her pulse hammered so hard in her ears she thought her ear drums would burst from the pressure.

The snake disappeared into the darkness, leaving behind nothing but a trail of water ripples. Evie kicked forward, getting closer to the bar each second. She could make out three steps above the water. There was about a foot, maybe, left between the porch and the river. She swam harder, keeping the gun over her head.

She sensed the large object in the water right before it slammed into her side. Pain exploded down her ribs and she dropped the gun. Evie made a frantic grab, but as soon as she stretched out her arm, agony erupted in her side. She tucked into a ball and rolled. The life vest pulled her onto her side, giving her a high-def view as her only source of protection sunk into the muddy river.

Evie stayed in that position, knees tucked to her chest, arms wrapped around her middle, and just floated. Her face dipped half-in and half-out of the water. Her eyes watered. Misery took a leading role over the pain. She wasn't sure how much time had passed, but she couldn't move. Didn't even want to try. Her awareness shrank to the small area around her body and the fact that she was floating.

Nothing else registered.

Then she hit something, only this time it was the top of her head. And it wasn't awful. She bumped it again. Evie blinked, coming back to full consciousness, and realized she had floated right up to the bar's front steps.

All she had to do was get to the door. Up the steps. Three agonizing steps.

Carefully, she stretched out an arm, but the pain was unendurable. Not a good idea. She took small, quick breaths and tried her other arm, the one on her uninjured side. Fire licked up from her hip to her chest.

Painful but doable.

She dug her left elbow into the wood plank of the next step up and pulled. The sharp wood corner of the step below the water scraped her shin. Evie continued to drag herself up one step at a time, using her knee, her elbow, anything that would get the job done. Finally, she collapsed onto the porch and rolled to her side.

Evie inhaled, deep and slow. More pain. Too much rib movement. She took small, deep breaths, almost panting, barely taking in enough air to expand her ribcage, and prayed she hadn't broken a bone.

When she thought she could move without passing out, she got to her knees. Each movement brought on a fresh wave of torture, and by the time she was on her feet, the night was fading in and out. Evie stumbled to the door, drunk on pain.

Her bar was dark. The door swung shut behind her and she fell to her knees, barely managing to catch herself with her left hand. Splinters dug into her palm, but she didn't move. Not yet. She had to wait for the fresh wave of white noise in her head to pass. She thought briefly about checking her side, but then discarded the notion. She didn't want to see.

A minute later Evie got to her feet again and surveyed the bar. Enough moonlight spilled through the windows to see the tables nearest her had been turned on their sides and most of the chairs were out of place and turned over. Barstools had been tossed across the room. It was like a freaking tornado had ripped through and demolished a ten-foot path straight through the place.

Evie dragged one foot forward. Then another. Breathing through the pain each new step cost her. She tripped over something in her path, turned and saw a pair of black army boots.

C.W. lay there on his back, blood trickling from his temple into his grey hair. A knife the size of her arm lay about a foot away. Evie stopped breathing, stopped everything, and dropped to her knees once more. She touched his neck, her whole body quaking and weak. She searched for a pulse and fell backward with relief when she found one. Strong and steady. C.W. had survived a POW camp for nearly twelve months. He'd been on three tours of duty. Had jungle rot. Malaria. He could survive a blow to the head.

She placed a kiss on his cheek.

She lifted her head and stopped. Something cold and hard had been pressed into her skull.

"Stand up and keep your hands out where I can see them." She knew that voice. Knew it deep in the bruises on her body.

Evie stood, careful to keep her hands out; the press of his pistol dug into her with each movement. Breathe. Just breathe.

"Now, turn around."

Evie complied, keeping her hands up. The wrong end of a pistol was aimed not three inches from her face. Evie stopped breathing.

"I knew you would show up here." Sheriff Lee Brown's gaze slithered down her body with venom.

"I knew all I had to do was get to your family. And since you got to your mom first, I took the next best thing."

Wait, he thought her mother was safe?

"You don't know?" Evie managed the words. It was impossible to swallow around the boulder in her throat.

"Don't know what? That if you don't do exactly as I say, I'm gonna put a bullet in your crazy grandpa?"

Evie cleared her throat, buying time to get her racing mind under control. "No."

"No?" Brown stepped forward and pressed the gun into the center of her forehead. Evie bowed backward under the pressure.

"I didn't get to her in time. Marcus has her."

Brown held her gaze, his eyes blood shot with fury. She didn't see him move, so the slap caught her by surprise. She'd been so focused on holding it together she hadn't seen his curve coming from the right. But this time she didn't fall. She stood up straight and wiped the blood from her face.

"Call him if you don't believe me."

"If you're lying, you'll regret it." Brown, his hand not as steady as before, pulled his phone out of his pocket, dialed it, and held it up to his ear.

"Do you have Maxine?" Brown said without any introductions.

Evie couldn't hear Marcus, but she could see the blood leave the sheriff's face. "What do you mean? Dammit, we had a deal."

Evie took a small step back, hoping to cash in on his distraction.

"Don't you fucking move." Brown lifted the gun back to eye level. Evie froze.

"You want me to bring her to you? Well, we need to talk about that. The way I see it is, I got what you want. And if you want her so bad, you should be willing to pay for it."

Brown held her gaze, his face turning red. His lips pressed together in a tight line. The phone was pressed to one ear, the gun held to her head.

"How about I put a bullet in her skull right now? Then how will you find your precious revenge?" Brown stepped forward and pushed the nozzle into her forehead again. Evie swallowed, fear freezing her thoughts. Her body.

"That's better. I thought you might come around to my way of thinking. I get my cut. I just want what I was promised. You can have the girl."

He hung up the phone, slipped it back into his pocket, and then grabbed Evie's arm. He yanked her to the door and out onto the back porch. Her boat bobbed in the water, tied to the porch rail. It was still there.

Brown let go of her arm, but the gun he held didn't waver. "Get on the boat."

Her muscles pulled taut as a stretched rubber band ready to snap. Tremors threatened to overtake her entire body. She went out the side door, stiff and scared, and climbed into the boat.

Brown boarded behind her. "Drive. You know where we're going."

Evie headed into the covered cabin. Betsy was spotless. Metal. Dark green and brown. Familiar. Only now she wasn't taking a pleasure cruise, she was driving to her doom.

The cab was lined with very small head-high windows. Bulletproof. The original 50-caliber had been removed and stored, but Betsy still had her machine gun mounted inside the cabin. Nothing and no one could see the weapon unless they boarded the boat without permission.

And no one boarded Betsy without permission.

She could open a hidden slot in the cab and slide the nozzle out if needed. The middle of the boat opened into a hidden compartment more than capable of hauling a very large load of weapons.

How was she supposed to get out of this?

"I said get going," Brown said.

Evie turned and gave the sheriff a frown. "I can't until you untie us from the porch."

He stepped forward, instead of back, and grabbed her jaw. "You sass me again and I'll make sure you suffer. Got it?"

Evie managed a nod and Brown let her go for long enough to untie the boat. Evie worked her jaw, making sure she still had movement in the joint.

She spun back toward the wheel and turned the key. Betsy turned on with one try. Smooth and predictable.

The boat was a small gun ship that had been perfect for taking out enemies down a river or canal in Vietnam. Maybe it would help her take care of her own river rats.

Brown's boots clanked on the metal floor. He grabbed her hair and ripped her head back. "Just because I can't kill you–*yet*–doesn't mean I can't cause you serious pain." He yanked back to emphasize his point. "Got it?"

Evie ground her teeth together. "Got it."

Brown all but threw her against the steering wheel and Evie had to grab it to keep from falling. Pain, sharp and instant, punched her side. She gasped and hunched forward.

Brown stalked off and patrolled the edges of the boat.

When she could breathe again, she flicked on the overhead lights and steered Betsy away from the bar. The water was littered with all sorts of obstacles. Limbs, hub caps, yard decorations. She drove through huge clumps of debris at a speed beyond sanity, all the while keeping her eye out for killer trees.

She had to hurry. If they didn't get to Marcus within thirty minutes, he would start in on her mom.

Evie forced the threatening panic attack down and increased the boat's speed. Betsy could take a little damage. She had to.

Her gaze fell on the small glove box hidden beneath the steering wheel. Holy crap. C.W.'s pistol. He held a firm belief in keeping himself and his vehicles armed.

"You remember the last time we were at Marcus's lodge?" Brown moved closer.

Evie scrambled to think. When?

"If I remember correctly, you were a big hit that night." Brown was right behind her now. His hand sliding up her hip.

Revulsion turned her stomach. Evie's grip could have crushed the steering wheel. She remembered all right. Most of it, anyway. The last half of that night had been masked in total blackness.

"I remember how beautiful you were." Brown's voice was right at her ear, sending a chill down her spine.

Evie eased toward the glove box and turned the latch.

"How bad I wanted a turn instead of just being the camera man." Brown bit her neck. Hard. Evie gasped and thrust her hand forward. Her fingers wrapped around the butt of a pistol.

"You know what? I think Marcus has held out for long enough. It's my turn. Right now. Shut off the boat." Brown's hand slid to her breast and tightened. She struggled to keep from dry heaving as she slowly pulled the gun to her stomach. Then she turned the boat off.

"You're right. It is your turn." Evie spun around in a quick motion and raised the pistol. Brown's weapon was still holstered at his side.

"You know what I remember about that night? I remember how you laughed when he hurt me. How you egged him on." Evie took a step forward. "I remember the humiliation."

Brown edged backward and held up his hands. "Now, Evie. Calm down. I was just playing."

"Playing?" She was on the verge of hysteria, but she didn't care. This man had been there for almost half of her beatings. Her torture. And he'd enjoyed every minute.

And he'd killed her father.

Her finger tightened on the trigger. Brown's gaze fell to the gun and he swallowed. "You shoot a law officer and you'll be on death row."

"Not if they don't find your body." Evie took another step forward. And another. Brown's feet shuffled backward.

She didn't miss the quick glance he gave to his pistol.

"Don't even think about it." She kept a few feet between them. "Turn around."

"You're gonna shoot me in the back?" Brown said. But he turned anyway, his hands slipping down to his sides.

"I mean it, touch that gun and I'll put a bullet in your head." Evie aimed at his back. She didn't want to kill him like that. It would be way too easy. But she would if he gave her no choice.

"You won't do it. You're too soft hearted." Brown kept edging his hand down toward his gun.

"You killed my father. I will kill you. I have the video, the evidence. Thanks to you. I know where Marcus is keeping my mom. The way I see it, I don't need you anymore." Evie held ready. Waiting on him to move. She didn't need to tell him she'd lost the phone.

"What do you want?" Brown asked.

"I want you off my boat. Right. Now."

"You're crazy. I get in this water, I'm as good as dead."

"It's a chance. It's more than you gave my family." Evie answered. Her hands clenched tighter around the butt of the gun.

"Let's talk about this. I can help you. I can get rid of Marcus for you," Brown said, his voice groveling.

Evie smiled. "Now that's just how I like my men. Begging."

Brown stiffened and she knew she'd struck deep. "You bitch."

Brown's hand fell to his pistol. He spun around so fast she couldn't think. Gunfire exploded and Evie fell back.

Chapter Thirty-one

He'd gone to Maxine's. Found it empty. Now Hunter was parked behind his dad's truck in front of The Wharf. The door was open, but it was empty.

His fist slammed into the vehicle's back door. "Dammit." He shook his hand, blood trailing from his knuckles. He'd left a dent in the new metal.

"You should save that for the bad guy." Hoyt approached, Jared and Hank following right behind him. The moon was tucked behind the clouds again, and there were no vehicles on the highway this close to the river. The river kept moving, her rushing water filling up the night.

"I'm just warming up," Hunter said.

Headlights appeared on the road. Ranger. He parked his bright red truck on the shoulder behind Hunter and got out.

Hank lifted a spotlight overhead and surveyed the slope from the highway leading down to the river. "I see a pair of boots."

"Lights on at The Wharf," Hoyt chimed in.

Hunter didn't wait, but ran down hill, stopping just above Evie's discarded boots. "Shit. Dad, shine that light on the bar, see if you can make out a boat."

"No boat, but I can see someone moving around in there." Hunter was in the process of kicking off his boots when Ranger's hand fell on his arm.

"Hey, instead of doing this the hard way, why don't we just take that?"

Hunter followed Ranger's pointed finger to right below the bridge, where a shiny Bass Tracker Pro had floated.

Hunter took a deep breath. He had to get his head on straight. Thinking like this, or not thinking, was what got people killed.

"Thanks, bro," Hunter said.

"You good now?" Ranger asked. His brow was raised, but the look in his eyes was understanding. And damaged. They shared a connection few others could conceive of and Hunter knew how bad Ranger was hurting right now. Probably more than Hunter. But his brother had sucked it up and thought of the mission first.

And so would Hunter. "Yeah. Let's move."

They loaded onto the boat and Hank steered them to the front door. Hunter grabbed the porch rail, tied them off in a makeshift anchor, and all five men climbed onto the porch, guns ready. "Me first, then Ranger. Jared, Dad, you take rear. Hoyt, keep watch."

Hunter knew his dad would chafe at being left outside, but he didn't care. He wasn't letting him walk in blind.

After slamming a shoulder to the door, Hunter burst inside, gun held high, his team right behind. He scanned the room quickly, took in the disarray, and then saw C.W. sitting back on a couch in the corner, legs spread, head tilted back with a Ziploc bag of ice pressed to his eye.

"Figured somebody'd show up sooner or later." C.W. didn't even lift his head.

"How do you know we weren't gonna shoot you, old man?" Ranger holstered his gun and Hunter did the same.

"Cause I knew it was you. And I know what you're here for."

"How the hell did you know it was me?" Hunter asked and crossed the room to squat down in front of him. "Jared, come check him out."

Jared was not only one of the best marine snipers on record, he was also a top-notch medic. He approached and lifted the ice from C.W.'s face and let out a low whistle. "Bet you got one hell of headache."

"I've had worse." The old man's eyes were black and small in his wrinkled face, but they were also intelligent and cunning. And his gaze was narrowed on Hunter. "So, you wanna tell me what the hell you're really doing here? Because you sure as shit didn't come back to make up with my granddaughter."

Hunter felt all eyes fall on him. Hunter rubbed a hand over the back of his neck, unsure of what to reveal and at the same time awed by C.W.'s vigilance. But at this point, he didn't care.

"We're here because Marcus and Brown are trying to move a load of weapons and they're setting up the MRG to take the fall. They want to use your bar to launder the money. And Evie to transport."

C.W. didn't move. Didn't look surprised. "Shit. I didn't see Marcus, the weasel, but his little lackey Brown was here waiting."

Hank, who'd joined them in the main room

once it was clear there weren't mercenaries awaiting them, took off through the kitchen only to return a few seconds later. "She's gone. The office is trashed." He turned to C.W. "Did you hear him say where they were headed?"

Had Hunter thought the man's eyes were black? Now they were like pitch-black holes of death. "You need to tell me right now-did you make a deal with Marcus?"

C.W. wiped the blood out of his eye. "If you're looking for me to feel guilty, you're gonna be lookin' a long time. Me and Maxine made the deal with Marcus. We told him we could move his shipment. But no one else knew we did."

"You son-of-a-bitch. You know what he did to Evie and you worked with him anyway?" Hunter said, his tone harsh, his voice loud. He stalked forward, towering over C.W., ready to shake the old man until his bones snapped.

"You think you know what's going on, but you don't. So sit down, shut up, and listen, if you want any chance of getting my girls back."

C.W.'s command stopped Hunter in his tracks. That wasn't the tone of a beaten man. "You've got two minutes."

"I figured out Marcus was responsible for Tom's murder. He and Brown set my boy up. Maxine knew too. We made the deal with him for revenge. We planned to steal the drugs and turn him over to the FBI. No one else knew. But then he involved Evie and our plan went to shit. That's why me and Maxine were here tonight, figuring out what to do next." C.W. held Hunter's gaze, unflinching.

"Drugs? He is moving goddamn weapons to a radical terrorist."

"Shit," C.W. let out under his breath.

"How do I know you're even telling the truth? That this wasn't some big money-making scheme gone wrong?" Hunter said.

"You can ask our FBI contact. He was the one who got in touch with us in the first place." C.W. placed a gnarled hand on the sofa armrest and rose on shaky feet. "I haven't heard from him in a few months, but he was the one who helped orchestrate this whole thing."

"And just who is this agent?" Hunter said.

"He went by Mr. J."

Chapter Thirty-two

"Mr. J?" Hunter echoed.

What the hell? Why would his mentor, his coach, have set up a sting connecting the MRG and Al Seriq without telling anyone? Why would he have endangered Evie that way? Mr. J was one of the few men who knew about her and how much leaving her had torn Hunter up inside. And pretending to be FBI?

Mr. J had fed Task Force Scorpion information. He'd taken care of his team. Hell, he'd been the one to form TS-F. To set up their last mission. The mission they'd lost Shane.

"He was dirty." Ranger spoke first. Hunter was still stuck between the hard place of knowledge and the rock of disbelief.

"Yeah, weird fella. Always wore sunglasses. Black hair. Beard. Real quiet. But he had credentials and I can tell an agent when I see one."

"Not agent, old man, operative. Mr. J was our CIA contact. We found him dead over three months ago," Hoyt said.

Three months of torture and guilt...only to find out Hunter's mentor was a traitor.

"You must be wrong. Mr. J made us. Made me. He wouldn't have betrayed us to the one man we've been hunting." Hunter tried to reconcile the idea of Mr. J as a traitor, but couldn't. He could see him laughing, pushing, driving them forward. Relaxing on a fishing trip. Grabbing a six-pack on his down time.

"Wore this big black ring on his right hand. I wouldn't have paid it much attention, but it ain't normal for men to wear rings," C.W. said. "I take it he didn't plan on intervening at all. Well, hell's bells, you can't trust anyone these days."

Hunter wanted to deny the truth. Deny that a man who was almost as close as family had sold them out. But a huge ax of evidence was wedged into his chest.

"He must have been the one funneling the weapons all along. He knew he could use the MRG to move more weapons," Jared said.

"He knew I would turn a blind eye to Mercy." Betrayal, swift and sharp, nearly cut Hunter in half.

"So he kept us busy. Too busy to figure it out." Ranger said.

"When did Mr. J make contact?" Hunter's revelation was quickly morphing into rage. His hands shook.

"Over a year ago. Shit like this doesn't happen overnight." C.W. grunted and then walked to the bar. He grabbed a whiskey bottle, twisted the cap off, and took a swig from it like it was water.

"Look, boys," Hank interjected, "we have to move, or it won't matter. Marcus isn't the kind of man to keep people around who have betrayed him."

"You're right. We need to figure out where he would have taken them." The cold hard truth was that Marcus had Evie. And Maxine. And he would hurt them.

Rage, familiar and welcome, flooded into Hunter's veins. Forget betrayal. Mr. J was dead and rotted. Hunter cared about one thing–Evangeline Videl.

"I know where we need to go." C.W. took another slug of whiskey and then slammed the bottle down. "But we're gonna need a boat."

Hunter glanced at Ranger. "We've got one."

"Good. Let me get my knife." C.W. went back to the couch, dug a hand in between the cushion and armrest, and pulled out a knife the size of a man's arm.

"Looks more like a sword." Hoyt snorted.

C.W. smiled and turned the knife in his hand before sliding in into a leather holster strapped to his thigh. "I've found the Bowie knife can accomplish more than a gun in close combat. It's silent and can slice a man's head off his neck in one motion."

C.W.'S grin spoke of experience. But the man had to be in his seventies, no way he was going with them. "Listen, C.W., I appreciate your experience, but I think it would be better if you let us handle it."

"I was killing before you were out of diapers, boy. No way am I staying behind when my girls are in danger. Save it. Besides, I know where we're goin'. And you don't."

Shit. He didn't have time for this. He could move his team undetected. Just like always. But not if they didn't have a destination. "We're gonna need another boat."

* * *

A few minutes later, Hoyt and Jared returned with a second boat in tow. This one was even better than the last. "Found it just upriver, still bobbing on the rope." Ranger jumped out and tied it off on the porch.

Jared throttled behind in the Bass Tracker. "This thing costs more than my freaking truck. I hope whoever owns it doesn't mind, but I'm taking her."

"That's John Redman's. Don't worry. He got extra insurance on it." C.W. and Hank climbed in with Hoyt.

Jared pulled up and Hunter and Ranger loaded in with him. They could move twice as fast on the water with less weight. "C.W, where we headed?"

"Five miles that way." C.W. pointed downriver.

"That's closer to the freaking dam," Hank said, his voice carrying over the water as if he were right next to Hunter.

"Yep. And I caught a conversation on the radio that there's a crack in it. So we need to shut up and drive."

Hunter assumed C.W. was referring to the type of radio a man could use to listen in on other people's conversations, but this wasn't the time to ask questions. He throttled the motor and shot into the middle of the river. Swerved just in time to miss a fucking trailer. *Jesus.*

Hoyt fell in behind, following in his wake, and they floored it, topping the Mercury motors out at full speed. Jared sat at point, keeping his light on the water in front of them. They dodged more debris.

"Damn, this place is a mine field," Jared yelled over the roar of the engine.

Hunter didn't answer. He could not focus on anything beyond saving Evie.

There had been a funny feeling in the pit of his gut when he'd realized Maxine's house was empty, but that pit had opened up and swallowed him whole at The Wharf. He knew Evie had overheard their conversation. He'd seen the look on her face through the window of Hank's truck.

He had to find her. Tell her he was sorry. Tell her he didn't mean it.

Tell her he loved her.

The thought didn't catch him off guard. The knowledge had been creeping up on him for a while. He knew it just as surely as he knew she was in danger at this very moment. More debris floated past and Hunter steered around it. The last thing he needed was to get distracted and put a hole in the hull. He wouldn't be able to help her if his boat was at the bottom of the river.

Hoyt whistled behind him and Hunter killed the motor.

C.W. piped up. "We better find somewhere to pull off and kill the engines if you don't want him to hear us coming. We got about a half-mile to go."

Hunter nodded. "Okay."

He would slow down. The element of surprise was worth more than gold. That way he could slip up behind the bastard, stick a knife in his back, and have the pleasure of twisting the blade.

A scream ripped across the water and Hunter jerked his head in the direction of downriver. "Evie."

Chapter Thirty-three

Evie stared in horror at Colette's dead, mutilated body on Marcus's covered porch. She covered her mouth, but it was too late to take back the scream. Marcus had killed her. Why? Why would he do that?

"Nice work, huh? That bitch mouthed off to me one too many times."

Evie looked over her shoulder. Marcus leaned against the door jam, arms crossed, the pistol in his hand hanging loose in his grip.

Evie stepped back, stumbled over Colette's leg, and hit the ground. Snake. Monster.

"And guess who I've got waiting inside?" Marcus pushed off from the door, his slacks pleated and his shirt without a wrinkle. Like killing was...easy. Pleasurable, even.

"Let her go, you bastard." The words scraped her raw. "Let her go now."

Marcus waltzed toward her, his movements as indolent as his tone. He stopped at her feet. "Why don't we go inside and visit a while first?" His sickly-sweet façade disappeared in an instant. "I said, get up."

Evie grabbed the rocking chair behind the dead body and lifted herself up. She recognized this side of him too. The one that itched like poison ivy to cause pain, and she knew to keep silent. Or it would get worse. A lot worse.

She followed him inside, head down, keeping her posture meek. Subservient. Just like he preferred.

"Good girl. Now, how about a drink? I think I'll have my favorite."

Evie walked past Marcus on wooden legs. He leaned against a velvet-backed barstool in front of the granite island. The wet bar, a masterpiece of mirrored tile and stone, stretched along the back wall of the kitchen.

Evie poured him a Crown and coke, measuring the amounts by memory and put in three cubes of ice. Brought it to him. Marcus took a sip and sighed in appreciation. "That ditz out back never got it right." Marcus sifted a hand past her cheek and into her hair. "Not like you."

Evie went cold at his touch. Ice-statue cold. He held her there as he took another sip. She wished she had filled it with poison.

"Now, where is Brown?"

Evie couldn't tear her gaze from his steel grey eyes, but she wanted to look away so he couldn't see her terror or disgust. When she tried to pull back, he tightened his grip.

"He...went for a swim." The image of Brown grabbing his throat, blood pouring through his fingers, filled her mind. She knew she should feel guilt. Or at least regret. She felt neither. She'd felt his bullet whizz by her ear. He'd tried to kill her. Too bad he didn't know C.W. had taught her how to shoot...and she was good. Really good.

Marcus threw his head back and his high-pitched laughter grated across her nerves like a cheese grinder. It took every ounce of her willpower to hold still. "You killed him? You?" He shook his head.

Evie eyed the revolver on the island behind him.

"My, my. Haven't we changed?" Marcus sat his drink down, followed her gaze, and picked up the gun.

She swallowed. "He tried to shoot me. I just got to him first."

Not that Marcus would care unless it affected him in some way.

"I'll have to thank you for that. That little pissant was getting on my nerves. I was planning to kill him when he brought you to me. Now I don't have to bother." He leaned in and kissed her forehead. Evie smelled his cologne. The same one he'd worn while they were together. Her stomach churned. "My little pet has turned into a stone-cold killer."

"Marcus." What could she do? She had to get him to take her to her mother. Had to get his gun. *Think, Evie, think.* She'd almost married the man, so she knew things about him no one else knew. She knew he liked to hurt people. She knew he liked power and money. But what he loved more than anything else was himself.

Evie laid a hand on his chest, gently, and he let her push him back. She cleared her throat. "Marcus, your shirt is clean. I've been in that filthy water outside. I don't want you to get dirty."

Her disgust was too obvious. Crap. Evie dropped her eyes, hiding her gaze. *Breathe, Evie.* Compartmentalize. Put it in a box. Marcus had taught her how to do that.

When she looked up, her eyes held a smile

like her lips, thin and fake, but real enough for him to buy it. He had no ability to recognize real happiness. To do that, he would have needed a soul.

"How thoughtful of you." But he didn't put down the gun or take his assessing gaze from hers.

"Why did you send that sleazebag Brown in the first place? I can't stand him. He is so coarse. So...ignorant."

Marcus's chest puffed up. A chest that didn't hold a candle to Hunter's. "You know I don't deal directly. Besides, he'd been effective enough before."

"Brown was going to kill you when we got here. He was planning to take the drugs himself." The lie slipped past her lips without even her conscious design. Marcus's grip on her hair tightened ever so slightly.

"So you killed him to save me?" His tone was disbelieving and Evie knew he would never buy it.

"No. I killed him because he pointed a gun at my head."

Marcus pulled her in close. Her scalp burned, her side burned, but she ignored the pain. "I know when you're lying. I've always been able to tell."

His eyes had gone light grey and angry. He tightened his grip more and Evie let the tears sting her eyes. He wanted to see her cry. She would let him. And then she would blow his head off his shoulders.

"I'm not lying. I did kill him. Shot him in the throat and he fell into the river." She gasped and grabbed his hand, her natural reaction to fight barely suppressed.

"So now, my ex-fiancée, the killer, is worried about my shirt getting dirty." His eyes went hard.

Shit, she was losing him. Evie let the tears fall. "No. No, Marcus. I just know you don't like to get dirty. And...and...the bar is sinking. We're running out of money. I know I held back at first, but I need this deal to go through."

"You need me. Say it, Evangeline. Tell me you need me."

Evie pushed words past the bile lining her throat, past her trembling lips. "I need you, Marcus. Please. I need you. I should have never left you."

He smiled then. That smile reserved for those special nights. The nights that haunted her nightmares. "I know you need me. You've always needed me. I was the one who caught you when that idiot ran from you in the first place. I was the one who taught you to be a lady. I was the one who gave you a nice house, a nice reputation."

He threw her back and Evie fell to the floor. Marcus stalked after her, leaving the gun on the counter. "And now you've come running back after you've been slumming at that trashy...bar." He said it like the words were filth and he couldn't believe he'd let them past his lips.

Evie scrambled back, flipped to her knees, and crawled frantically into the dining room. He planted a foot on her behind and pushed. Evie sprawled forward, her arms out, legs behind, her injured ribs taking the brunt of the fall. She blacked out long enough for him to pull her to her feet by her hair. "Please. I was scared. You branded me. I didn't know who to turn to after that."

He didn't slap her like Brown had. No, that

was too subtle for Marcus. He punched her, her head flew sideways, and her body followed. Evie landed on her arm and hip, the impact sending pain through her entire body from face to feet.

"I blessed you with my mark. And you acted like it was a disease. My mark!" Marcus roared and Evie had enough awareness to scramble through the dining room door and into the living room. Marcus had always skated the line between sanity and insanity, but he seemed to have finally chosen his side.

He grabbed her shirt; she felt the cool blade of a knife, followed by cold air on her back and chest. He cut her shirt off and yanked her to her feet, his arm wrapped around her middle, a knife pressed to her side. "This. This will stay with you forever. You will always know who you belong to."

Marcus traced her scar with the tip of the knife and Evie froze again, afraid he'd want to re-open the wound. "Marcus. I was just scared. I know I screwed up. Please let me have another chance."

He spun her then, his fingers digging into her jaw, his face suspended an inch from hers. "Why should I give you another shot? I can have any woman I want."

"I...I brought my boat. I can transport the drugs. I can launder your money. Whatever you want."

He shoved his lips to hers and invaded her mouth with his tongue. This time she couldn't stop herself from gagging. When he pulled back they were both panting. She could see the desire in his gaze and prayed he couldn't see the disgust in hers.

"Yes. You can. But it won't be drugs, my

dear. You will transport a shipment of weapons to Mexico. And, you will service me in any way I see fit." He let the words hang between them, power radiating from every square inch of his body.

"Yes. Yes, I will," she whispered. Oh. My. God. It wasn't innocent pot. He didn't have drugs. He had weapons. Weapons that could kill Americans.

He squeezed her jaw until she cried out and then pushed her away. His gaze raked hot coals over her body, but she shivered. "But not like that. You smell disgusting."

Marcus grabbed her again and dragged her upstairs. Evie followed, compliant. She knew he wouldn't touch her like this. Not intimately. She wasn't surprised when he pushed her into their old master bathroom. "Shower. You have five minutes."

"Please, let me see my mom." Evie covered her chest and hunched forward.

"When I'm satisfied, you will be allowed to see her. Now clean up." He shut the door and she heard the lock fall into place. The room had no windows. No other exit than the solid six-panel wood door.

Evie turned around in a frenzied search for a weapon. Any weapon. He'd left the gun downstairs. She just had to knock him out for long enough to get her mom. Or the gun. Her gaze fell on the two-foot bronze statue in the corner next to the walk-in shower. He'd always been so proud of that piece.

Evie turned on the shower, grabbed the statue, and flattened against the wall beside the door. She knew Marcus wouldn't wait. He wouldn't be able to resist torturing her with his hungry gaze. His touch.

She waited. And waited. Time stretched out so long it felt like thirty minutes had passed rather than two. The door latch clicked and she lifted the weapon overhead. Held her breath.

He slinked inside slowly, the smile curving his lips apparent in the mirror. Oh shit. The mirror. She saw his smile disappear as she slammed the statue down. He ducked to the side just in time and her blow glanced off his shoulder.

Evie threw the statue and ran through their old bedroom and out to the staircase. Marcus's footsteps pounded behind her. "You'll pay for that." His yell filled her ears but she kept going down. Down the grand staircase. So many steps. She reached the bottom, tripped, but righted herself. She couldn't help but glance over her shoulder. Marcus was right behind her.

She gasped and took off, running for the gun. She almost made it.

Marcus grabbed her hair and yanked backward. Evie's feet flipped up and she slammed into the polished hardwood floor. All the air left her lungs in a whoosh and she lay paralyzed. Marcus grabbed her hand and dragged her into the living room. She heard a drawer open and started to struggle. Too late. He latched an iron cuff on her wrist.

She tried to get to her feet, but he pulled the chain attached to the cuff and her momentum drove her forward. She hit her knees. Marcus had the other cuff on her before she could move. He pulled her, on her stomach, down the hall attached to the living room.

Evie's stomach bottomed out and she screamed. She knew where he was bringing her.

He'd had the room built just for her. She screamed again.

"Keep it up. No one will hear you. Well, except for your mother. You wanted to see her, right?" His smooth golden voice had disappeared into a snarl.

He yanked so hard it felt like he'd pulled her shoulders loose. He stopped at the third door on the left, inserted a key, and pushed the door open. The lights were on, low and barely bright enough to highlight his torture chamber. He dragged her inside, used her hands to pull her to her knees. He grabbed her jaw and forced her head to the side. "Look. She's been waiting on you."

Maxine's brown hair was tangled and her eyes were wild. Duct tape covered her mouth. Her hands and legs were tied to a chair. Tears fell down her cheeks and Evie felt a sob rise in her chest. Her mom was alive. For now.

Maxine leaned forward and yelled behind her gag. Evie realized how it must look. Her daughter shirtless, beaten, bound and bloody.

"Keep it up. I'll start in on you when I finish with her." Marcus's voice was pure menace. Evie tried to get to her feet, but he just dragged her forward again, throwing her off balance, and her stomach scraped against the floor. No more smooth hardwood. No. He'd wanted something easy to clean, easy to bleach free of blood. This floor was polished concrete.

Marcus pulled her up and she fought. Evie summoned every reserve of strength she had left. But he was too strong. He got her hands overhead and she managed to aim a kick at his groin. He deflected the blow with his thigh and yanked her hands overhead. Latched the chain on her cuffs to a hook dangling from the ceiling.

Evie spat in his face, unable to hold back her disgust. Marcus merely pulled a handkerchief from his pocket, wiped her spit off, and calmly returned the cloth to his pocket. He kept his arms at his sides. Loose. Then he punched her in the stomach.

She couldn't bend forward, but brought her knees up and gagged.

"Looks like we will have to start over with your lessons." Marcus walked away and Evie frantically looked at her mother and shook her head. Maxine needed to keep as quiet as possible. He wouldn't hesitate to hurt her now.

He crossed to the wall nearest Evie and selected the longest, thinnest cane from the group.

Oh no.

"That's right. You remember this one. This one leaves the best impression."

Chapter Thirty-four

No matter how hard he listened, he couldn't hear her screams any more. He prayed it meant she was safe. But in reality, he knew it meant she was either dead or unconscious.

He prayed silently for the latter.

"Fuck, row harder," Hunter ground out. Tension coiled his entire body tight.

"Take a left between those two cypress trees," C.W. called out from behind them.

Hunter plunged the oar into the water on his right and steered the boat between the trees. As soon as they rounded the corner, he saw the lodge. Lights lit the inside, but the front porch was bathed in shadows. Even so, he couldn't miss the empty boat floating in front.

"That's Betsy. Evie is here," C.W. said. Hunter could hear the alarm in his voice. It was the same alarm crawling up his spine. They glided silently beside Evie's boat and tied off to the porch. The men unloaded one by one onto the porch.

"Dead woman." Jared kneeled over a body, hiding her from view.

Hunter's heart plummeted into his feet. "Evie?" he croaked.

"No. Brunette. Pale. Tall," Jared said.

Hunter reached out for anything to hold himself up straight. His hand landed on C.W. He nodded, got his feet straight and they eased their way to the door. Hunter tried the knob and found it open. He nodded to his team and they fell into place, Ranger behind him. Jared and Hoyt ran around to the other side of the house.

"Dad, C.W., follow us in. Stay down. Keep your gun down, but be ready." Hunter waited for their nod of understanding before proceeding. The door swung open silently. He stepped inside, pistol raised, and walked into a gourmet kitchen complete with stainless steel appliances, granite counter tops, and a pistol on the island.

Hunter swept right into the dining room, and Ranger swept left, through the open door out of the kitchen. C.W. and Hank split up and followed. The kitchen led to a grand dining room, complete with a crystal chandelier, then continued around into an open formal living room. Dark leather couches were placed in perfect lines. A stone fireplace dominated the main wall and climbed up the vaulted two-story ceiling. Ranger and Hank started up the staircase to their left. Hunter and C.W. moved through the living room, heading toward the connected hall.

Slow. Cautious. Careful.

Evie's scream ripped through the house and Hunter stiffened. He wanted to take off running, but he forced himself to continue easing down the hall slowly, his feet silent. Hoyt and Jared appeared through a small back door.

Hunter held his hand to his lips. He heard a snap, then Evie screamed again.

Hunter kept moving and pointed to a door

they had not yet opened. The men fell into line behind Hunter as he eased the door open and peeked inside.

He saw Maxine first, tied to a chair, her eyes red and filled with tears. Her screams were muffled by a gag. Hunter swung the door in further. When he saw Evie, he almost snapped. Almost raised his gun and shot the bastard holding the whip in the back. But he would have risked hitting her.

And fuck all if he could hurt her.

C.W. gripped his shoulder. Hunter turned, barely able to restrain himself, and took the bowie knife C.W. handed him. And Hunter knew what he would do.

He waited until the bastard pulled his hand back. "Have you learned your lesson yet?"

Marcus's words gut-punched Hunter. He grabbed the middle of the long black whip and yanked. Marcus stumbled around in surprise and Hunter lifted the blade, ready to kill. Marcus stumbled right, barely missing Hunter's knife.

"Drop the whip. It's over."

"And if I don't?"

"I'll put this knife in your fucking throat." Hunter kept his gaze trained on Marcus as he circled back left, getting closer to Evie. "Stop now, this is your last warning."

"You think I'm scared of your little knife?" Marcus cracked the whip and took another step to the left.

Hunter pulled the knife back, readying to throw. "You should be."

"Trash. You never deserved her. She's mine. I'll kill her before I let you touch her." Marcus dropped the whip and dove back, grabbing the shelf behind him. His hand wrapped around a pistol.

Hunter threw the knife, its whisper barely audible as it flew through the air. The blade sunk into Marcus's flesh with a thud and the sound of a single gunshot echoed through the room.

Marcus went down, the knife protruding from his throat. Blood pooled around him. Hunter felt something warm trickle down his face. He touched it and when he pulled back, blood covered his hand.

"Shit man, you're hit." Ranger appeared in his peripheral.

Hunter felt his temple again, the burn running across the whole right side of his skull. But he still stood. He could talk, walk and breathe. What did it matter if he was bleeding?

"I'm good." Hunter rushed to Evie and yanked on the cuffs that restrained her hands, but they didn't move. Evie was panting. Shivering. Blood ran across her back in thin strips. *MC* was bold on her hip. He clenched his jaw, wanting to throw up at the sight of this violence that had been done to her, and ran back to Marcus.

He was still gurgling on the floor. Hunter ignored him and rifled through his pockets. Nothing. Then he spied the small chain around the man's neck, pushed his shirt to the side, and spied a key. Hunter tore it from his neck and ran to Evie without looking back.

His hands shook as he tried to find the hole. Fuck. He couldn't get it.

Jared, who'd entered the room after him, stood across from him and took the key. "You catch her." His voice was gruff with emotion. Hunter cupped her beneath the arms. Her head hung limp. Jared turned the key. One hand dropped and Hunter caught it and draped it over his shoulder. When her other arm fell, he did the same.

"I'm going to pick you up, honey. Okay?" Hunter leaned in and whispered in her ear. She nodded, a tiny motion, but he felt it. Hunter carried her to the kitchen, careful not to touch her back, and sat on a stool, keeping her body draped chest-to-chest over his.

Evie hung limp in his grip. He prayed she had passed out.

"Hunter?" Her voice was hoarse and barely audible.

"Shhh. I'm here. Don't talk. We're getting you out of here." Hunter held her as tight as he could without touching her back. Each time she shivered, he cringed.

"My baby! Where is she?" Maxine rushed into the kitchen and ground to a halt. Her normally perfectly-teased brown hair hung askew. Mascara trailed down her face. She approached them cautiously. "Is she...okay?"

Hunter nodded. Maxine touched Evie's shoulder. "Baby?"

Evie lifted her head from his shoulder. "I tried to make it in time."

"Hush. You did fine. Just fine." Fresh tears tracked down Maxine's face and Evie's head hit Hunter's shoulder. He knew she was exhausted.

Hunter avoided looking at Evie's back, which would only make him lose his mind with rage. Rage that would have no outlet now that her attacker was dead. "Get Jared. He's a medic."

Maxine nodded and took off for the living room. He heard murmuring voices then Jared strode into the kitchen. "Jesus Christ."

Hunter clenched his jaw. "How bad is it?"

"Sorry, man. I just don't like seeing women treated like this." Jared leaned in and touched Evie's bare back. She tensed and hissed out a breath.

"It's bad, but she'll be fine. We need to disinfect the wounds. Treat them and cover them with some bandages. My bag is in our temporary headquarters at Hank's farm."

Hunter lowered his head to Evie's neck and inhaled her scent. "Do you think you can make it?"

Evie mumbled something into his skin.

"Baby, speak up. I can't hear you."

Evie leaned back, using his chest for leverage, just enough for her gaze to meet his. "Yes. But not with you."

Her words tore through him, ripped him from stomach to sternum. Hunter clenched his jaw. He saw the pain in her gaze. Not just physical. Emotional. Pain that he himself had caused.

"Evie, I..." His tone was harsh with despair.

"Don't. Just don't." She fell back to his chest, panting like she'd run for miles.

He wanted to hold her forever. Never let her out of his sight again. But right now, he had to let her go. And Hunter knew it would be harder than hearing her screams of pain.

His eyes found Ranger, who had joined them in the kitchen. He couldn't do it. He couldn't willingly hand her over to someone else when she was in this condition. Half-naked and half-dead.

His gaze snapped to his brother's. "Find me something to cover her with."

Ranger left and Hunter heard him running

upstairs.

Hank stood off to the side, holding Maxine, and she willingly returned his embrace. He'd never seen his dad look at a woman like that. With adoration and love.

Ranger returned with a bed sheet, which the two of them draped over Evie. No matter how careful they were, she gasped and jerked with pain.

Hunter clenched his jaw as Ranger slipped his hands under her legs and shoulders and lifted her gently. When he cradled Evie to his chest, Hunter bit back a roar of possession. Of pain. She was his woman. His.

And he'd fucked it up. Again.

Chapter Thirty-five

By the time they reached The Wharf, Evie had passed out. As soon as Hunter realized she was unconscious, he took her back, unable to stand seeing her in someone else's arms. Even if they were his brother's.

Hunter sat in the backseat of Hoyt's truck, Ranger beside him. Jared and Hoyt were in the front. Hank and Maxine were in Hank's truck.

They made record time back to Hank's house. Hunter carefully carried her inside to his old bed and Jared met him there with his medic bag. "Pull the sheet straight up, slow. Try not to re-open any of her wounds."

Hunter inched the damn thing off centimeter by centimeter. Blood had already dried in a criss-cross pattern on the material.

When her back was bare, he almost exploded. Where there weren't welts, there was blood. And then there was the fucking brand. Hunter stood and stalked across the room, barely resisting the urge to slam his fist through the wall. Rage ran through his veins.

He needed an outlet.

"Hunter. You need to get it together. For her." Jared spoke slowly, his words measured.

How could his buddy expect him to calm down? Evie's back was a battlefield of bloody stripes.

"You choose. Your needs or hers." Jared met him stare for stare, not backing down. And Hunter's anger deflated, and he sat on the mattress, feeling regret well in every cell in his body. He'd let this happen.

"I didn't trust her. And because of that, she's like this."

Jared nodded but didn't argue. "You fucked up big time."

Hunter shot him a glare.

"Hey, don't be mad at me. I support you. But you screwed up, and you're gonna have to work your ass off to get her back."

"And I get to sit back and watch you squirm," Hoyt said from the doorway.

Great. Here he was, sweating over the love of his life, and his men were giving him shit. Well, he deserved it.

"Just make her better," Hunter bit out. He didn't have a clue about how to win her back. He had set out to charm her and use her. He had thought her a cheater. Now he knew the truth. *He* was the reason she'd ended up in Marcus's arms.

And she'd suffered there.

Fuck. He wanted to scream. To tear something up. Anything to release this beast of self-loathing. But that would be too easy. He needed to suffer.

He deserved it.

* * *

Evie woke to sunlight streaming through sheer curtains. She was in her mom's house, in the guest bedroom, on her stomach. Hunter held her hand, his face a mask of worry. Elation filled her as she met his gaze. But then she remembered his words and her elation turned to sorrow.

He had lied. He had used her. And...she loved him. She still loved him.

Evie wrested her hand from his, the slight movement pulling the skin across her back. Pain made her cringe.

"Can I get you anything? How do you feel?" The questions came rapid-fire and Evie struggled to keep up.

"I'm okay. The pain isn't anything I haven't dealt with before." Hunter cringed and Evie felt a pang of guilt, but she quickly squashed the emotion. Why should she care about hurting him after what he'd done to her?

"Do I need to call Jared? Let him check out your back?"

Evie bit her lip and shook her head no. She didn't want anyone to see her like this. Broken. Battered. Bloody.

"Where is Mom? Is she okay?"

"Yeah. She left about ten minutes ago. It's the first time we've gotten her to leave your side. Hank drove her to town to get her a Dr. Pepper."

Evie smiled. Her mom's idea of a pick-me-up had always been Dr. Pepper. Personally, Evie couldn't stand the sweet syrupy taste. But whatever made her mom happy...

"So I took over," Hunter finished.

A piece of hair fell over her eye and he brushed it back. Evie cringed. She couldn't handle him touching her. Not now. Not when the wounds were fresh. So raw.

Hunter pulled back and she saw the pain her action had caused him. First she felt sorry for it. Then she felt angry. "Dammit. Don't sit there making me feel bad for you. You screwed me, remember? I heard you. I heard every word. I was just a means to an end. A mission."

His skin paled and he leaned forward like he wanted to argue, but Evie cut him off. "Get out. Now."

"Evie, just give me a chance to explain," Hunter pleaded.

"I don't want to hear it. I don't trust you. You lied to my face." And she had fallen for it. Just like she had fallen for the gentle giant next to her. Only he wasn't gentle. He was a liar. And he'd hurt her. She felt the tears start but was too tired to wipe them away.

Hunter did it for her.

"Leave. Please." Evie forced the words out.

Hunter pulled back. "Evie..."

"No! Get out!"

The effort of yelling at him had cost her dearly. What little strength she had left vanished and her skin pulled tight across her back.

But it had the desired effect. Hunter stood and walked to the door. He turned. "I'll be back, Evie. I'm not giving up on us."

Her laugh was bitter. "There *is* no us."

Hunter left. Evie laid her head back on the pillow and let exhaustion claim her.

* * *

The next time she opened her eyes it was dark. The lights were off. No sunlight. Evie glanced at the clock on the bed stand. Five a.m.

The sun would rise soon. Her mom would get

up by six. The woman had always been an early riser, unlike Evie, who could easily sleep past nine.

The lamp was turned on at the lowest setting, casting a dim glow across the room. Evie moved and this time her back didn't scream in pain, so she tested her strength. She pushed up, locked her elbows, and held herself like that—her knees and hands supporting her. She caught her breath and eased back into a sitting position on the bed, her feet tucked under her.

Each movement pulled and squished the sores on her back, but it was tolerable.

What was not tolerable was the man asleep in the recliner three feet away from her.

But as much as she wanted to tell him to leave again, she couldn't wake him and destroy the look of peace on his face. His face was relaxed, almost boyish, and she found herself drawn to him.

"Don't wake him." Evie turned to see Maxine, dressed in a robe and long satin nightgown, standing in her doorway. Her mom crept into the room and gestured for Evie to follow her out. She helped Evie from the bed and into a robe and they quietly walked from the room. Evie had to hold onto her mom for support, and was out of breath by the time they reached the kitchen.

She eased down into the kitchen chair, careful to keep her back from touching the back of her seat. She pulled her robe together and put her head in her hands. Maxine started a pot of coffee, then sat down beside her and took her hand.

Maxine stayed silent as she stroked Evie's hand. She started to speak before stuttering to a stop, and Evie could tell she was fighting back the tears. Evie was about to say something, but Maxine held up a hand.

Evie gave her mom time. When Maxine finally spoke, her voice was ragged. "I should have known, baby. I'm so sorry. I can't believe I let you stay with that monster for so long." Maxine started crying.

Evie felt her own tears rise. "It's my fault. I kept it secret. I learned how to hide the bruises. You couldn't have known."

"I'm your mother. It's my responsibility to know when my only child is in trouble." More tears ran down Maxine's cheeks and Evie realized this was the first time she had seen her mom without make-up in years. Small lines had grown around her brown eyes and mouth. She was paler. Her cheeks redder.

"Mom." Evie squeezed Maxine's hand and scooted closer, even though the action sent a wave of fire shooting across her back. "Mom. You couldn't have known. No one did. Cheri just happened to find me one night. If it hadn't been for her, I would probably still be with him. Or dead."

"Oh, baby." Maxine leaned forward, crying hard, her head bent over their entwined hands. Evie soothed a hand down her mom's head.

"Please stop. It's not your fault. It's no one's fault but mine."

"No. It's mine." Hunter's deep voice dragged her attention from her mom.

He filled the doorway, his shoulders almost touching the frame. His T-shirt and sweatpants were rumpled from sleep. But his gaze was alert. Focused on her. He stepped into the room. "I left you. I let my past cloud my judgment. It's my fault you ended up with him."

Evie lifted her chin and held his gaze for just a second before looking away. His expression was raw and open and filled with longing.

Maxine patted her hand and stood. "I think you two need to talk."

"Mom..."

Maxine shushed her and leaned close. "I think you should listen to him, honey." Then her mom was gone and Evie was alone with Hunter.

The liar.

She turned from him, unable to look at him for fear that she would relent.

Hunter took her mom's seat. "Evie, I have to tell you something."

She still couldn't look at him, but he took her hand anyway, his touch sending sparks up her arm.

"I should have trusted you. I should have known you wouldn't cheat on me with Marcus."

Evie gave him her attention then, her anger too hot for her to hold it back. "That may be true. And it's forgivable. But not this. You used me. You used me and didn't care if I was hurt." Her lips trembled and she ripped her gaze from his, unwilling to let him have the satisfaction of seeing her cry.

Hunter turned her chin gently until she faced him again. "You're right. In the beginning, my intention was to use you. But after we talked, after we touched, after I spent more than five minutes in your presence, I knew I couldn't do it. I couldn't use you and turn you in."

"Do you think I'm stupid? I heard you at your dad's. I heard you tell them." Her words weren't tinged with bitterness. They were filled with it. She jerked her hand from his and stood. The familiar pain shot up her back.

"If you'd stayed a minute longer, you would've heard me tell them I knew you weren't involved. That I planned to keep you safe no matter what." Hunter rose, his voice desperate.

"You expect me to just believe you? After everything you've done?" Evie's chin rose even as tears fell.

"You should believe him. He's telling the truth."

Evie turned to see a sleep-rumpled Hank in the doorway. He walked to the coffee pot, poured two cups, and met Evie's gaze head-on. "Can't you see how much he loves you?"

With those words, Hank left the room and Evie slowly turned back to Hunter. Her whole body shook. Could it be true? Or was Hank just covering for his adopted son?

Hunter cursed and paced the kitchen. He looked awful. Tortured. Dark circles under his eyes. A couple days' growth of beard on his cheeks. But it was his eyes that held her. There was torment in their dark depths.

"Evie, I know I screwed up, but I swear on my mother's grave I'm telling the truth." He strode over to her then and took her hands in his, his eyes pleading.

Evie felt her heart melting as she searched his gaze.

"Please, you have to believe me." Hunter dropped to a knee.

Evie touched his cheek, his hair. He closed his eyes and leaned into her touch. "Okay."

Geez. She needed a new brain. But her heart

screamed for him. Was drawn to him.

Hunter looked up then, his expression filled with hope, and Evie nodded.

"I love you, Evie. I've loved you since I first met you."

"I love you too, Hunter."

Epilogue

A few months later, Evie and Hunter stood on a sandbar of the Mississippi, holding hands in the very spot where they'd first kissed. The sunset cast warm hues of gold and amber on the crowd gathered behind them.

"I now pronounce you man and wife." C.W., it turned out, was not only a POW, but an ordained minister. For the first time that Evie could remember, he wasn't wearing camo pants. The pressed jeans looked good on him, if not weird.

"I love you."

Evie tilted her face up to her husband, Hunter James. The fierce possessiveness in his dark gaze stole her breath, but not as much as the consuming kiss that followed his declaration.

When they broke apart, her husband's lips broke into a huge grin and he turned her to face their friends and family. "My wife."

Everyone clapped and cheered. Maxine stood with Hank, his arm anchored around her waist. Ever since that night, Hank had barely let her mother out of his sight. The only family member absent from the crowd was Hayden, Hunter's little sister.

Maxine   strode   forward,   her   arms outstretched and pulled Evie into a fierce hug. "I'm so happy for you."

Hank approached and held out his hand to Hunter. Evie stepped back, just as he pulled Hunter into a hug. Evie's cheeks hurt from smiling so much.

Ranger came next, squeezing his brother tight. He leaned down and kissed Evie on the cheek. When he stood, she caught his quick glance away and followed it. Amy stood off to the side, her arms wrapped protectively around her middle.

Evie felt a pang of regret. Amy had lost her husband and brought his child into this world as a single mother. If it hadn't been for Hunter's insistence on such a quick wedding, Evie would have put if off longer. But her man gave the word stubborn a new meaning.

Amy's gaze caught Ranger's and a blush stole through her cheeks. A scorching look passed between them. *What the heck?*

Evie didn't have time to question her new brother-in-law, though. The rest of Hunter's team filed through, offering their congratulations. Even Greer and Rayland Wilde, her cajun cousins, were here to give their congratulations.

Cheri marched up, her short dress drawing the attention of Hunter's entire team. "Remember what I said about fish bait?"

Confusion sliced through Evie. "What?"

"Ask your husband." Cheri grabbed Evie into a hug and turned to Hunter.

"You don't have to worry. She is my life." Hunter held out a hand.

"As long as we're straight." Cheri slid right past his hand and hugged Hunter.

"Would you two tell me what you are talking about?"

Hunter let go of Cheri and pulled Evie into his embrace. "Just a little conversation about fish and balls. Nothing important."

"Time for the party!" C.W. said. "Hoyt, hit it."

Hoyt started the music. Hunter and Evie shared their first dance together as husband and wife. "How can he do that with that little speaker?"

Hunter shrugged and then dipped her. "I have no idea."

Evie swayed with the beat, warm sand squishing through her toes and the man of her dreams in her arms. Her friends and family joined in, forming a loose group around them. "I love you, husband."

Hunter leaned down and rested his forehead to hers. "I love you too, wife."

* * *

Sherriff Lee Brown lay limp in the river. The dull roar of the boat barely registered as Evie sped away, leaving him to bleed out in the river. Brown floated on his back, staring up at the night sky, waiting for the blackness to swallow him whole.

His whole life he'd been a follower. He'd followed his brother and nearly ended up in jail. He'd followed his friends and nearly ended up addicted to drugs. He'd followed Marcus, and all for the promise of money. And now he would die. Alone.

Two boats sped by, not ten feet from where he floated. Brown saw Hunter James in one, surrounded by his friends. Another boat followed, full of more reinforcements. Good. At least Marcus would die too.

Leaving nearly ten million dollars worth of weapons to rot where no one would find them.

Ten million. What he could do with that kind of money. Fuck, he could do anything with half that. But he'd never get the chance.

Or would he?

How was he still alive?

Brown lifted a hand to his neck, feeling the hot sticky blood there, dripping into the water. Dripping, not squirting out.

Realization dawned. She'd missed his artery. Fucking hell, the bitch missed.

Steeling his resolve, he turned his head to the side to take in his location. Pain, white hot and burning seared across his neck. His heart thudded hard in his chest, working overtime to deal with the surge of adrenaline. He was almost to the shore. The current moved swift, carrying him along the shoreline.

Slowly, testing his strength, Brown struck out with one hand, the other held tight over his wound. He dipped below the surface, but forced himself to come back up for air. He could do this. He could survive.

His hand hit solid ground. He pulled himself out of the river, collapsing face down onto the muddy bank. His feet remained submerged, but he couldn't move another inch. His arms and legs were numb, cold seeming to creep into every pore of his flesh.

But he was alive.

And he knew where the weapons were.

Before you go...

From the author: I hope you enjoyed Redemption River, I want to thank you for joining the adventure. ***I would like to invite you to post a review on Amazon or Goodreads.***
****
****
As a bonus for signing up for my newsletter you'll be entered for monthly $50 gift card drawings, as well as receive exclusive promotions and excerpts available only to subscribers.
www.lindsaycross.com
–Lindsay Cross

email: lindsaycross@lindsaycross.com
facebook: Lindsay.cross.author
twitter: @lindsaycross101

Resurrection River
MEN OF MERCY, BOOK 2

Ranger James accepted his best friend's death like a good soldier. With guilt. Regret. Vengeance. But a forbidden desire keeps pulling him from his mission...

Desire for his best friend's widow.

Killed in Action. That's why Rachel Carter's husband wasn't coming home.

A war widow, alone and broke, Rachel struggles to revive her family's crop dusting service to survive. Now she takes to the skies to find escape. Escape from the pain. From the guilt. From the earth-shattering desire for her husband's best friend.

Rachel and Ranger can't fight the attraction between them any longer. But one fateful night cleaves their new found love in two...

Can they find the will to fight for true love? Or will an evil so shocking destroy their lives for good?

Chapter 1

Amy's day started at sunrise and ended after midnight. Feed the chickens. Feed the cows. Feed herself. Then, after five, feed the alcoholics.

The rest of the time she spent pretending her

husband hadn't left for deployment with a good-bye fight instead of a good-bye kiss.

Six months was a little long for a stand-off between husband and wife. And if Shane were home, that time would shrink to hours. But the damn man hadn't called. Hadn't written. She'd gotten nothing but a cold shoulder from a third world country. And Shane should have been home from deployment two-weeks ago.

She paused painting the new nursery pink and put a hand to her aching back. She'd been on her feet for five hours straight trying to finish painting before her shift at the bar. Over three hours ago her feet had swollen past the confines of her tennis shoes and she'd switched to flip-flops. Now she just had to make it through the night without some drunk stepping on her feet and mashing her bare toes. Amy probably should have taken a break, but she was determined to make a place for her daughter.

Someone knocked on her front door. Eight o'clock. Who would be knocking on her door this late? Most of the residents of Mercy, Mississippi considered this bedtime. Her hand immediately went to her belly, covering her unborn child. Amy was seven months along, only finding out about her condition the week after Shane left. If he were regular military, she could tell him. Let him know he was going to be a father. But when Task Force Scorpion, TF-S, an elite branch of Special Forces deployed, they went off grid.

Nothing and no one could contact them.

They knocked again. Amy carefully balanced her wet paintbrush on the open bucket at her feet and headed to the front door, stopping for a quick peek in the mirror. A few smudges of paint dotted her cheek and her ponytail sagged a little. They knocked again. This time more forceful. *Two-weeks late.*

Could be someone needed help or her best friends wanting to drag her out of the house and make her pretend to be happy.

Could be an all-together different reason. One she never wanted to know.

Don't answer it.

Don't answer it.

Don't answer it.

"Amy, it's me."

Ranger James. The man she should have married.

Why was he on her front porch and not her husband? They were both in the same unit. If Ranger was home and not Shane...

Her unborn daughter, Chloe, shoved an elbow into her ribs and Amy rubbed soothing circles over the skin. She took a calming breath. Her doctor told her no undue stress. It's okay. He's just letting me know Shane had to stay in the country longer than expected...

She pasted on her I'm-sure-it's-nothing-important smile and opened the door.

The roar of the battering rain immediately surrounded her. A drenched and dripping Ranger stood on her front porch, his truck headlights shining through the downpour. His blond hair plastered to his head. His t-shirt plastered to his chest.

Do not look at his chest.

"Amy." Ranger's voice still had that edge, the one that always managed to scrape across her nerves. But right now his voice had something else. Something frightening.

She stepped onto the porch. Lighting flashed, highlighting his expression, and she jerked like she'd been struck in the chest. The raw pain in Ranger's gaze made her tremble. "No."

"Shane." His voice slammed through her with the force of an eighteen-wheeler.

Her heart stopped.

"Shane. He's…"

Ranger's words faded under the roaring in her ears. Her hands went numb. He kept talking, but she couldn't hear. Couldn't process anything but the oxygen seeping from her lungs in horror. Just because she hadn't talked to Shane recently didn't mean something had happened to him.

Didn't mean he was dead.

She wanted to run. To close the door, curl up in a ball and sob. Instead, Ranger's eyes filling with tears trapped her. "I'm so sorry. The condolences officer showed up at headquarters. I beat him here. I thought you should hear it from me."

No. No. No.

Not her. Not him. Not her husband.

Shane. Shane hadn't failed to call because of their fight. Not because they were flirting with separation. Not because he didn't love her. He hadn't called because he was dead.

Oh God.

Her stomach twisted, and sharp pain ripped across her back. Amy doubled over and Ranger grabbed her arms, barely keeping her from falling. "Amy, holy shit. You're… you're…"

Pregnant.

A stabbing cramp ripped through her stomach again. She gasped out loud. "Something's wrong."

Lindsay Cross is the award-winning author of the Men of Mercy series. She is the fun loving mom of two beautiful daughters and one precocious Great Dane. Lindsay is happily married to the man of her dreams – a soldier and veteran. During one of her husband's deployments from home, writing became her escape and motivation.

An avid reader since childhood, reading and writing is in her blood. After years of reading, she discovered her true passion – writing. Her alpha military men are damaged, drop-dead gorgeous and determined to win the heart of the woman of their dreams.

FOR YOUR **FREE COPY** OF DAVID, A MEN OF MERCY NOVELLA, SIGN UP FOR MY NEWSLETTER AT WWW.LINDSAYCROSS.COM

Also by Lindsay Cross

Resurrection River: Men of Mercy Book 2
Reckless River: Men of Mercy Book 3
David: Men of Mercy Novella, Book 4
Raylan: Men of Mercy Novella, Book 5
Ravaged River: Men of Mercy Book 6
Coming in 2016:
Merc's story- Men of Mercy
Ethan's story - Men of Mercy, in Desiree

Holt's Team Omega Kindle Worlds
Sheriff Bo Lawson's story - Men of Mercy